ACORNA'S SEARCH

ANNE MCCAFFREY
& ELIZABETH ANN
SCARBOROUGH

CORGI BOOKS

ACORNA'S SEARCH
A CORGI BOOK : 0 552 15076 2

First publication in Great Britain

PRINTING HISTORY
Corgi edition published 2003

1 3 5 7 9 10 8 6 4 2

Set in 11/12pt Palatino by
Phoenix Typesetting, Burley-in-Wharfedale, West Yorkshire.

Corgi Books are published by Transworld Publishers,
61–63 Uxbridge Road, London W5 5SA,
a division of The Random House Group Ltd,
in Australia by Random House Australia (Pty) Ltd,
20 Alfred Street, Milsons Point, Sydney, NSW 2061, Australia,
in New Zealand by Random House New Zealand Ltd,
18 Poland Road, Glenfield, Auckland 10, New Zealand
and in South Africa by Random House (Pty) Ltd,
Endulini, 5a Jubilee Road, Parktown 2193, South Africa.

Printed and bound in Great Britain by
Cox & Wyman Ltd, Reading, Berkshire.

To Nelda Wythe and Doris Saario
with many thanks for help during hard times

ACORNA'S
SEARCH

ONE

Home! The word sang in Acorna's mind, a song of chiming silver streams and drumming water-falls, of wind fluting across the tops of bending blue-green grasses and through the spade-shaped leaves of gigantic trees in vast forests. The song echoed in the minds of every Linyaari present as they beheld Vhiliinyar-that-was.

The first homecoming place was on a high plateau, overshadowed by a conical mountain. Among deep purple and azure wildflowers lay a sprinkling of snow, while a pinkish cap of glacier frosted the distant peak, silhouetted against a delicate violet sky. A cascade flowed majestically from a plateau, the water forming a roaring curtain that plunged down to the mountain's base, ending in a froth of rainbow mists and white water that smoothed out into a broad plum-colored lake.

Acorna felt instinctively that this lake had tremendous significance for her but she didn't understand what that significance could possibly be. She wanted to stop and stay there, gazing into it, looking for something she was sure she could find if she just had time to look for it, but the world

11

around her swooped onwards, as if she and her traveling companions were flying through it in an open-topped flitter.

The violet skies of Vhiliinyar arched overhead, edged by the scalloped beauty of snow-covered mountains, as the spectacle swiftly segued from one glory to another.

Acorna almost forgot to breathe. This was the world she had dreamed of for so very long. She didn't hear the thoughts of the others, not even Aari or Neeva, nor did she seek them out. Surely they were as overwhelmed as she was by the sheer beauty of Vhiliinyar.

Abruptly the sky darkened, the moons rose, and sunset-colored words blazed overhead:

Brought to You Courtesy of Harakamian Homeworld Holograms and Terrestoration – Making Any World a Better One®

A collective sigh went round the room as the images faded. Everyone began talking, aloud and with thought-talk, all at once, so that the resulting words were little more than confused babble.

Despite all the verbal confusion, Aari's communication was very clear. He was trembling and looked rather greenish. His jaw was firmly clenched and his brimming eyes stared straight ahead.

'What is it, *yaazi*?' Acorna asked, using the Linyaari term for 'beloved'. Taking Aari's arm, she led him quickly to the main exit from the holo-bubble. She felt, rather than saw, Aari's parents,

12

his sister Maati, and Thariinye, who had become Aari's friend, following them.

Aari's answer to her question came into her mind in a wave of shock, the sort of emotional trauma he had seemed to be free of for some time now. Acorna placed her gleaming horn against his cheek to reassure him. Normally, among Linyaari, this caress would have been horn-to-horn, but Aari had been mutilated during his capture by the evil Khleevi. His horn had been destroyed. Thanks to hard work by some of the best Linyaari healers and a tissue donation from his younger sister Maati, Aari's horn had regrown to a short, twisted knot protruding an inch or so from his forehead and in time would be fully restored, but horn-to-horn gestures weren't possible for him yet.

His friends and family, emerging from the holo-bubble that had been temporarily transformed into their lost home, sensed Aari's anguish and joined their horns with Acorna to try and soothe him.

Hafiz Harakamian bustled out, the silk panels of his robes flying behind him like the wings of varicolored butterflies. His round face retained its geniality, but Acorna, raising her head to watch her adopted uncle's approach, felt a subtle blend of pique and embarrassment beneath his surface cheer, and saw the right half of Hafiz's mustache twitch irritably.

'How is it that my small conjuring trick to bring to life your once-exquisite home world has so distressed our heroic Aari that all of you must leave so precipitously, O She Who Is Closer to My Heart than Any Daughter of My Flesh Could Ever Be?' Hafiz complained, addressing Acorna.

But it was Maati, a youngling not afraid to rush in where diplomats feared to tread, who raised her horn from her brother's chest and answered, 'The Khleevi made him watch while they destroyed it all, Uncle Hafiz. It was awful. They killed all of those beautiful animals for sport, and ate every living plant and tree. Then they fouled the lakes and streams with their horrible excrement before they blew the mountains apart and filled the valleys with rubble.'

'Yes, yes, these regrettable circumstances are common knowledge. But have we not just demonstrated with our science which is so much like magic how the damage can be repaired and the planet reterraformed so it is as good as – nay, better than – new? You cannot but be aware of the extensive interviews we have conducted with Linyaari who lived on Vhiliinyar, in order that we may gather their memories of the place so that our scientists' efforts can bring them to life once more? Now all that remains is a simple aerial topographical mapping expedition and . . .'

'Nothing remains to map,' Aari said, his voice flat with a lack of emotion that was painful to hear. 'How will you know where to put a river when there are no mountains to feed it or seas for it to flow into? Even Joh Becker could find nothing to salvage from the planet except the bones of our ancestors.'

Acorna considered this statement as the holo-bubble emptied of the rest of Hafiz's Linyaari guests. From them she heard random snatches of troubled thought.

(I don't remember that mountain as being quite so high.)

(No, and there was always a summer settlement near the mouth of the Paazo river. The channels were all wrong.)

'There is still at least one recognizable landmark,' Acorna said thoughtfully. 'Maybe more than one . . .'

Liriili, the former *viizaar* of narhii-Vhiliinyar, was standing nearby, waiting to find fault, as usual, and to contradict anyone who seemed to have something positive to contribute. She was that rarest of creatures, a Linyaari with very little empathy for her fellow beings. She snorted, broadcasting her thought not only to Acorna but also to all the other Linyaari near enough to receive it.

(How would you know, Khornya? You have never been to Vhiliinyar.)

(That's not quite true,) Neeva defended her niece. (Khornya was born in space, that is true; but my sister and her husband brought their babe back to Vhiliinyar while Vaanye finished his work on his new defense system. However brief that sojourn, and however young she was during it, Khornya *was* there.) Neeva turned back to Acorna. (So what landmarks remain, dear Khornya?)

'The cave where Aari and his brother Laarye were,' Acorna told them all. 'And the final resting place where the bones of our forebears were once buried before Aari and the captain brought them to narhii-Vhiliinyar. We could use them as a starting point to rebuild the planet just as it was.'

Hafiz wrung his hands. His wife Karina, arriving in a drift of lavender draperies and scent, cooed solicitously and massaged his shoulders.

Hafiz protested in a wounded tone, 'But rebuilding it just as it was will take a very long time. We certainly can recreate the most beloved portions of Linyaari topography, my dear girl, as you have seen with your own eyes. Surely it is enough to replicate only those features best remembered by your people. How can they possibly miss that which they cannot recall?'

The *aagroni* Iirtye clearly understood enough of this to make his opinion on the matter known. He pushed to the front of the crowd and cleared his throat. 'Human recollection has nothing to do with what is necessary for a planet to function,' he said in an authoritative voice, though in the Linyaari language. 'Appearances are only an outward manifestation of the processes that enable life to grow and develop naturally upon a plantetary body. Restoring the vitality of a world is much more complicated than providing pretty mountains and panoramas of rivers, Lord Harakamian. It is based to an equal or greater part in getting the most minute and fragile details of the ecosystem right, many of which are virtually invisible to us. I have said this repeatedly to those who have interviewed me, Khornya. If our planet is to flourish again, it must be fully restored biologically as well as topographically.

'Your uncle promises to reproduce those land-marks that are stored in the memories of our

16

people and in what few records of our planet that now survive, but he also says that he cannot replace them exactly as they once were nor with a full suite of native flora and fauna. He would merely give us vistas, and try to make them live without the forests, the fields, the hills, and valleys, and indeed the very grasses, lichens, mosses, and ferns that colored their beauty. He would give us rivers and waterfalls, but not the associated swamps with all of their myriad microorganisms, plants, and animals that were once so essential to our world. But the greater beauty cannot exist without the life that once gave it form, for biology as well as geology brings its vital contributions to our ecology. And even the right geology is essential to its function.'

Acorna translated this to Hafiz. From his blustering growl and defensive posture, she shrewdly suspected, knowing her adoptive uncle's piratical nature, that while he realized on some level the truth of the *aagroni*'s arguments, Hafiz had his own agenda. His bursts of altruism frequently had a deeper commercial motivation that was not immediately apparent.

In the case of the restoration of the Linyaari homeworld, Acorna did not need her telepathic abilities to guess that Hafiz had it in the back of his mind that eventually he would convince the Linyaari to allow off-worlders to visit. Maybe he was even plotting something as crude as an intergalactic attraction called *Ki-Lin* Land or something similarly exploitative. Although the need of some Linyaari for peace and privacy in an inviolate world of their own had been explained to him repeatedly, such feelings were so foreign to Hafiz's own nature that he found them inconceivable. A master of hologrammatic illusion, he was himself deeply involved in surface appearances and loved an audience for his work, and thus felt that the same was true of everyone else.

Seeing that his niece was reading, if not his mind, at least his character, Hafiz protested, 'Acorna, dear girl, have I not moved heavens and planets to help your people? I am willing to pour out my fortune for them, to beggar my house in order to help them, but how can I restore those areas of Vhiliinyar no one can describe to me, much less provide images for or specimens of the native lifeforms? In my employ are the best terra-forming engineers in the universe, but without detailed maps or charts or biological samples, they can hardly be expected to revivify Vhiliinyar with such precision as your so-eminent scientist insists upon.'

Acorna nodded slowly and turned to the *aagroni*, to whom she had been transmitting Hafiz's remarks after translating them into Linyaari. (*Aagroni*, I know that most of the written and visual records of Vhiliinyar's features were destroyed in our battles with the Khleevi, but perhaps with your help, and the help of your fellow scientists, I can help locate the original positions of these landmarks upon our old planet using the resources available to us. Once we have these features in place, we can gather further information on the location of other less prominent areas. It won't be perfect, but it will be a good

18

start. Then we can start thinking about the biological issues).

(And just how do you intend to locate those sites, young lady?) the *aagroni* demanded.

Acorna smiled. (I have my methods,) she said. (We have promised the memory of Grandam Naadiina that her home will be again what it was and her people will thrive upon it. She died so that we might have this opportunity.)

The *aagroni* hung his head respectfully. (Did you think I would forget? But believe me, Khornya, the restoration of Vhiliinyar must be done properly.)

Suddenly Karina Harakamian's body swayed and her eyes turned up in her head. She spoke up in an eerie far-off voice. 'Ground surveys,' she said, in a rasping practical tone that was far removed from the dramatic voice she used when she was purporting to be, as she put it, 'a conduit for the Other World.'

Karina continued to speak in a voice and a language that was not hers. 'Everyone who once lived on Vhiliinyar must walk its ruined surface to participate in ground surveys. Vhiliinyar will be healed only by the love in the hearts of those who once inhabited her surface. Perils will be many, but you will – aaaaaaah . . .' Karina sagged and flopped somewhat gracefully into her husband's arms. Since he could not entirely support her ample form, not being an athletic sort himself, Hafiz staggered backward to lay his beloved on the ground. Aari intervened, however, swooping up Lady Harakamian in his arms and gently lowering his new stub of a horn to her cheek.

Karina, who did not speak more than a few phrases of Linyaari, had been speaking it fluently. Furthermore, distant and eerie though her words had sounded, they were readily recognizable as being in Grandam Naadiina's voice. Since Karina did not know Grandam, this was no mere imitation of a voice for effect. Karina claimed to be psychic far more often than she actually showed any evidence of psychic ability, but this was one of those rare times when her claims would appear to be true.

Hafiz, who like Karina had never met Grandam, was the only one unfazed by his wife's behavior. 'Excellent suggestion, my little couscous,' he said, patting his wife's hand and giving the others a look that seemed to say, 'Isn't it adorable how she comes up with these things?'

Captain Jonas Becker, the only non-Khleevi who had the coordinates for Aari's cave in his data banks, took time off from salvage gathering in the ruins of narhii-Vhiliinyar to assist the remaining Linyaari space vessels in transporting survey crews to the site on their old home world.

In the cargo holds of the *Condor* were a dozen House Harakamian flitters. As Acorna, Aari, Becker, and the android Mac unloaded the last of these, Becker said, 'I wish I could go with you kids, but Mac and I have a shipload of work to do back at NV. I got a favor to ask you though, Princess,' he said.

He and Acorna stood on the robolift deck, Becker holding his feline first mate, Roadkill the Makahomian Temple Cat, while Acorna scratched the cat behind the ears. Roadkill, who usually enjoyed such attention, squirmed mightily, kicking out with his back paws, which were securely tucked under Becker's left elbow. RK's front paws tried to jerk loose from the grip of Becker's left hand. Every striped hair on the beast's body was standing at attention, and the cat's eyes, barely slitted open, had a ferocious glint.

RK was purring, but woven into the purr was a thin stream of growly whine. The cat had been behaving wildly all during the journey to Vhiliinyar, leaping from deck to deck, racing along the tops of the Linyaari passengers' heads with a recklessness that had seemed likely to get him impaled on a horn at any moment.

'A favor? Certainly, Captain, if it is within my powers to grant it,' Acorna said.

'I was hoping you'd say that,' Becker growled, and shoved RK into her arms. 'Take the cat with you.'

Several of the Linyaari passengers, no matter how fond they had been of the *pahaantiyir* species native to Vhiliinyar that RK was said to resemble, had been happy to finish their journey simply so they could leave the cat and his erratic behavior behind them on the ship. Those Linyaari who read animals well reported that RK's thought patterns were deranged and unpredictable – not at all to the surprise of those who normally did not. Just now, the calculating appraisal RK gave Acorna, along with the paw full of claws he used to leave a lasting impression on Becker about a

F/ 1035292

WEXFORD
COUNTY
LIBRARY

cat's opinion of being held against his will, bore testimony to that.

'Why would you ask that, Joh?' Aari asked, a little nervously. 'Do you not need RK with you?'

'Normally, you know me, I'd hate to let the little guy go, but I need to get him off NV so he can dry out.'

'Dry out?' Aari asked.

'Yeah. You guys got some *baaad* catnip there on narhii-Vhiliinyar, and it didn't get all burned up when the Khleevi trashed the place. Old RK can't keep out of it, and it keeps him drunk as a skunk and it takes darned near forever to wear off. I can see I don't have to tell you that he's a mean drunk. He's always been a pretty shrewd character about keeping his tail screwed on straight, but while he's around that stuff, I'm afraid he's gonna get one of us killed. It's a temptation he can't resist, and it's driving him mad – and me with him. I'd leave him with Nadhari but, uh, we had this little disagreement.'

'I see, Captain,' Acorna said, and lowered her horn to scratch RK's forehead where a horn would be if he had one. Tearing loose a paw from Becker's grip, he made a swipe at her nose with his claws. The moment her horn touched him and her healing powers reached out to him, however, he detoxified. He lowered his paw, waggled it at her, relaxed to boneless limp serenity, and purred with deep contentment. 'I will be happy to take care of Roadkill for you,' she said.

'That's the ticket, Princess,' Becker grinned, offloading the foolishly grinning beast into Acorna's embrace. 'Your buddies on the ship would have done the same thing if they'd thought of it, but nobody could catch the little monster. See ya!'

Shortly thereafter, the *Condor* lifted off the rock-strewn blasted surface into the bruised purple sky of Vhiliinyar. A rush of anguish flooded across Acorna's mind, though the pain was not her own. She looked up at Aari. He seemed to be fairly composed, his eyes perhaps a little hard, his jaw a trifle set as he watched his friend's ship leave. But the other Linyaari were the ones having a difficult time of it as they explored the broken ruins of their former home.

'There must be some mistake,' Liriili said. 'That stupid man set us down on the wrong world. This can't possibly be Vhiliinyar. The scouts told us our home had been ruined, but they never said the destruction was this bad! Even the sky is the wrong color! Vhiliinyar's sky was a beautiful shade of violet, not this . . . this . . . putrescent purple.'

'Yes, well, it darkened when the debris from all of the explosions and the smoke from all the fires filled the atmosphere,' Aari said matter-of-factly.

Liriili snorted. 'Those scouts did not do a very good job of reporting the true extent of the damage. That is all I have to say.'

Beyond a forlorn wish that her last words would be true for a long time to come, the others ignored her, but her observation triggered disturbing recollections for Acorna, who had seen this blighted world through Aari's eyes and knew that Liriili's pessimism was probably justified in this case.

In the next shipload, more of the *aagroni*'s

23

assistants and apprentices arrived, as well as Aari and Maati's parents. They came equipped with portable laboratories, that they set up near the cave along with a base camp. Once the camp and laboratories were in place, the Linyaari began to organize survey parties for their mission. All of the survey parties were to transmit reports back to the base camp via the flitter com-units on a regular schedule or, when rest breaks from the survey work were needed, in person.

Acorna, Aari, Thariinye, and Maati chose to go out and survey the ruins of Vhiliinyar together. Neeva, Melireenya, Khaari, and Liriili, the present crew of the *Balakiire*, were to have been the second survey team, but Liriili suddenly balked. 'I have no wish to go out into the destruction of this world I so loved,' she declared with so much feeling that, in Liriili, it had to be counterfeit, since she was widely known to be the most unfeeling of Linyaari.

The rest of the *Balakiire*'s crew were not entirely unwilling to spare Liriili's 'feelings' – and their own.

(How I wish we could leave her behind!) Khaari thought with great fervency. (I grow so weary of her grousing and sarcasm, her contradicting everything anyone says. I feel almost that the *Balakiire*, once such a pleasant vessel, has become like Vhiliinyar itself since the Khleevi came. *Much* despoiled!)

Neeva laughed. (If you feel that way, I'm sure we can manage without her. I suppose she could run errands for the scientists and perhaps question their findings. They should not mind. They adore critical analysis. They do it to each other all the time.)

Turning to the *aagroni* Iirtye, she said, (What do you think? Could you make use of Liriili's talents here?)

(She is a bureaucrat, isn't she?) the *aagroni* said gruffly. (We will have a great deal of paperwork and accounting to do, once your findings start pouring in. And reports to send to Mr Harakamian and test results to transmit to Dr Hoa regarding meteorological conditions. She could be quite useful. Yes, certainly. Leave her.)

With great relief, they did. Maati laughed. 'That'll be a perfect place for her,' she told Acorna and Aari. 'Once these scientists get to work, they don't notice anything that isn't a specimen. They won't even see her, much less allow themselves to become annoyed by her.'

Relieved of their unwanted crewmate, the *Balakiire's* crew, supplemented by Melireenya's lifemate, boarded their flitter and lifted off to begin their work.

Acorna handed RK to Maati after the younger girl had climbed into the flitter's four-seater cabin. The cat, exhausted from his 'catnip'-induced shipboard acrobatics, melted into a furry puddle across Maati's knees. Thariinye boarded the flitter next. Acorna took the helm and Aari, as the person who knew this planet best and needed to be able to focus all of his attention on the terrain, sat in the navigator's seat.

Given its location on the star maps, Acorna knew intellectually that the planet under the shadow of their flitter had once been Vhiliinyar,

'Home of the People,' but it was hard to believe, as they skimmed the surface of this desolate place, that it had ever supported any sort of life.

The planet's remaining sun, 'Light of Our People,' was an amorphous gray-blue glob of smoky light in the sky, little resembling the brilliant orb she remembered from her dreams and from the descriptions Neeva had provided.

Remembering those descriptions, Acorna realized that some of her recent experiences were at odds with them. She turned to her lifemate – perhaps he could shed some light on the inconsistencies.

(You know, Aari, for a long time I had the impression from the other Linyaari that you were the only one left behind when the evacuation ships fled Vhiliinyar. But I've recently discovered that there were other Linyaari who chose to stay behind rather than leave their homes, as well as scouts who remained to relay information on what the Khleevi were up to. I wonder what happened to them. The scouts claimed that all living beings on the planet appeared to have been killed – that their bones were piled up by the Khleevi as monuments and yet, so far, I have seen no such monuments.)

Beside her, Aari moaned. The memories her question brought back were undoubtedly terrible for him.

(Laarye and I were the only youths lost in the chaos, certainly. There were others, mostly Linyaari who were reaching the twilight of their lives, who chose to remain behind on Vhiliinyar, *yaazi*, rather than adjust to a new world. Almost

26

all of them resided in distant settlements. I believe they were exterminated before the Khleevi found me. Certainly the Khleevi thought so. The Khleevi showed me their bones to torment me, but in the end, all of the chaos the Khleevi let loose on our world scattered those charnel piles along with the stones of our mountains.)

(You survived. Do you think it is possible we will find others?)

(They would have starved here, with nothing left to eat,) Aari told her. (It was only because our Ancestors' graves were near my cave, purifying the blighted land around it and enabling the plant life to continue to grow and thrive, that I was able to find the resources to sustain my own life.)

(I wonder . . .) Acorna said, and toggled the connection to Neeva's flitter.

'Yes, sister-child,' Neeva responded. 'Is everything well?' Then she added wryly. 'Relatively speaking, that is.'

Considering the devastation below them, Acorna could understand her aunt's disquiet. 'I am as well as can be expected, Aunt Neeva. But I have a question. You once told me that our people had scouts who risked being caught by the Khleevi in order to send back reports to narhii-Vhiliinyar of what happened here following the evacuation. Are the surviving scouts among us now?'

'Just the parents of your lifemate, Khornya. The scouts who stayed behind to see what the Khleevi did to our world sent in reports of conditions on Vhiliinyar as long as they could. But only Aari's parents survived to rejoin us. None of the other scouts were ever heard from again after those initial reports. Because we received no images of them being tortured by the Khleevi, we assume that they made use of the substances they were issued to end their lives before they were captured.'

'Oh,' Acorna said. She was so distracted by that revelation that she was hardly aware of breaking the connection.

Then Maati pointed out the windscreen and cried, 'Look! Those long lumpy trails, aren't those—?'

'Khleevi scat,' Thariinye said, disgusted. 'Maybe it's my imagination, or bad memories, but I think I can smell it from here.'

'I smelled it back at the cave,' Maati said.

Aari snorted. (The stench has not left my nostrils since we first landed.)

(It has been so for me, as well.) Even as she replied, Acorna tried not to broadcast the other disturbing recollection she'd had from the scout reports she'd reviewed. The reports had spoken of Khleevi Young being bred in the rivers and streams of Vhiliinyar. She shuddered, recalling her own single encounter with the Young, so voracious and vicious as to form the driving force behind Khleevi conquest. But surely all of the Young were dead now, killed on their horrific home world where they were both protected by and avoided by the adult Khleevi.

Aari picked up her concern and, to her surprise, *he* was the one to comfort *her*.

(I can sense when the Khleevi are close,) Aari told her. (And I do not sense them now.)

Acorna sighed. (Yes, they must have moved on once they had destroyed all the resources here, and returned to their home world. I'm sure you're right.)

(They're gone now, *yaazi*,) Aari repeated. (Nothing of them remains to harm us or others.)

Gratefully, she allowed her special talent for sensing the mineral composition of any substance she chose to probe – something she'd developed while working with her asteroid-miner foster parents – to preoccupy her with the data it fed her senses. Instead of smelling Khleevi scat she smelled, tasted, mentally touched, each major mineral deposit in their flight path as they passed above it. This was a vital part of her plan to map the planet. The few survey maps they had were short on biological detail, but extremely precise when it came to mineral deposits. She could take what she learned on their surveys of Vhiliinyar as it existed now and use it to reconstruct the planet topology as it had been before the Khleevi had attacked.

The work was a welcome distraction from the ugliness below her, and from the cold bleakness that overcame Aari as he withdrew to that inner place where he found protection when reminded too forcefully of his ordeal among the Khleevi.

Long stretches of alluvial deposits containing copper, gold, garnets, agates, and other, rarer gems indicated riverbeds, and when Acorna sensed these she noted their coordinates on the flitter's computer. The distribution of these minerals and gems would help her trace the rivers to their origins in the mountains and their endings in the seas. Limestone deposits in large quantities indicated former ocean floors – even recent ocean floors, since the Khleevi had diminished as well as befouled the planet's oceans until they were turgid, lifeless swamps.

Salt deposits provided another indication for the oceans, and basalt deposits often outlined original shorelines. Acorna's talent for sensing minerals, a trait apparently unique among the Linyaari, was invaluable here. She could use it to help Hafiz and her people reverse engineer Vhiliinyar from the mess it had become and return it, she hoped, to something at least approaching its original beauty and vitality.

The terrain abruptly changed and she increased the flitter's altitude to avoid the vast ranges of tumbled boulders before them. This landscape was in constant motion, like a terrified animal pinned down and writhing to escape torture. Showers of stones plummeted from precipices, landing with puffs of dust on the hills newly formed from the avalanches. These in turn were blasted apart by subsequent slides. Plumes of ash and smoke rose from three vast craters gaping in the range like festering pockmarks on the planet's face.

After the calderas were some distance behind them, the ground finally stabilized a bit. For the first time they could see vegetation growing, low and scrubby at first, and then a thick parrot-green jungle rising from the battered ground.

At the edge of this jungle, Aari indicated Acorna should set down the flitter, which she did.

'Ouch,' Maati said to RK as she tried to pry him

from her lap. The cat's ears were flat and his tail was poofed into something that looked like a massive feather duster.

'I don't think he likes it here,' Thariinye said.

'But it's *beautiful*,' Maati replied as she was finally able to dislodge RK and dump him onto the flitter's deck. She followed after him, climbing out onto the scarred stone surface of Vhiliinyar. 'Isn't this wonderful? This is the first sign we have seen that the planet is finally starting to heal and grow things again.'

'Hmmm,' Acorna said, noncommittally, 'but what kind of things?' Something scuttled across the edge of the greenery, but disappeared before they could determine its nature. It might have been an errant breeze moving a plant frond, though the air here was inert and stagnant right now.

Actually, the whole planet was, for the most part, stifling, with much of its protective ozone layer punctured by volcanic explosions and toxic chemical reactions from its unstable land masses and destroyed seas. Add to that the effect of the hazy atmosphere, which served to trap and reflect the energy from Vhiliinyar's sun, and the planet's climate was far hotter than it used to be and likely to get worse before it got better. Acorna suspected that the lush greenery before them was a valiant attempt on the part of this world to restore its own much-depleted atmosphere.

A sudden, happy thought occurred to Acorna. This survey might well have positive conse-quences for their ravaged world. The presence of the planet's native people might well speed its efforts to recover, even before Hafiz's terraformation could begin. With so many Linyaari horns available to purify the waters and the air and to cleanse much of the poison inflicted upon Vhiliinyar by the Khleevi, the planet might well heal a little each day they were present, just as a wounded creature would heal with the application of the horn's power.

The Linyaari were superb healers, and their horns could detoxify nearly any substance that they came into contact with. The powers of their horns were not unique to the Linyaari, nor had they originated on Vhiliinyar. They were a legacy from their Ancestors, the *ki-lin* of long ago Terra, often called unicorns. An ancient spacefaring race the Linyaari knew only as the Ancestral Friends had saved the *ki-lin* from primitive and brutal humans who were hunting them to extinction on Terra, and brought them through the cosmos to Vhiliinyar, where they had thrived once again.

Though the *ki-lin* still existed as a separate race, many of them had blended genes with the Ancestral Friends, and the result of that fusion was the Linyaari people. The powers were the same in the Linyaari as in the Ancestors themselves.

But that was all ancient history – this was now, and they were in the midst of a terrible ecological disaster, one that needed all the healing power the Linyaari could muster.

Maati frowned. The caution displayed by all of her friends, right down to RK the cat, in the presence of the lovely greenery before them confused her. Still new to thought-talk, she addressed the silence of the others with a perplexed protest. 'But that forest *is* pretty. And alive! Why aren't the rest of you happier that it's growing things and – and – pretty?'

Aari glowered at her, the first harshness he had shown to his little sister.

Thariinye, picking up on Aari's thoughts, pointed out, (How is she to know what is wrong? She was not born here! She has never been here before. She has nothing but some stories, a few thought-pictures, and Uncle Hafiz's holos to compare it to.)

(True,) Acorna agreed. To Maati she said, 'You remember that place we were in within the holo-bubble, right at the beginning? With the beautiful mountain and the waterfall and lake?'

'Yes. Are we going there tomorrow?'

'We are here now. This is that place,' Acorna told her.

'But – it is so flat,' Maati said, bewildered. She was not at all stupid, but the concept of total terrestrial destruction was a large one to absorb, especially in the presence of the reality of the thing. This rather savage and uncertain 'pretti-ness,' first vestige of life among the ruins of Vhiliinyar though it might be, was a far cry from the deeply spiritual beauty of the mountain with its glorious waterfall and wine-hued lake that she'd seen in Hafiz's holo.

'It's not as flat as it appears. We had to climb quite steeply to land here. And the vegetative growth is no doubt due largely to the residual moisture from the lake. Perhaps not even the Khleevi could destroy it entirely.'

'Its very waters were known to have healing powers akin to those of our horns,' Thariinye said.

'That is clearly no longer the case,' Aari said, with a snort to dislodge the stench of the place – a mix of rotting vegetation and who knew what else – from his nostrils.

'The presence of the plants means that there is water here,' Acorna said. 'We should purify it, but perhaps it would be wise to explore this forest a little at a time at first, until we can analyze just what it consists of, and what pollutants are present in the water and the vegetation.'

Aari nodded. 'There are chemical combinations that could eat right through what we're wearing before we could purify it with our horns. There are even chemicals the Khleevi developed that can eat through Linyaari horns themselves.'

Maati and Thariinye exchanged startled glances. The idea that any chemical could be so strong as to counteract the purifying effects of their horns, and harm the horns themselves, was totally alien to all they knew about their own abilities. And more alien was the thought that such hostile strangeness could exist here, on what had once been the safest place in the universe to be Linyaari.

The pallid sun drooped near the scarred horizon, and Acorna said, 'Let's settle in for the night here. For now, we should perhaps use only the water and food we brought with us from MOO.'

Her opinion was unanimously accepted, and after a quick meal of water and dried grasses, they spread air mats over the rocks and arranged the flitter's attachable awnings as tents over their small campsite.

The flutter of useful activity served to calm Acorna's nerves, which were, if not exactly jangling, at least on red alert. An air of menace pervaded this spot, the very place, however unrecognizable, that had seemed to be the epitome of peace and serenity in Hafiz's holo. At least she wasn't alone in her concern. Aari was alert to the slightest change in air currents, the least nuance of shifting current in the miasma of rot and waste simmering around them.

RK, too, that veteran of a thousand adventures, clearly was displeased with the place. He stayed near the Linyaari, slinking with his belly dragging the rocks, his ears rotating constantly, his whiskers and fur bristling, his upper lips raised above his fangs in a snarling expression that uncovered the scent glands on either side of his muzzle. He looked like a creature from a nightmare.

Maati reached out to stroke him. He allowed the small caress after almost taking off her hand. He rubbed it with his head in apology, but continued to slink and prowl about after she released him.

Thariinye, meanwhile, was lamenting, 'We could have brought our traveling pavilions if the Khleevi hadn't destroyed so many homes on narhii-Vhiliinyar. They would have been much more comfortable than these makeshift shelters.'

'I thought you were the rugged adventurer,' Maati chided, 'used to surviving in the worst possible circumstances with nothing but your wits, never mind a pavilion.'

'These *are* among the worst possible circumstances, would you not agree, Aari? Khornya? Even with these sleeping pads, we are unlikely to find a rock level enough to rest our flanks upon, much less our shoulders. I cannot imagine that any of us will be able to sleep.'

Acorna said, 'Nor can I. So I will take first watch.'

'Watch?' Maati asked. 'Watch *what*? This planet can't sustain sentient life. I thought we'd established that. Well, except for these jungly plants and that scuttling thing and – I guess I see your point.'

'I will watch, also,' Aari said. 'It may be best to do so in pairs for now.'

'I might as well watch with you also,' Thariinye said, 'because I cannot imagine that I will sleep a wink in this place.' But he did, and almost immediately. The sound of his snoring soon filled the air. It was a calming, familiar noise.

Acorna and Aari sat, relaxed, each with one knee drawn up to their chins, each with one leg dangling over the side of the largish rock on which they perched. They gazed toward the jungle growth slightly above them, instead of back in the direction from which they had flown. The leaves and fronds of the strange forest were not outlined black against the night, as they might have expected, but instead glowed in the darkness with a greenish iridescence. A small wind stirred the leaves. Otherwise all was silent.

Acorna almost expected to hear a birdcall, or the snuffle of some smaller creature in the woods around them. Neeva had told her once of the endearing furred creatures that lived in the forests of Vhiliinyar before the Khleevi came – but they were no longer here, and the jungle was nothing but mutated weeds and brush grown very tall. The creatures of old Vhiliinyar sang in lovely voices and delighted all who heard. The grace of their forms entranced all who saw them. Acorna wondered – had *aagroni* Iirtye managed to save specimens of all those creatures, or even samples of their cells to clone them from later on? What a wrenching loss it must be to have known such creatures well, and to lose them, along with all of the other wonders this planet had held when it was beautiful and whole.

Absorbed in her thoughts, it took Acorna a moment to realize she was hearing a noise, a soft snuffling sound, from beside her. Trails of tears ran down Aari's face.

She took his hand. (Penny for your thoughts, or was I broadcasting, and you were responding to mine?)

He sniffed again and turned a chiseled manly countenance to her. (What is a penny?)

(A primitive coin used by one of the nations of humankind before it became so devalued it was not worth the materials needed to create it.)

He gave a short laugh. (Ah, a coin worthy of my present thoughts, indeed. Which are that we would have a better chance of re-forming narhii-Vhiliinyar into a semblance of Vhiliinyar than we have to transform Vhiliinyar to its former state, as the *aagroni* wishes. Who would have thought even the Khleevi could so mutilate the landscape that its own people could not recognize it? I was

37

wondering where the mountains were, where the lake was, and the waterfall. I see nothing here that resembles them.)

(And yet they are here,) Acorna pointed out. (I sense the iron and granite of the mountain, and the plateau – the bones of that formation run beneath us and all through the area. Also the waters of the lake and cascades are here, though there are elements of sulfur and mercury and other contaminants in them. I do not think it will destroy our horns to purify that water. But there is something worrying about those plants . . .)

They heard something then: the thump of paws jumping down and a scattering of small stones beneath soft footpads. Looking in the direction of the sounds, they saw the movement of a dark plumed tail hovering at the edge of the plants. RK, Acorna realized, had decided to relieve himself and he wished to perform his duties unobserved, but he was not happy about the only available cover. The cat emitted grumbling growls and plaintive meows to show what he thought of the feline sanitary facilities available at the campsite. Instead of plunging into the growth, he began to skirt it, his ears still flattened, his tail twitching with frustration, searching for a way to conceal himself without having to actually step between the plants.

Acorna and Aari observed their former shipmate, amused. (We won't watch,) Acorna promised RK.

This produced no visible change in the cat's behavior, but in a moment he disappeared from sight and the Linyaari couple concluded he had found what he was looking for.

Then an earsplitting yowl burst from the greenery several yards to the left of the campsite.

Acorna and Aari jumped to their feet, stumbling over the rocks in the dark. Acorna fell heavily and scraped the skin from her right arm and knee.

Aari turned back to her, his horn lowered to help with the healing, but Acorna waved him on urgently.

(This will keep. See to RK. Help him!) she insisted above the cat's caterwauling as she climbed painfully to her feet. (That does not sound like a cat bellyache to me.)

She brushed her wounded arm over her horn but the cat screamed before she could touch her leg. Her wound could wait. Something was very wrong with RK. She moved as fast as she could toward the noise. Sounds of thrashing and howling, snarling and more shrieks and screams rang through the night as she limped forward to see one of the tall plants whipping a furry tail back and forth in the air. Nothing remained evident of RK but his furious cries and his tail. A huge green bulbous protuberance on the plant concealed the rest of the cat.

Aari leapt for the lashing tail but it whipped out of his grasp.

They had no weapons handy, no implements or utensils that would be useful in destroying the plant. And RK's cries were growing weaker, strangled, more pitiful. They had to do something . . . now!

Acorna grabbed the stalk in both hands and plunged the tip of her horn into it, deeply. Her assault split the stalk. Thus weakened, its top half dropped. Acorna caught the broken plant bulb in her hands, preventing it – and RK – from hitting the rocks.

Thariinye and Maati, awakened by the commotion, joined their friends, which was just as well, since it took the strength of them all to pry open the bulb of the plant from around RK.

First they saw nothing but his tail, then his writhing back end, the legs jerking and claws churning. But the cat's legs and flanks were denuded of fur, and raw looking. They could scarcely bear to look as they pried the rest of the plant loose from the animal.

Digestive acids had caused great burns on poor RK's affected hide. But the cat wouldn't give up the fight. He still had the strength to squirm so hard that it took all four of them to restrain him while pulling him free of the plant.

(We might have known the only living things the Khleevi would leave behind would be carnivorous plants!) Acorna said. Some of the other plants seemed to leer at them in the dark.

They pulled the injured cat back onto the rocks with them, where all four began laying on horns to poor RK's denuded and sore-covered body. His ears were the worst casualties of his adventure, and his nose was deeply burned. The cat choked and coughed, making strangling noises, as his throat swelled.

Naturally, for RK's mouth had been wide open as the cat shrieked his anguish and rage while the plant's digestive juices poured in to make a meal of him. Acorna, as gently as possible, pried the cat's muzzle open and inserted the tip of her horn to heal as much of the damage as she could.

In order for all four well-grown Linyaari to bend over one Makahomian Temple Cat, how-ever large and fierce it was for its species, it required a certain amount of contortion that would have been comical to an outside observer. Acorna squatted down so that she put no pressure on her horn as it healed the cat's mucous membrane, lungs, esophagus, and other internal organs damaged by the juices. Aari rubbed the nub of his still stunted horn gently across the red and weeping stumps of RK's ears. Maati and Thariinye used their horns to close and heal all of the lesions and restore life to the cat's damaged exterior, though Thariinye winced in sympathy as he did so.

As RK's breathing returned to normal and his pulse grew stronger, he began to shiver, and Acorna stripped off her shirt and wrapped it around the cat. 'Even though the night is warm, he's chilling without his fur,' she fussed mater-nally, and felt a brief flash of affectionate amusement from Aari. Handing RK to Maati, who rocked the cat as if he were a baby and crooned to him, she and Aari returned to the plant she had horned. She sank her horn into it again, stabbing it repeatedly, while Aari pulled and tore at it, until they wrenched the top half of the plant free from the rest of its stalk and carried it back to the flitter.

Thariinye had already begun to strike camp.

The Linyaari had needed no thought-talk to be in common accord that they would not remain in this spot for another moment. They were better off in the destroyed stone canyons than here. They needed a less exposed area for RK to finish healing in. Besides, the *aagronis* should have the specimen of the plant they'd found to analyze immediately. It was time to head back to the base camp.

Was the strange plant that had nearly killed RK a mutation of some more benign plant that had once grown on Vhiliinyar? Or was it perhaps an infestation that had been a farewell gift from the Khleevi? Best to have it analyzed while the sample was still fresh.

En route, they tried several times to alert the base camp of their unexpected arrival, but surprisingly could rouse no response on their com unit.

'Why doesn't anyone answer us?' Maati asked the first time their hail was ignored. 'That's funny. I thought Mother said they were going to monitor the com around the clock. Maybe the scientists got their noses into experiments and are ignoring it.'

But their subsequent attempts at communication were also unanswered. Acorna once hailed her aunt's flitter to see if their com unit was functioning. It was – Neeva replied in a sleepy voice. Their party had not tried to reach the base camp and so far their assignment had proven uneventful. Her aunt offered help and shared her concern, even though she tried to sound reassuring.

'I'll try them from here and let you know if we

reach them, Khornya,' Neeva promised. 'Your site is a great deal farther out than many of ours. Perhaps we miscalculated the range of the flitter transmitters?'

But even as the flitter neared the base camp their hails went unanswered.

When they touched down on the site of the former Linyaari graveyard, everything was as still as it had been when the bones of the ancestors were the only inhabitants of the place.

The base camp was dark, the double pavilion provided by House Harakamian for the laboratory silent except for the vague snatches of dreams Acorna caught coming from the inhabitants. Normally Acorna was not able to pick up dreams, but Vhiliinyar was so abnormally quiet, the unguarded thoughts of those who slept were like sharp bursts of song from startled birds.

'They posted no guard,' Aari said. 'Unbelievable.'

(Son! Maati!) His mother woke all at once and sat up on her sleeping pallet. He could see her in his mind's eye, and through him, Acorna saw her, too. (What is it?)

(We need your advice, Mother. A hostile plant attacked RK and nearly devoured him.)

(What sort of plant?) This was the *aagroni*, his thought voice husky with troubled sleep, and brusque with trying to separate what he was hearing from his dreams.

(Not of Linyaari origin that I can tell, *aagroni*.) Aari, the only one of their team to have lived extensively on Vhiliinyar, was the obvious one to answer. (Perhaps it is a mutation?)

43

(Or some Khleevi monstrosity left behind!) the *aagroni* said.

(There is an entire forest of them on our site. We will need to remove some portion of that forest in order to safely examine the area,) Acorna said.

(Not before I've had a chance to study it!) the *aagroni* declared.

(No, of course not, but could you please study RK, too, and perhaps find a way to hasten the regrowth of his fur?) This was from Maati in an aggrieved tone. (He is cold and – embarrassed – without it.)

(Why were we not informed of your arrival?) the *aagroni* asked. (You should have sent word. We are wasting valuable time.) As he said this he was pulling on his robe with one hand and setting up beakers and trays with the other.

(We tried to send a message, but no one was receiving,) Aari informed him with an edge of disapproval, (probably because you were all asleep.)

(Liriili didn't answer? But she was standing sentry, supposed to answer any hails. How often did you try?)

They assured him they had tried often enough that if Liriili had been alert, she would have heard them. It occurred to Acorna that the contrary former administrator might have ignored them simply because she disliked all of them – except that Acorna had been very specific about the carnivorous plant and the terrible injuries to RK. Liriili had an odd partiality for the Makahomian Temple Cat – odd because she liked almost nothing else, not because RK wasn't loveable. The former *viizaar* might well berate Acorna's team for failing to take proper care of the feline, but she would hardly ignore requests to stand by to assist with his emergency treatment.

The mystery of Liriili's absence was temporarily forgotten as the *aagroni* took charge of RK, who, with four Linyaari horns to heal him, was purring madly most of the time, except for growls when he went to lick his furless body. His sudden condition clearly perplexed and upset the cat, and he glared at the anxious faces around him, his expression murderous, as if demanding to know who had made off with his coat. Maati stroked the cat's head with one finger while the *aagroni* analyzed the fur on his tail to see if it could be restored more quickly than nature alone would permit.

The plant specimen commanded the attention of the other scientists.

Acorna, still uneasy, wandered around the laboratory and sleeping quarters, but nowhere did she see Liriili curled up in a corner, neglecting her duties in favor of sleep.

As she left the pavilion, Aari emerged from the cave where he had once taken refuge until rescued by Becker and RK.

(She's not there,) he answered Acorna before she could ask. (It is as if the planet has swallowed her up, Khornya. I know every rock in this area and she is simply not here. I cannot see, hear, smell, or read her. Of all the places on Vhiliinyar, this is the one where I would most feel our people could be safe. And yet . . . she's gone.)

They combed the area around the base camp, continuing to call Liriili with their voices and their thoughts, to sniff for her scent, to listen for an unconscious movement or moan.

Then Acorna suddenly realized they hadn't checked the base camp flitter, which was where the com unit would be. Feeling foolish, she headed for it. Surely not even Liriili would be so inconsiderate as to enter the relative comfort and privacy of the flitter and, while she was supposed to be standing sentry, turn off the com unit so her rest would be undisturbed. But with the ex-*viizaar*, one could never be certain.

As Acorna opened the flitter hatch, she could plainly hear, however, that the com unit was on, and the base camp being hailed.

'Base camp, this is the flitter *wii-Balakiire* (small *Balakiire*). Come in, please.'

Acorna flipped the toggle. 'Melireenya!'

'What's happened, Khornya? We've been trying to raise the base camp for hours. We were so worried we were about to abandon our mission and board the flitter and investigate ourselves. Has some freak storm wiped out the base camp already? Or maybe it was a massive equipment failure that prevented them from responding?'

'Neither,' Acorna answered. 'The base camp is fine, for the most part. Everyone here was asleep. Liriili was in charge of the com unit for the night shift, but she seems to have abandoned her post. None of the scientists have seen her since they retired for bed. We've been looking for her, but wherever she went to avoid her work, it is a good hiding place. We have looked extensively, and as far as we can tell, she isn't in the laboratory or the cave, and we can't find her anywhere in the vicinity. She appears to have vanished.'

'Oh, dear,' Melireenya said. 'Isn't that just like Liriili? She can't even handle a simple task like com duty without causing an uproar. She's our shipmate, and we foisted her on the scientists. I suppose that makes her our responsibility. We'll be en route at once and come to help you search. Normally, I'd guess she just wandered off to avoid working, but if you cannot find her, something might be wrong.'

Acorna, still scanning the area, nodded to the com unit, then realized that it did not actually have a video component. 'That will be fine,' she said. 'We will be glad of the assistance. We should find out what has become of her. If it were anyone but Liriili, I would be frantic. I'm beginning to wonder if the Khleevi haven't left behind a number of nasty booby traps for us.'

'I'm afraid you might be right,' Melireenya said. 'We'll be there as quickly as we can. Now that I think about it, just disappearing without a word or a trace is completely unlike Liriili. She would never be so accommodating.'

Acorna smiled at her aunt's small joke, but was inclined to agree.

TWO

Many hours later Acorna looked at her gathered friends and shook her head. 'I have nothing to report. We can find no trace of Liriili, or of her body. Our infrared sensors pick up no trace of her heat signature, and our DNA scans of the planetary surface are negative. She apparently never left this camp. She can't have been buried in an avalanche, or have fallen into a crevasse, or have been engulfed in a volcanic cataclysm, or been consumed by any unknown lifeforms that might have survived the Khleevi, as traces of her skin or hair or bodily fluids would have been found on any path she would have taken to the areas where those disasters might have occurred. And, though the scientists were sleeping when she vanished, surely they would have heard any mental or vocal calls for help if Liriili had issued them. I believe that, whatever happened to Liriili, it happened with her cooperation, and perhaps at her instigation.'

'Hm,' Miiri, Aari's and Maati's mother said, 'I agree. Knowing Liriili, I think it is far more likely to assume that somehow or other she has left the planet than that she has managed to vanish into thin air as a result of foul play. I do have one possibility to suggest. The equipment we brought for this mission is aimed at detecting objects on or below the planet's surface, not ships overhead. The flitters and shuttles have the standard suite of detection devices, certainly, but our attention has been concentrated here, upon this planet. It is possible that somehow an orbiting ship might have sent down a shuttle and that Liriili boarded it.'

'Why would she do that?' the *aagroni* asked.

'Well, look around you,' Miiri answered, indicating the rough and barren landscape surrounding the makeshift encampment. 'Liriili was not exactly one who liked to do without the amenities. And surely she made *some* friends and contacts while she was *viizaar*. And she *was* in charge of the com unit for the night. Perhaps she hailed a passing, friendly ship whose signal she recognized and begged to be "rescued." I wouldn't put it past her, would you?'

The silence that followed her statement was telling. None of them could say for certain that they could.

'Whatever the explanation for her absence,' Neeva concluded, 'she knows where we are. We will continue to look for her, of course, but it seems unlikely that she has stumbled into trouble out there on Vhiliinyar somewhere. If she is on this planet, she has a camp to return to, a camp that I think she left of her own free will. We can remain alert when flying over the surrounding terrain for traces of her. Meanwhile, we all have a mission to perform, and it will be dark again soon.

We should continue to perform our assigned tasks.'

'I have reported Liriili's disappearance to Council representatives on the Moon of Opportunity, who will relay the message back to those still on narhii-Vhiliinyar,' the *aagroni* said. 'I hardly think they can provide any assistance in this matter, but it is best that they be told of all important developments on this world. I also informed them of the injury to Riidkii – and, for the information of Captain Becker, of Riidkii's recovery.' The *aagroni* gave Roadkill's name its closest Linyaari pronunciation, which was a word with a meaning far dissimilar to the cat's name in Standard Galactic Basic. Whereas Roadkill meant 'Randomly Squashed Formerly Living Being Now Refuse Lying Disregarded on a Thoroughfare,' Riidkii was the Linyaari term meaning 'Noble Protector.' The *aagroni* said RK's Linyaari name as if he believed in the meaning of it, despite the cat's behavior aboard the transport ship.

'I think we had best leave RK with you, *aagroni*,' Acorna said. 'Those carnivorous plants are a terrible threat to smaller beings and he is still healing.'

But Acorna had not discussed this issue with Roadkill, who had his own opinions on the subject. As they climbed into the flitter, the cat bounded out of the laboratory bubble and leaped through the door of their vehicle. The cat settled onto the flitter deck with his tail wrapped around his front paws, planting himself so solidly that it seemed as if a nuclear explosion could not dislodge him.

The cat certainly looked fit enough for the mission. His burns were completely healed and his fur, while a bit shorter than it had been, once more covered his entire body.

Aari laughed. 'I can translate that, Khornya. RK is not going to let any overgrown vegetable keep *him* down. In fact, I think we must be vigilant to ensure he does not attempt to attack the plant when we return.'

'*I* think we had better rig up a cat box so he doesn't have to go near those horrible plants if he needs to relieve himself,' Acorna said, patting the cat.

'What is a *cat box*?' Maati asked, sending out a mental image of a cage with an angry RK trying to rip his way through the bars.

'No, no, that's not it at all. Don't you remember seeing something like this aboard the *Condor*?' Acorna asked, and sent the image of RK's shipboard sanitary facilities.

Thariinye flared his nostrils. 'Oh. That.'

'I have one more piece of news for you,' the *aagroni* said. 'While you were searching for Liriili, we analyzed the plant specimen you sent, and we have manufactured a repellent that seems to work.' The *aagroni* thought for a moment, then continued, 'I believe we will try devolving the plant to its original form to determine whether or not it is a mutation of a species native to Vhiliinyar or if it is something brought to our world in Khleevi spoor. If it is the former, we can simply devolve the plants to their original harmless state prior to terraforming. If it is the latter, the plants will have to be eradicated.'

'Have you considered the possibility that they may be a hybrid of domestic and alien?' Miiri asked.

'Which doesn't matter,' the *aagroni* said dismissively, 'since our options are the same. We would still need to either reverse engineer the DNA to the original parent species native to Vhiliinyar or to eradicate the plant entirely.'

Kaarlye said, 'Yes, and I agree that it must be done before the terraforming process begins. A very aggressive plant, given the stimulation inherent in terraformation, is likely to totally dominate all plant life on the planet once the process is complete.'

'Yes,' Acorna said. 'I can see where that might happen. I can hardly bear to contemplate the results for Vhiliinyar if such a plant is left in its original carnivorous state. In the meantime, we thank you for the repellent. It will be useful for us as we explore our sector.'

'Tell us how it works,' the *aagroni* said. 'My associates worked hard to produce it for you.'

'Very well, we'll keep in touch,' Acorna said.

'Keep in touch with us, too,' Neeva said. 'We're a bit closer to you than base camp if you should have any other trouble.'

'Thank you, Mother-sister,' Acorna said, and with an affectionate embrace, took leave of her aunt and the *Balakiire*'s crew to return to the pilot seat of her own crew's flitter.

They arrived at the weed-ridden site once more

at twilight, but this time set down a bit further away from the plant life. RK permitted his fur to be powdered with the *aagroni's* repellent and did not even try to lick it off. The others made camp once more, using a fire pellet to make a nice open fire. It lent a homey touch to what should have been a homey place, but seemed instead to be hostile to their very existence.

RK snuggled against Maati's side as she fell asleep under one of the thermal blankets. Thariinye also slept. Acorna and Aari had resolved to stay awake. They didn't speak. Instead they sat together listening to the hiss and snap of the fire, and the sounds of the leaves of the carnivorous plants rubbing together – in anticipation of another chance to eat a cat, no doubt. For a long time, Acorna simply sat enjoying the fire's light and the sight of Aari's profile, outlined by the fire and the phosphorescence of the leaves. Then her head slowly drooped, finding a place to rest on Aari's shoulder. Finally, despite her best efforts, her eyes closed and sleep took her . . .

Together they sat quietly on the ledge overlooking the waterfall, watching the waters rush from the mountains to give life to the valley below. He nibbled a few strands of ginger grass, a worried frown creasing his noble brow just around his horn. The white of his star-clad skin was startling in the night, and she longed for the day when her own red-and-golden coloring would soak in the starlight until it, too, was as white as his. Her sister Neeva was already on her first mission.

53

(You know how I feel about you, Ferilii, but they may not allow us to be together: Your parents disapprove of my work.)

(But you devise weapons for our defense, Vaanye. Not weapons at all really – barriers to intrusion. And my parents loathe the idea of intrusion.)

(So do most of our people. I suppose they think that if they just ask hostile aliens nicely to please go away, that will be enough to send them fleeing to their homes. But I have seen things in my travels, Ferilii. Horrible things, sometimes. And I don't want them to touch our world, ever, even if my work means that I am myself alienated from our world because of it.)

The silence stretched out before them as the moon rose above the waterfall, its rays elongating on the great lake that filled the basin at its bottom, gilding the ice of the mountain tops with pearl.

Her heart swelled with courage and love and she reached for his hand, and found it.

(We should wake the others now, love,) Aari's thoughts brushed her mind as softly as a flick of RK's tail. (They should take over the watch. We are exhausted. We need to sleep.)

(Oh! I slept. Aari, I saw my father. I mean, I was my mother. I mean they came to me here. I saw them in my dream.)

His hand stroked her mane back from where her curls had tumbled and tangled with her horn. (Did you, love? That's good. They must have come here when they were young and courting. It was a famous spot for lovers' meetings, I think. I'm glad your dream was a happy and peaceful one. Let us turn our duties over to Maati and

Thariinye, and perhaps you'll find your parents again in your dreams.)

(I hope so,) she said.

But Acorna had no more dreams during the rest of the night. It was a quiet one, with none of the alarms and emergencies that had marred their last stay at this place. Even Roadkill stayed out of trouble, using his new commode when the occasion arose, disappointing the plants.

In the morning, the four Linyaari, machetes and toporecorders in hand, and their cat, his claws and fangs ready for trouble, began to survey the area.

As cold as the night had been, the day was hot. The thin atmosphere made for extreme temperatures in both directions and the plant cover seemed to emit heat of its own as the day drew on. The plants also emitted something else, something that made all of the Linyaari itch. In the end, they controlled their reaction by healing each other with their horns periodically. RK was not so troubled. When he accidentally brushed against one of the carnivorous plants and felt it shrink from him, he amused himself by charging it, clawing its stem, and peeing on its roots. If his smug expression was any indication, he enjoyed the process mightily.

The tasks they were engaged in were tedious, the whole process of the survey was slow going, and being where they were was depressing because of all of the associations the Linyaari had with this place. To see it in its present state and contrast that with what had once been there was heartbreaking.

*

'We used to swim in the lake,' Aari said. 'Laarye and I would jump from the ledge at the top of the waterfall and dive into the pool at its base. It terrified my parents when we did that. We'd have big parties there – here.'

'I think we're about in the middle of where the lake once was now,' Acorna told him. She was shin-deep in some sort of itchy slime she hoped, for everybody's sake but especially RK's, was not terribly toxic. The cat was sulking a short way away, pretending to bask in the sun and sending resentful looks toward Maati, upon whose shoulders he had been riding until the girl shooed him away with an unusual show of irritability. The cat, even with his coat grown back to only half its length, was an uncomfortable neckpiece to wear in the heat of the days here. This place was right on the equator of Vhiliinyar, even though their altitude saved them from some of the worst effects. Acorna pitied the teams at the lower elevations who would be getting the worst of the heat. They were suffering enough right here.

At least it would cool off later. During the cool nights they'd spent in this place, the stars had shone brightly in the thin atmosphere, and the bright sphere of the Moon of Opportunity had reflected the glory of Vhiliinyar's sun with a comforting glow. It had seemed a remarkably stable and benevolent beacon compared to the planet's volatile surface.

Just as Acorna thought that, the ground rumbled and trembled beneath their feet and suddenly a great jet of water burst from the

56

surface into the air, spewing the smell of rotten eggs into the skies along with thousands of gallons of yellowish water. All around them, including from one nasty vent just under Acorna's feet – feet which she had to shift in a hurry – smaller eruptions imitated the large one, as the earth suddenly boiled with scalding hot mud and water.

Suddenly there was a cat-colored blur as RK streaked back toward the flitter.

The Linyaari didn't even stop to think. RK clearly had the right idea. They took off after their cat, moving as fast as they could through the unstable ground. Suddenly Thariinye cried out. They turned around to see that he had become much shorter – or rather he appeared to have done so. A closer look revealed that he had sunk into the ground, and his struggles were only sinking him faster. By the time they'd all worked their way over to him – carefully – he was already in up to his waist.

'Quit moving so much. You are just making it worse. Spread yourself out,' Acorna told him. 'Try to float on your back.'

(What do you think I was *trying* to do?) he asked, with an insulted feeling in the thought.

(It is just quicksand,) Aari said, kneeling within about three yards of Thariinye's foot.

'What's that?' Maati asked.

'What he is sinking in, apparently,' Acorna replied.

'Yes, you find these sorts of things on developing worlds,' Aari said. 'The carnivorous plants, the geysers, bogs, sudden caves, quakes and volcanic eruptions. Very common. Just unsettling to see them where home used to be. But still, we're used to challenges. We'll get through this in the end. But for right now, we'd best get him out of there.'

'Yes,' Maati said. 'The poor planet is polluted enough.'

Thariinye stuck out his tongue at her. It was instantly coated with grit that made him spit and sputter and thrash about and start to sink. Maati smiled at him smugly.

'Careful,' Aari said, 'Thariinye, you just keep your head and keep calm. And right now that means keeping your tongue where it belongs – in your closed mouth. I have a plan. Hold out your hands, Thariinye. Khornya, I will hold onto your knees if you can stretch forward, reach out, and pull him to us.'

'I don't think she can reach that far,' Maati said. 'But I have an idea.'

'What?'

She looked up at the stalks of the carnivorous plants surrounding the pool. Very carefully, she used a fallen branch to bend one down and maneuver it toward Thariinye. The plant folded and unfolded its petals a couple of times and sent a green shoot of a tendril growing, snakelike, toward Thariinye. The green stem latched onto his hand and pulled.

'I figured that the liquid in the sand washed off his killer plant repellent,' Maati said with rather ghoulish satisfaction. 'And since the plant knows lunch when it sees it . . .'

'You sadistic little brat, I'll get you for this!'

Thariinye threatened, beginning to flail again, resisting the gentle pull of the plant-predator.

'Shush, Thariinye,' Acorna told him. 'She's right. It's working. Don't just stand there, Maati. Help us haul on the stalk and pull him to shore before the plant starts digesting him wholesale.'

There was little chance of that, unless the plant had a taste for the various synthetic materials from which Thariinye's shipsuit and gloves were manufactured. In any case, the plant never got a chance to find out whether it liked synthetics. Aari plucked the younger Linyaari from the bog and the plant's grasp at the same time.

Their group returned to the flitter to find RK washing his fur in the sun and looking at them, especially Thariinye, with a disdain that suggested they might need baths, too.

They built another bonfire before following the cat's advice. After they'd cleaned off the worst of the grunge covering them, Thariinye, covered to his calf curls in a metallic blanket, washed his shipsuit off and laid it near the fire to dry.

'I will take watch tonight,' he said. 'I might as well stay awake while my clothes and I dry off.' They left him staring moodily into the fire, while his shipsuit steamed in the cool night air.

In the morning the sky was a cauldron of curdled yellow-green clouds, occasionally extruding tentacles of brownish funnel-shaped whirlwinds toward the ground.

Despite the weather, they had a job to do, and a limited amount of time in which to accomplish it. They headed out to work on the survey, casting wary eyes at the angry sky.

That day they saw nothing of the Harakamian vessels, staffed with Linyaari, which regularly overflew the planet on aerial mapping expeditions. They heard from them, though. Periodically these crews would ask for descriptions of the terrain at such and such coordinates and Acorna's team and the other Linyaari teams responded with both verbal descriptions and uploads from their toporecorders if they had the information requested.

That afternoon, Acorna heard in thought-talk that Aarkiiyi's flitter had been caught in one of the whirlwinds, then dropped and smashed many miles away. This was not a good day to be airborne.

They waited anxiously for a report from the Linyaari survey team nearest the crash site, hoping that despite the crash, Aarkiiyi and his team would be all right. It was the first crew loss they'd suffered on this mission, other than Liriili, and there was some question as to whether that was a loss or merely desertion. No one had seen any sign of Liriili at all, even though all crews had been instructed to keep an eye out for her.

Acorna wondered if the former *viizaar* had somehow escaped the base camp undetected that first night, and was now lost in the wilderness of this harsh planet in the storm. As she and her team retired for the evening back at their little camp, Acorna could not escape the feeling that something was wrong. She shivered in her blanket as she dreamed of Liriili calling for her people to find her. Awakened by the image, she listened intently, but heard nothing. She snuggled closer to the shelter of Aari's body for comfort and fell asleep again.

THREE

During the second week of the mission, Acorna's survey party had visitors.

A flitter set down a short distance from their own and two Linyaari elders stepped out. Acorna didn't recognize either of them, but Maati did.

'Maarni, Yiitir!' she squealed, and ran back through the partially destroyed shrubbery to join them. '*You* came!'

'Ah. Yes. Yes, we did,' said the male, whose mane was a bit less luxuriant between the ears than average, and whose stray chin whiskers were forming a long thin beard that bespoke considerable age. 'Us and an entire great *herd* of others, all whinnying and complaining and thinking so loudly we couldn't hear *ourselves* think.' His grumbling was completely belied by the twinkle in his eyes and his wide grin as he held out his arms and said, 'Young Maati, my goodness, child, what a treat to see you again! And in such illustrious company. And I don't mean you, Thariinye, you scamp. But the most talked-of couple in Linyaari current events as well, Khornya and Aari. You young people *must* tell me the real stories of your lives, you know. You owe it to posterity.'

Acorna must have looked puzzled, because the female of the pair gave her mate a swat on the bicep and said, 'You should introduce yourself, Yiitir, on they'll think you're nothing but a nosy old blowhard.'

'But, my dear, as you well know, I *am* a nosy old blowhard,' he protested.

'Yes, but you are a very distinguished and eminent nosy old blowhard, entrusted with the task of being chief keeper of the stories of our people.'

'She means I teach history at the academy, my dears,' Yiitir told the others.

'He's a great teacher, too,' Maati said. 'Everyone says he's brilliant. Grandam always said if the Council had paid heed to Yiitir when the Khleevi were first spotted in Vhiliinyar's vicinity, we'd have had a defense ready. He knows all about great space battles and things.'

'Quite bloodthirsty for a member of the gentle sex of a pacifist people, isn't she?' Yiitir said, looking down beneath his scraggly brows at Maati. 'Always did say she was a splendid child.' He turned to Maarni. 'Put that down in the biography along with my other deathless utterances, will you, m'dear? Yiitir always said that Maati was a splendid child. That way perhaps the Council will remember and consult her before appointing an idiot like Liriili as *viizaar* again.'

Maarni shook her head and rolled her eyes. 'It's completely gone to his head that the Council has suggested he write his own memoirs as well as the volumes he's already written on the history of our people. By the way, that's why we're here. In case you have any questions about Vhiliinyar as it once was.'

'Maarni is as much an expert on the unwritten stories of our people as Yiitir is on those that have been documented, or that occurred within his lifetime so that he can document them,' Maati told Acorna.

'And I'm nearly as old as Grandam was,' Yiitir said. 'So that's a great long time that I've been paying attention to what happens. Maarni is my child bride but she has more imagination than I, and loves a good story. That's how I caught her, you see.'

'Bored me into a stupor with a great long saga about the interclan trade wars and took advantage of me while I was unable to defend myself,' Maarni laughed, patting her lifemate's arm affectionately. 'Now then, can we do something of the sort for you? How are you faring with this – this – oh, dear, it's really rather a horrible tangle, isn't it?'

'Thought you'd never notice, my dear,' Yiitir said softly.

Aari said to Yiitir gravely and with considerable respect, 'This was the Vriiniia Watiir, Elder Yiitir.'

'Quite a mess they've made of it,' Yiitir said. 'But then, I suppose that's what we're all here for, isn't it? To clean up the mess? No sense standing about weeping over dried waterfalls when, with a bit of elbow grease and application of proper knowledge, we can help put everything right again, eh, my dear?'

'As you say,' Maarni said, her shrewd blue eyes

under tight curls of mane grimly surveying the landscape as a general might the bloody aftermath of a battle. 'Puts me in mind of when our twins were little and we returned to our pavilion after a day at work. Well, perhaps that's giving the Khleevi too much credit. Our twins were very innovative younglings.'

Maarni and Yiitir soon dug in and made themselves useful. Far from interrupting the work, the newcomers made it go much faster, and when Acorna showed them the approximate position of the falls, the mountain, and the pool, they began recalling other well-loved features of the area and asking if she knew yet where they might be. The trained memories of the two historians brought the dream of restoring Vhiliinyar to its original state much closer to realization.

Even the smallest of their recollections was useful. It was of great help when Maarni suddenly recalled that she used to enjoy diving for agates and garnets in the lake to use in her jewelry crafting and bead-making. Acorna was able to locate deposits of the minerals usually containing those stones several yards from where she had thought the boundaries of the lake had been – just where Maarni had indicated they occurred. That reinforced everyone's confidence in Acorna's mapping.

After another hard day's work, they shared an evening meal back at the flitter. They had all been so busy imagining the area as it had been before the Khleevi came that Acorna almost saw it that way now. Now she had the memories of the Linyaari Elders, very strong and vivid memories, in addition to her own recollection of how the falls had looked in Hafiz's holo. Though that, too, echoed in her dreams.

'Do you know the story of how the Vriiniia Watiir came to be?' Maarni asked, when they had finished grazing from their hands on the sweet grass Maarni and Yiitir had brought from the hydroponics gardens on MOO. It was a bit stale already, but a welcome change from the dried grasses they had with them. The problem with their usual diet was that the grasses didn't retain flavor all that well. One could freeze or dry them, and survive on the nutrients they contained, but it simply wasn't the same as grazing.

'The origin of the lake? I've heard some stories,' Aari said.

Maati said, 'Wasn't everything pretty much the way it was in the holos when the Ancestors arrived?'

But Thariinye said, 'No. It wasn't. The lake's beginning had something to do with lust, didn't it? Back in the bad old days, before everyone had evolved into the thoroughly superior moral beings we are today, of course.'

Yiitir gave Thariinye an approving glimmer from under his brows but said nothing. This was Maarni's area of expertise and Acorna suspected that even her eminent husband stole her thunder at his own peril.

'My, so many questions to answer at once,' Maarni said, gathering their attention as she might gather flowers for a banquet. 'Let me see. Maati, my dear, things have not always been as they were in the holos any more than they are now. Worlds always change. If people don't change them, planets rearrange themselves. Scientists can call it laws of entropy, or chaos theory, or whatever they will. *I* suspect planets change because they grow weary of always looking the same, and they find a good catastrophe a cure for boredom. Such change does make life quite interesting indeed for any lifeforms living on the surface of a planet at the time one of these makeovers occurs.'

Maati giggled. 'When they change, do the planets then admire themselves using other planets' oceans for mirrors?'

Maarni looked at her in surprise. 'Why, I shouldn't doubt it at all! That must be how they do it. Perhaps you should go into my line of work, with a mind that generates such images. Anyway, as Thariinye so shrewdly pointed out, we were not always as we are now. In the times before time as we know it there were no Linyaari. There were only those of the race we call the Ancestral Friends and there were, after the Rescue, the Ancestors here on the face of this planet along with the plants and all of the creatures unable to share their mind's thoughts. About this time we have only the stories the Ancestors handed down to us, and much speculation. None of the Ancestors alive today were alive then, nor were their dams or sires, or their dams or sires for many generations back.

'So if what I say now shocks you, Maati, for I know that Grandam took a very positive tone in her interpretations of our stories, please bear in mind that the People were Becoming back then, that they were finding their way, and that although they knew many things, they did not know then, any more than most people know now, how to treat their fellow beings.

'The Friends rescued the Ancestors from Old Terra. Perhaps they felt compassion for the Ancestors' plight on their home world, it is true, but it also said by some that the Friends had other reasons, or developed other reasons after the Rescue, for wishing the Ancestors to live near them. The Friends, you see, found our Ancestors very beautiful and they – *yearned* for them.'

'How?' Maati asked. 'They were different species, weren't they? Surely the Friends were anthropoid so that the mix between them and the friends produced – us. Oh, I see. It did produce us. So. Yes. The Friends yearned for the Ancestors. So what you're saying is that we came to be for other than purely scientific reasons?'

'Yes. The Friends loved the Ancestors and yearned for them. And the Ancestors in those days were different from the precious ones still among us today. They were four-legged as they are now, true, and looked very much the same, but their temperaments were different in those days. Wild and fierce, intelligent and capable of learning, but not very learned, and very strong-willed and stubborn.

'The Ancestors were very grateful to the Friends for the Rescue and looked upon them as protectors, but still they remained wary. They had been hunted nearly to extinction back on their home world, and trust came very hard to them.

'One Friend in particular conceived a great

passion for a particularly lovely Ancestor and followed her everywhere. She became alarmed and afraid of his ardor and one day, when she saw him, began running very fast, until she came to the edge of a great cliff. She was fleet of foot and nimble and turned aside quickly but the Friend went tumbling over the edge to his death on the rocks below. The Ancestor, with great remorse, began to weep, and her weeping became a great torrent that flowed over the cliff and formed the waterfall and lake. There used to be a rock formation at the bottom of the lake, we were told, that was actually the petrified remains of the hapless Friend.'

'Oh, dear,' Acorna said.

'Hmm,' Maati said, 'I never heard that one. But then, Grandam didn't like to tell stories of Vhiliinyar all that often – not the old stories anyway. It made her sad. I guess it affected a lot of the People that way.'

'That is unfortunately true,' Maarni said. 'Some of the oldest stories have never been recorded – too fragmented, too many versions, too unsubstantiated to pass on officially, I suppose. They're my personal favorites, however. I love to think about how to fill in the gaps in the information provided.'

The conversation around the campfire wound down as the night lengthened and their exhaustion caught up with them.

But before they slept, they called back to the base camp to see if there was news of Aarkiiyi and his crew, or of Liriili, but were told there was nothing.

That was disquieting. Maarni and Yiitir slept near them that night. Nobody wanted to be out of sight of the others, and they stood watch in pairs.

About two hours before dawn, their com unit crackled to life.

'Mayday. Mayday. This is the *wii-Balakiire*. We have a missing person in our sector. Fiirki Miilkar, the animal specialist, visited our site today and was staying the night here. He offered to stand the first watch. When the next watch came to relieve him, Fiirki was nowhere to be found. We heard no outcry from him during his watch, nor have we found any sign of foul play. But he has disappeared without a trace and all our attempts to find him have failed utterly. All crews, please be alert for any sign of him. Base camp, please advise.'

'This is base camp, *wii-Balakiire*,' said a voice Acorna identified as Aari's father, Kaarlye. 'Does this incident appear to you to be similar to the disappearance of Liriili?'

'Oh, no, Kaarlye,' Melireenya said. 'Fiirki is a very useful and respected expert on the evolution and habitats of Vhiliinyari creatures. He is not at all the sort of person to just wander off, although anyone can have a call of nature. He would never desert his post. If he is missing, it is because something happened to him, something he could not prevent or escape.'

'Perhaps Maarni and I should flitter over there and help them look for him, eh?' Yiitir suggested to Kaarlye. 'Of course, we won't see much in the dark, but we might pick him up on the infrared. Melireenya, could you use the assistance?'

'Oh, yes. We would be so thankful,' she replied.

'Sounds like a plan,' Kaarlye agreed. 'Keep us notified if there is any change to the situation, please.'

'Oh, that goes without saying,' Yiitir said in an airy tone that belied the grave expression he wore.

When he had signed off, Acorna said softly, 'We should come and help, too.'

'Nonsense, m'dear, no sense everyone rushing in. A crowd of hunters is more likely to obscure whatever sign of him there is; that is, if he's truly lost. You know how it is with these scientists, especially those who pursue the natural sciences. Get so involved in finding a special sort of fern or some such thing that they quite forget where they are. I'm sure he's fine. Besides, he's on your team, you know. Second wave. You've important work to do right here.'

'True enough,' Acorna said. 'But please let us know what you find out as well. When you find him, I mean.'

'Certainly, my dear Khornya,' Maarni said, laying a hand on Acorna's arm. 'In fact, we would very much like to return and speak with you further. You represent not only the youngest survey crew, but also have special knowledge among you – Aari knows more about the transition of this planet than any other living Linyaari, and you, thanks to your unusual upbringing, bring almost a totally alien viewpoint to our world that will provide a fresh perspective. Young Maati is heir to the greatest number of Grandam's stories of any of us. If you will permit it, we wish to spend quite a lot of time with you all.'

71

'And me?' Thariinye said.

'I'm sure you'll be a quick learner,' Yiitir said with a closed grin.

Thariinye's face fell for a moment, then he grinned back, showing plenty of teeth. Yiitir looked mildly alarmed, since showing one's teeth was a sign of hostility among the Linyaari.

'Just joking,' said Thariinye. 'When you're around people who have been raised by humans, as Khornya has, showing one's teeth can be taken as joviality and courtesy. Sometimes it's fun to confuse people.'

Yiitir did not appear to hear him, however, for the historian and his lifemate were already starting their flitter.

FOUR

Neither Acorna nor anyone else on her team got much sleep that night. They were too busy worrying. As soon as the sun shed its murky light over the landscape again, they resumed their explorations.

Maati was the one who found the artifact – the hard way. 'Ouch!' she cried, hopping around while trying to hold onto her foot.

'Maati, what's the matter?' Acorna asked. She quickly ran to the girl and knelt beside her, applying her horn to Maati's bruised flesh. The source of the bruise, an oblong piece of a hard black substance, protruded from the soil.

'That thing!' Maati pointed. 'It attacked me.'

'She means she stubbed her foot on it,' Thariinye said.

Acorna began digging the object from the ground. As she ran her hands along it, dislodging the dirt and plant life twined around it, she noted – much to her surprise – that it was not a natural rock. Nor did she recognize it as an artifact of Linyaari design – though she was hardly an expert.

'Can anyone tell me what this might be?' she

asked. 'It's definitely manufactured – see, how smooth and even it is in texture and thickness?'

Thariinye shrugged. 'Could be a broken bit of anything – a wrecked flitter, a piece of a pavilion support.'

Aari joined them and Acorna handed him her find.

'No, that's nothing I've ever seen from our people,' he said.

'Oh, come now,' Thariinye said. 'How can you be so sure on such a short examination? Maybe it's a piece of one of the off-world items the techno-artisans were working with before the planet was overrun.'

'No,' Aari shook his head, his mane flying up from his neck and shoulders and tossing in the wind. 'The techno-artisans took as many of their projects with them as possible and I am familiar with the things we were working on at the time we were invaded. This *is* natural to some extent, Khornya. It is a substance formed by the skeletons of small dead sea creatures. But it has been shaped intentionally by sentient hands.'

Maati leaned forward and touched the thing with a fingertip. 'There's something on the surface – it's very light, but it's there. Don't you see it?'

'Those are just the random marks made by passing fish or erosion,' Thariinye said, glancing at it.

'No, absolutely not,' Maati said. 'See, some of these marks are exactly the same. The designs are repeated.'

Acorna examined it more closely. 'Yes, yes,

they are, Maati. And here's another pair, and another. These ones look vaguely familiar. I think I have seen them somewhat larger, somewhere on narhii-Vhiliinyar.'

'That's *not* Linyaari,' Thariinye said emphatically. 'Maybe it's Khleevi. A fragment from one of their craft.'

'Their craft were all intact,' Aari said bitterly. 'As far as I could tell each and every one flew away from this place under its own power without so much as a scratch on it. Not one suffered by Linyaari hands.'

'Oh. Uh – true – true,' Thariinye agreed. He had come to like Aari and secretly regarded him with something close to hero-worship.

'I have seen something similar before as well, *yaazi*,' he told Acorna. 'This mark,' he indicated a lightly etched design that reminded Acorna of a stylized sun with long rays.

'And this one,' he said, pointing to a swirl with a hook on the end.

'Are they – Khleevi, Aari?' Maati asked.

'I don't know. I don't *think* so.'

'It does seem to be an artifact or a document or a sign of some sort,' Acorna said. 'It's covered with these symbols. Well, bag it and take it with us. As soon as we get to camp, we should consult with Yiitir and Maarni and base camp about it. Maybe someone will recognize it.'

They continued working, cataloging with an electronic tabulator all the various forms of plant life and minerals they came across.

When Maarni and Yiitir returned from helping Melireenya's survey crew search for the missing

Linyaari scientist, they had no news to report. The man was still missing, with no explanation for his absence. Still, the return of their friends was a welcome break for the four younger Linyaari, who showed them the artifact.

'Ahhh,' Yiitir said.

'You know what it is, then?' Acorna asked.

'No. But I sounded very much as if I did, didn't I?' Yiitir's eyes sparkled with good humor.

Maarni took the stone from him and examined it minutely, but her 'aaaahhhs,' and 'ummms,' and 'Oh, I sees,' were genuine.

'I can't be entirely sure without corroboration,' she said, 'but I believe this may be from the ancient culture of the *sii*-Linyaari.'

'Who?' all four asked at once.

'Another early race on this planet, also developed by the Friends. They were much like us,' she said. 'Except that they evolved into aquatic beings instead of two-leggeds who walk on land, as we do. This swirl here? The one that forms a row from smallest to largest all curling the same direction? That denotes the white spume of the waves of the sea, which were said to be the manes of the *sii*-Linyaari.'

'I never heard of them,' Aari said.

'Me, neither,' Thariinye agreed.

'The Ancestors don't speak of them much, although my understanding is that they were as much the descendants of the Ancestors as we are.'

'Grandam mentioned them once in passing, when she was telling a story,' Maati said. 'But when I asked about them, she said it had nothing more to do with the story and not to distract her.'

'That doesn't sound like Grandam,' Acorna said, mildly surprised. The eldest of Linyaari Elders had taken Acorna under her wing when Acorna first arrived on narhii-Vhiliinyar. Grandam was the only one willing to tell Acorna about parts of Linyaari society nobody else would speak of.

'There are overtones of something a bit shameful about them,' Maarni said. 'But they were long gone by the time the Khleevi came – the Ancestors say they vanished into thin air one day, or so their Elders told them. Though, in ancient times, from some of the stories I've heard, the seas were teeming with them.'

'Can you read their language?' Acorna asked, nodding at the long black artifact in Maarni's hands.

'I could probably translate it, with a little help. I'm afraid that many of the books and computer files that would have helped me were lost in the Khleevi attack. But I'll see what I can do.'

Thariinye had lost interest. 'So, tell us about hunting for the missing person.'

'Not much to tell,' Maarni told him. 'It was the same as with Liriili.'

'Hmph, not at all,' Yiitir said. 'Fiirki was respected and useful. *He* is much missed.'

Acorna was puzzled. How could Fiirki vanish so completely? All Linyaari except the very young were telepathic. Every Linyaari on this planet was able to hear and broadcast thought-voices. Surely any Linyaari in difficulties would send out a mental cry – just as Thariinye had done when he'd gotten stuck in the quicksand. Those mental cries for help would be heard by the nearby crews, if not by those farther away. Liriili's mental powers were somewhat less powerful than most other Linyaari, but mostly because being able to read minds had never endowed her with empathy for her fellow beings. But Fiirki surely would have the same abilities as most Linyaari.

'Has no one heard Fiirki's thoughts calling out?' she asked.

'No, apparently not.'

'But that's very strange, isn't it? My experience with Linyaari thought-speak is that we can sometimes, especially under emergency circumstances, read each other across great distances – even across the vastness of space.'

'Perhaps Liriili and Fiirki are no longer able to send their thoughts,' Maarni suggested.

'You mean they might be dead?' Thariinye asked.

'Possibly. This is a dangerous place since the Khleevi destroyed it. Or they might be unconscious,' Maati said.

'We should still be able to get a reading, even if they weren't conscious,' Aari said.

'Well,' Acorna said. 'It is clear our usual methods of locating the lost don't work on this planet. Just as a fail-safe, I think we should ask Uncle Hafiz to send us down some personnel locators that my human friends use in times like these – the tiny ones that send out constant signals. That way, if someone else disappears, we will have a backup means of communicating our position to rescue parties, regardless of whether we are conscious or not.'

'That is a very good idea,' Maarni agreed. 'I think it might also be a good idea for those of us on the survey teams to avoid being alone at any time – we should always be paired when we are apart from the main group. That way, if one person is unable to call for help, the other one will perhaps be able to take action or call for assistance.'

'I suggest Acorna goes to communicate that to the base camp right now, my dear,' Yiitir said. 'In the meantime, we will take our own advice, heh?'

So Maarni, Yiitir, Maati, and Aari continued their examination of the artifact while Thariinye and RK accompanied Acorna back to the flitter.

Before long Acorna was on a relay from the base camp to MOO, where an unexpected and familiar voice greeted her. 'Hey, Princess, it's me, Becker. I heard that the cat met something that eats even worse stuff than he will.'

Acorna had to smile. These borrowed flitters had no vid screens, but she could imagine Becker's bristling mustache and – in spite of his words – the worried expression in the back of his twinkling brown eyes. 'Your concern is most touching, Captain. I will convey it to your first mate, who now looks completely recovered, and is purring beside me as we speak. Ah yes, he understood your message. He is lifting his leg to cleanse his rump.'

Becker chuckled. 'That's my boy. What can we do for you?'

'When did you become the communications technician for the Moon of Opportunity, Captain? Have you run out of salvage?'

'Oh, no, I just brought a load in. Hafiz had arranged to have some buyers look over the goods when I showed up. They wanted me to send an inventory before they bothered to come all this way, so I came in to send them a message that I sold the salvage already.'

'Did you?' Acorna asked, as she could tell he wanted her to. Most of the time, it didn't require telepathic powers to know what cue Becker wanted you to take.

'Not yet. But I will. These guys are clowns. I don't think your ol' unk really understands the salvage business, Princess. He thinks it's just junk, so he thought he was helping me out when he asked these bozo buddies of his to take it off my hands. Cost me a trip to the MOO for nothing, except I think I may be able to supply one of his architects with a few odds and ends for the Linyaari pavilions.'

'I'm sure you will manage to prosper, Captain, despite my uncle's interference. It's very good to speak with you. As a matter of fact, I was calling to ask Uncle Hafiz if he would send down some personnel locators to Vhiliinyar. We seem to have mislaid two of the people who landed here.' She explained why she thought the locators might be useful.

'Well, don't that beat all? Liriili is missing and that other guy, too? Princess, Liriili can't still be on the planet. You can hear that woman grousing three solar systems away whenever she's conscious. If you can't find her, she ain't there.'

'Maybe not, Captain, but there is another person missing as well, and we cannot hear thought-talk from either of them. We need enough locators for every person here. Uncle Hafiz has the records from our expedition, so he will know the quantity of receivers to send. Do you think that can be managed?'

'I think if you think it's necessary, old Hafiz will make it so. He dotes on you, Princess. But it'll be better if you explain it to him yourself. Let me patch you through to his mobile unit. And – Princess?'

'Yes, Captain?'

'Look, in case there's some bogeyman or Khleevi scum left there kidnapping Linyaari, don't you take any chances. Mac has a few tricks that even some of your folks don't, as you know. You want me to send him down to help?'

'No, Captain, you *need* Mac to help you with the salvage.'

'Not really. I got whole messes of brawny young stallions wanting to show off their muscles to the Linyaari ladies by helping me out. And – I think Mac misses you. I'd feel better if he was there looking out for you and Aari and the little girl.'

'That's very kind, Captain. I think it best, however, if we try to solve this problem ourselves for now. You know how some of the traditional-ists can be about off-world people coming here.'

'Yeah, you'd think we all were Khleevi. But technically speaking, you should pardon the expression, Mac is not a people. Mac is a device. I mean, you and I know he's got a lot more person-ality than say, Liriili, but some folk wouldn't look at it that way.'

81

At that point Hafiz's voice said, 'Acorna, dear girl, how delightful to hear from you! Your scientists at the base camp let us know of the unfortunate disappearances. I certainly hope you are not calling to relate more such news to me?'

'No, but it is related to why I'm calling, Uncle,' Acorna said. Becker made a loud smooching sound into the transmitter and broke his own connection, and she told Hafiz her reason for calling.

Hafiz promised to send the locators at once to as many Linyaari as were on the planet's surface, and also assured her that all future personnel who came to Vhiliinyar would be similarly equipped.

Then Karina came on and said, 'Acorna, darling, be careful, be very careful. My spirit guides tell me there are mysterious forces at work on Vhiliinyar.'

Acorna thought of several things to say to the obviousness of Karina's 'prediction' and was very glad that Karina could not read minds as well as she claimed. Instead, she thanked the Harakamians, asked how her uncles and their wives were and where they were at the moment – all well but off planet – and signed off.

Or tried to. Immediately the light on the console was blinking for her attention again.

Aari's mother's voice said, 'Khornya, we cannot locate Kaarlye or the *aagroni*.'

'Miiri,' Acorna said, 'I'll get Aari and Maati. We will come and help immediately.'

She left the flitter and found Thariinye dozing lightly against the outside hull, RK fast asleep with front paws and chin laid proprietarily across

Thariinye's outstretched leg. There was no need to disturb them right now, of course. She could thought-call the others easily from here.

(Aari? Maati? Come back to the flitter. Your mother wants to speak to you,) she broadcast her thoughts into the late afternoon storm. The tops of the carnivorous plants dipped and bobbed in a freshening wind. The sky was boiling, and jagged bolts of lightning flashed green nearby. There was no rain yet. It was hard for it to rain with the surface water so diminished, Acorna supposed while she waited for her lifemate's answer.

As they terraformed, possibly they would need to bring in water from the outside first, to 'prime the pump' as humans said in some of the old books she had read, the ones about life in the desert.

There was no answer from Aari or from Maati. Acorna told herself to be calm, that they might be preoccupied or conversing with someone else, not receiving. She stepped back into the flitter and said in a carefully level voice, 'Miiri? I'll have them hail you as soon as I can. I know it's hard, but try not to let anyone go look for Kaarlye and the *aagroni* before Hafiz's ship arrives with the personnel locators.'

But the voice that answered was not Miiri's and was, in fact, strange to her.

'Khornya? Miiri said she had to join the search for Kaarlye and the *aagroni*, so I am now communications officer. This is Fiicki. Was there some message you wanted to give Miiri?'

'Fiicki,' she said. 'Try to call the search party back, please. Tell them to wait for personnel locators from the Moon of Opportunity. We must think of the safety of the searchers as well as of trying to find those who are lost. In fact, I may be missing two of my crew now.'

'I'll see if I can find them to tell them, Khornya,' Fiicki agreed, rather nervously. 'No one seems to be around at the moment, though.'

'Call them – with thought-speak,' Acorna suggested. 'Before you leave the building.'

'That's odd,' Fiicki said after a moment in which Acorna followed her own suggestion, calling out for Aari, Maati, Maarni, and Yiitir. She could still see the tip of Thariinye's toe and RK's tail out the flitter window. 'Silence.'

'That's what I'm getting too. Fiicki, there is something very peculiar going on here. Do not leave the com unit under any circumstances until those locators arrive, and call me at once when they do. Meanwhile, patch me through to Hafiz again, please, I am going to awaken the rest of my crew and do an air search for our missing people en route to base camp. No, no,' she said, feeling the panic in the erstwhile communications officer even through the vast distance between them. 'Please don't be overly concerned. Whatever is happening is certainly curious, and cause to investigate. But remember that we have heard no alarm or fear from any of those missing. Whatever is happening, it may not be at all harmful or dangerous. I think we should recall all personnel to base camp, dispense the locators when they arrive, then regroup and redeploy each team in continuous communication with MOO if possible. It's either do that, or evacuate – and personally, I have no plans to leave this place without my family and friends. We *will* find them.'

'I—'

'If you feel differently, then of course you must do as you think best,' she added quickly.

'It's as if they've been swallowed whole,' Fiicki whispered hoarsely, sounding as though he was afraid the very building could hear him. 'I have never felt such – silence, Khornya. Even in space there were the other crew members. Please don't sign off.'

'I won't. Monitor the unit during my hail to Hafiz, but please keep trying to contact the others through thought-speech. And stay at your post – other crews might be trying to call for help, too.'

'I – I will, Khornya. Please don't break the connection.'

She promised she would not. While the patch to MOO was relayed, she opened the flitter door, gave her sleeping shipmates a mental hail, and said to Thariinye, 'Please come aboard now, and bring RK. We are going to base camp.'

'It's not my shift,' he said, yawning. 'Can't a man get any sleep around here? Why do we have to go now? And where are the others?'

'I don't know,' Acorna said. 'Why don't you call them?' She watched his face as he did. His confusion when his queries went unanswered was all too evident.

'Khornya, I don't understand. I hear nothing. No answer, no other thoughts, nothing.'

'Exactly,' she said. 'It happened while you were sleeping and while I was speaking to Captain

85

Becker and Hafiz. Just like that. I remember watching them walk away from the flitter toward the bog and then I became involved in the conversation. Then, just a few moments later, when I tried to call, nothing. They've vanished. It is apparently happening all over. So get in. We will do a quick fly-over where they are supposed to be, and see if we can pick up any clues. I do not expect to find easy solutions. The *aagroni* – and from the sound of it, nearly everyone else at base camp – is gone. And we'll be no help to the people back at MOO or our friends if we find out where the missing persons are only by joining them.'

FIVE

The fly-over of the territory they had been covering on foot for the last few weeks showed no signs of any Linyaari, or of other animal life of any kind.

Acorna flew low and in a zigzag pattern three times, covering the entire area of their study and somewhat beyond those boundaries before she would give up. Yiitir, Maarni, Aari, and Maati were all gone, if she could believe the evidence of her own eyes and the instruments of her flitter. She double-checked to make sure they had not returned to their camp or Yiitir's and Maarni's flitter, but both were sitting as silent and empty as they had been all during her conversations on the com unit.

The weather was not good for flying. Although the flitters, once airborne, had shields to protect them from lightning, the small craft was buffeted by the wind and twice lightning crashed against the shield. The flare of energy was so bright that Acorna was nearly blinded. RK huddled on the deck behind her, and she was sure his fur must be standing at attention all over his body. Thariinye said nothing, but his eyes rolled to the sides a bit, his nostrils flared, and the white of his star-clad skin blanched even further around the knuckles as he held onto the control panel while the flitter dipped and bobbed and took heart-stopping plummets in the storm.

At last they landed at the base camp, leaving the worst of the storm crashing and booming behind them. The large laboratory bubble looked as quiet as the former graveyard upon which it was set.

Night gathered even more rapidly than usual, the storm clouds bunching with other more innocuous ones, bullying the planet's pallid sun into seclusion. Acorna feared that they would find the base camp entirely deserted, but at the sound of the flitter, Fiicki emerged from the lab bubble and pulled the flitter door open before the engines had shut down.

'Khornya! Thariinye, I am so glad to see you! Oooooh, and poor little Riidkii,' Fiicki said, impeding Acorna's exit to reach behind her and scoop up the bristling, growling RK.

'At least *he's* not missing yet,' Thariinye said with a trace of annoyance.

'True, true,' Fiicki said. 'But everyone else is. Please don't leave me alone here again. The silence is enough to distress and depress me – and worse, there are the noises.'

'Noises?' Acorna asked. 'What sort of noises?'

'Underground growlings I hear through my sleeping mat, like the beginning of an earthquake, or a volcano about to erupt or – as if the ground was *digesting* something. Or someone.'

Acorna laid her horn against the side of Fiicki's

head, but since his fear had a reason and was not pathological, it could hardly be cured as if it were a mental illness. He did grow calmer, either because of the effects of her soothing thoughts or because they gave him the reassurance that he was not completely alone.

'Underground noises? Now that's something to consider,' Acorna said thoughtfully. 'I wonder – could there be underground Khleevi installations? Or is this just another sign of Vhiliinyar's unstable geology?' She got on the com unit and began hailing the other crews, asking them if they had any further cases of missing persons or if anyone reported hearing unusual subterranean noises.

It was no surprise, and in fact confirmed her worst fears, when she learned that many more people were missing, several from some crews, one from others, and none from still others. Altogether, in the last afternoon twelve more people had vanished from Vhiliinyar as if they had never been there at all. But no one mentioned underground rumblings other than the usual ones, which seemed to be related to volcanic eruptions.

When she reached MOO and gave her report of what had happened, Hafiz said, 'You must evacuate at once.'

'What about our mission here?' she asked, because she knew none of the others back on MOO would. 'What about our friends?'

'There is no wisdom in reviving a planet to house a race that becomes extinct in the effort,' Hafiz said.

'That's true,' Acorna said, 'and I think it would be smart to evacuate most of the crews and all nonessential personnel, but I believe I can discover what is happening. I want to stay here, Uncle Hafiz. I need to find Aari and Maati and the others. I have no evidence to give you at all, but I can't believe they're dead. They're simply – not here. If they were dead, or even in terrible, terrible trouble, I'd know that. Even if I didn't pick up actual thoughts, I'd be feeling *something* if I'd lost them. I feel nothing but the certainty that I can find them if I continue to look.'

Hafiz, wily old merchant that he was, said reasonably, 'Of course, of course, my dear Acorna, I understand completely how you feel and you may certainly stay behind to look to your heart's content and the blessings of the Three Prophets and the Three Books be upon you. But only on one condition.'

'What is that?' she asked, sounding vague and distant, even to herself.

'That you promise on the lives of my nephew Rafik, his ugly first wife, and Giloglie that you will not yourself become lost.'

'I cannot promise that,' she said. 'In fact, being – lost – taken, whatever happened to them – myself, may be the only way to find them.'

'You are far too precious to risk on a maybe, my dear sweet Acorna. Come now, for once listen to the wisdom of your elders, and return with the others while you are able. We will not abandon your friends and loved ones. Once you are here, we will form a plan to search for them, using all the considerable resources at my command.

But – please – leave before you vanish with the others. When all have had a chance to compare impressions without disappearing in the next instant as if at the will of some evil djinn, when from this you have gained perhaps insight, formed an idea that may have some outcome other than the sacrifice of yourself, done perhaps some research into this matter, then shall you return with all of the assistance it is within my power to give you.'

Acorna's protestations that meanwhile her loved ones could be in deeper peril were met with a philosophical, 'If it is God's will, they will survive until we can assist them. It is my will that you now put your head before your heart in this matter.'

She knew he was right, but leaving Vhiliinyar behind was the most difficult thing she had ever done. When they had arrived on this planet, she had finally been part of a real Linyaari family – her lifemate, his parents and sister, her aunt and crewmates. Now, all of them were suddenly gone as if they had never existed and she was alone again.

The enormity of it was completely unreal to her. She could not grasp it, and did not want to. Despite what she'd told Hafiz, she felt no fear for her companions, because she could not feel the truth of it at all. The people she loved couldn't possibly be *gone*. They weren't lost forever – or surely they would have broadcast some kind of distress call that she could have heard. There had to be some explanation for their absence. Perhaps they all were suddenly taken on a voyage off-planet together, and were waiting for her elsewhere. Her feelings were leading her thinking, she knew, but she realized that she had often gone with her gut feeling in solving problems. She just didn't have any idea how to proceed in this case. So, even though she hated to leave Vhiliinyar, Hafiz's counsel was good. It was time to hold a planning council and decide what to do next.

Neeva and Melireenya were among the missing, though Kaari and Hrronye remained to bring the *Balakiire* back to base camp. The remaining Linyaari survey members straggled in with their flitters, along with their data and the precious specimens they had gathered for the *aagroni*. Under the supervision of Fiicki, all samples of material from Vhiliinyar were carefully packed. Aside from her personal losses, Acorna knew that *aagroni* Iirtye's absence would be a crushing blow to any hope of restoring Linyaari life as it had once been, if he was not found again. Especially when not only the rather gruff old scientist but all of his colleagues had been taken at once. They had to find the missing Linyaari, not just to ease her own heart, but also to save her people's hopes.

For all her conflicted feelings about leaving Vhiliinyar, she was incredibly glad to see the Moon of Opportunity again, and to be crushed in Becker's bear hug. She had been holding RK, but the cat simply prowled back and forth between her shoulders and Becker's for the duration of the hug, kneading his claws in and out and purring louder than the *Condor*'s engines.

'I sure am happy to see you, Princess,' Becker said. 'Good thing I sent that cat along to look after you. And I know it's hard, but try not to worry about Aari too much. He is what we call one tough hombre. I mean, the Khleevi messed with him, and he came out of that and look what happened to the Khleevi! Nah, anything takes a bite out of that boy is gonna need a big chunk of something else to take the taste out of their mouth! We'll find him. Mark my words.

'Hafiz has got a feed and a bunk organized for all of your folks, but Mac and I would really rather you'd come back aboard the *Condor* with us when you're done eating.' He winked at her. 'You could bring some chow with you if you really love us,' he said. She could tell he was as worried as she was. He was talking nonstop – as fast as if he was selling salvage, and mugging as he did so. With that last request he batted his eyelashes, ridiculously long and curly on such a rough-looking character, to cajole her. His efforts to distract her drew one corner of her mouth up slightly.

'Okay. I'd like that,' she said.

Thariinye, who had been consoling a young female who had lost three members of her team, left her being cosseted by a bevy of Linyaari females who had remained on MOO. He caught up with Becker and Acorna just as she was about to go eat.

'How about me, Captain?' he said. 'Can I come back on the *Condor* as well?'

'If you think you can make yourself useful in other than a supervisory capacity, yeah,' Becker said. 'Just kidding,' he added, seeing, as Acorna did, that Thariinye appeared to be genuinely upset.

'Don't worry about Aari,' Thariinye said. 'I think I've figured out what happened, Khornya. Something went after those elders and you know how Maati is, she would have been in the middle of whatever it was before it knew what hit it. And Aari wouldn't let anything happen to Maati so he went, too. To tell you the truth, I'm glad in a way that, since the others disappeared, Maati and Aari are with them. They can take care of themselves, and save the others, too.'

'Your confidence in our friends is very sweet and I know they would both be touched by it,' Acorna said.

'Sounds good to me,' Becker said. 'I hope for once you're right, fella.'

The captain strode off toward the *Condor* with RK wrapped around his neck.

Hafiz and Karina enveloped all the returning survey personnel in scented silken robes and solicitude as soon as they entered the dining gardens Hafiz had created especially to cater to Linyaari tastes.

As she grazed, Acorna kept both her ears and her mind open to conversation and nuances of thought around her. The verbal conversation was perfunctory, but the thoughts she could overhear spun in circles of wonder and fear.

(How did it happen? I'm sure I didn't take my eyes from him for more than a moment – not even that – yet he simply was nowhere. No sound, no word . . . How could he leave me like that?)

(But there were three of them! How could three people vanish? Why would they, or why would anyone else want them to?)

(No sinkholes, no avalanches, no eruptions there. I checked before I went there. Liriili checked, too. Gone into the air, as if they had been vaporized. And yet, if that were so, surely we would have heard fearful thoughts, perhaps – a moment of startled recognition of what was happening, a cry for help from one who saw it happen to another. Surely something! I don't see how it could have happened without a trace.)

(How? . . . How? . . . *How?!*)

Everyone's thoughts eventually turned to that one question. No one questioned why it had happened. They assumed that the vanishings were involuntary, under the influence of some irresistible force. No one seemed to believe that any of the missing had reasons to vanish, or that anyone could possibly have a reason for wishing them to do so. They assumed that something was behind the events on Vhiliinyar, drawing them all along an unknown and possibly hostile path.

But how had it happened? Even if the ground or the heavens had swallowed their friends up, there would have been a thought-cry, an instant's panic, something that might have brought help, or at least a witness to the disappearance. Surely their vanishing would leave a sign of some kind on all their instruments monitoring the planet. But it hadn't. Every single instance was traceless, leaving not a single clue behind, not even a blip on the energy or heat sensors, or the slightest joggle of the seismic detectors. No unidentified ships had been in their skies, and even the identified ones had remained just as they were in position and population before their friends had vanished.

The Linyaaris' unguarded thoughts at the banquet clearly demonstrated that they were as puzzled as she was, and that no one had any more information than she did to explain what had happened. But perhaps they knew things they were not aware of, had observed connections no one had yet put together. When the grazing was finished, she went to each member of the survey teams with the map of Vhiliinyar she had downloaded from the ship's computer, detailing their various work sites.

She asked each crew where they had last seen the missing people, where were they working when the disappearance occurred. She checked to see if the missing were in areas of the planet new to the survey teams, places that they had not been working before.

Few could exactly pinpoint for her the spots where their comrades went missing, but Kaari at least was able to give her the location of the relatively small area where Neeva and Melireenya had been seen conversing right before they had vanished. And she discovered that Fiirki, when he disappeared, had been only a few meters from the flitters, on ground everyone had walked over hundreds of times as they unloaded equipment. She herself knew, within a fairly close range, where the people in her party had vanished. It was close to their camp, again in a place that they'd all traversed many times.

Little was decided at Hafiz's banquet that night. Everyone was too tired and distraught to even think, so the planning meeting was postponed until they had a little time to recover from the shock of it. Acorna gathered all the information she could, and took it back to the *Condor* after dinner, where she showed the maps to Becker and Thariinye. 'What I'll have to do first is backtrack to the site where each of the disappearances happened and thoroughly investigate the terrain.'

'But people did that when they searched to begin with!' Thariinye said.

'Not in all cases. The largest numbers of disappearances happened just before the evacuation. No one has searched properly for those people. And no single person has yet searched *all* of the sites. So I—'

'We,' Thariinye said. 'I'm going, too.'

'Me, too,' Becker said.

'Captain, you can't,' Acorna told him. 'The Council won't allow it, even now. You know how they feel about humans on their planet.'

'Blessed Mother of Invention!' he roared. 'I've been there already – probably more than most of your folk. Who brought the bones of your people from Vhiliinyar to narhii-Vhiliinyar? Me! Who saved Aari from that cave after the Khleevi got through with him? Me, that's who!'

'It makes no sense, I agree, but even so, it is how they feel.'

'You're taking Mac with you, then,' he said.

'He's not as good as me, but if he loses you, he knows I'll dismantle him and short out every circuit he's got.'

Becker had one of the command chairs turned around to face the two secondary seats he had installed at the *Condor*'s helm. Acorna and Thariinye each occupied one of these, with RK perched behind Becker's head, on the back of the chair. Now the fourth chair turned and Mac, who had been monitoring the control panel, said, 'The Captain is very strict.'

'Well, please don't be too hard on him, Captain,' Acorna said. 'He might not be able to stop matters. After all, Aari, Maati, and the elders disappeared from right under *my* nose.'

'If you go, he'd better plan on being with you if you vanish,' Becker said with a pugnacious jut to his chin as he folded his arms across his chest. ' 'Cause Mac won't like what happens to him if he comes back alone.'

'I'll take care of Khornya, Captain, have no fear,' Thariinye said.

Becker rolled his eyes and didn't dignify that remark with an answer.

'I *will*,' Thariinye said. 'And we'll get Maati and Aari back, too, and the others. Won't we, Khornya?'

'We'll try, Thariinye,' she said. 'You know, Captain, Uncle Hafiz mentioned something about research. I can't help but feel that whatever is causing these disappearances has nothing to do with the Khleevi. It doesn't have their touch – the terror and destruction that are the hallmarks of their inventions. I am beginning to wonder if it is keyed into our own people's history on the planet. It seems to me that if this – problem – is happening to us now and yet, if what Aari observed was true all over the planet, it did not trouble the Khleevi—'

Becker snorted, 'Not much troubled the Khleevi. They weren't exactly sensitive little things.'

'No, but Aari felt fairly certain that they were unmolested in their destruction of the planet. It seems to me that the destruction our enemies visited upon Vhiliinyar itself may have stirred up some forces from long ago, from back when the Friends first brought life to this planet. Remember what Maarni told us about the *sii*-Linyaari vanishing into thin air? Maybe these disappearances are related – following the same path as the *sii*-Linyaari. Perhaps the Ancestors would have some clue about this. I wonder if an interview with them might be illuminating.'

'Oh, yes,' Thariinye said. 'The Ancestors are older even than Grandam was. If anyone knows about the olden days they do. I think Joh—'

'Captain Becker to you, punk,' Becker said.

'All right – Captain Becker, then,' Thariinye said with a pout, 'must take us to narhii-Vhiliinyar to see them. The Ancestors no doubt already know what is happening here and why, and will be able to tell us what has become of our friends in that sarcastic, cryptic way they have. Maybe it is possible they know how to get our friends back. Yes, going to see them is a very good idea.' He said this with a great deal of self-satisfaction, as if it had been *his* idea, which was exactly the sort of thing Thariinye often did that irritated people. But Acorna was glad to think they'd agreed on any valid course of action, no matter who thought of it first.

She would consult with Hafiz, and head back to narhii-Vhiliinyar as soon as possible.

SIX

Unlike their descendants, the Linyaari, the Ancestors needed none of the trappings of civilization to live their lives in a happy and fulfilled manner. As soon as the funerals on narhii-Vhiliinyar were over and the losses counted, the Ancestors retired to their accustomed hills, and began to heal the damage left behind by the Khleevi. They had only to apply their horns to the scorched and scored soil to make it flourish again, green with shoots of their favorite grasses. They were content in their place.

The Ancestors' Linyaari handlers needed almost as little as their charges: a place to store the ceremonial trappings, a pavilion for when the weather was inclement, grazing privileges on the newly restored fields, and they, too, were satisfied.

Becker landed at the site of the old spaceport and began accepting loads of salvage again from Linyaari who had been picking through the ashes for it. The sale of such gleanings would help to offset some of the Linyaari debt to Uncle Hafiz for the reclamation of both Vhiliinyar and narhii-Vhiliinyar, although in the long run the Linyaari

101

services to Hafiz as healers and psychics would be far more valuable than the more tangible goods they were unearthing. But it felt good for them to be doing something physical, while they were cleaning up the mess the Khleevi had left behind.

Linyaari began lining up, their arms full, some of them pulling makeshift carts and wagons also full of debris, as the ship set down. Becker greeted most of the waiting Linyaari as old friends, but Acorna spared little more than a nod for most of them as she passed. Already her thoughts flew ahead of her feet, as she moved quickly toward the hills and her forthcoming visit to the Ancestors.

Thariinye trotted along beside her, occasionally bursting into a flurry of distracted chatter. This told her that he was as profoundly disturbed by the disappearance of their friends as she was. She knew he had grown to admire Aari and was, though he would deny it, genuinely fond of Maati.

They traveled for three days from the spaceport before reaching the hills where the Ancestors lived.

Acorna realized as they came down over the brow of one of the hills that the 'hills' were actually a single ridge – the rim of a very old volcanic crater. A beautiful blue-green lake filled much of the basin, surrounded by flowering blue meadows and groves of young trees. The Ancestors had done a fine job at restoring their homeplace to normalcy.

Two of the Linyaari Attendants walked toward them across the meadow where the four-footed, goat-bearded unicorns from whom the Linyaari were partly descended stood grazing, sleeping, or simply enjoying the day. The weather of narhii-Vhiliinyar seemed unusually fine after the storms of Vhiliinyar, with high fleecy pink clouds and warm sunshine. At nightfall a light rain would mist the fields for about an hour, just to cool things off, before clearing off so the individual stars could be counted and clearly identified.

'Greetings, Khornya and Thariinye,' said the female Attendant wearing fuchsia and lime silks. 'You are troubled and your news is troubled. Grandmother says you have come to ruin her day.'

'Well, I might do that, but it's not why I've come,' Acorna said, dredging up a small smile. 'We need help. We need to draw on the wisdom of the Ancestors and their memories of things past. Some of our people have come into danger. We feel that it might be due to things that happened long ago. Only by learning more about the past can we determine what has now become of these people and how best to help them.'

'You can ask,' the other Attendant said. He wore yellow and sapphire silks and was perhaps a head shorter than Acorna. His voice held a wry twist to it.

When Acorna had conversed with the Ancestors before, the Attendants had served as interpreters most of the time. This time, however, she caught commands from the Old Ones themselves as they approached.

'Hurry up, Children. I'm trying to save you some of this but it isn't easy around these other old goats. Nobody has any manners these days.'

'Never mind her, Younglings. You're troubled. Come graze and tell us what's on your mind and how we can help.'

'Of course they're troubled. They've been gallivanting around the universe in one of those ridiculous contraptions. It's enough to unhinge anybody.'

'That's not it, you old fool. I can hear already that it's something far more serious. If you will just quit sending so much perhaps we could read why they've come to see us.'

Acorna couldn't tell which thoughts were coming from which Ancestor, they came so quickly, but she settled herself in the middle of a group of three. Four more ambled casually to the edge of the group and put their heads down to tear up some grass.

She waited for them to raise their heads and begin chewing before she said, 'People are missing. A lot of people. We were mapping on Vhiliinyar, trying to make sure that during the terraforming we put things back where they belong, just as they were in the old days. On the first day of our survey, Liriili disappeared. Some of us thought she might have found a way to leave the surface. But then in a few days, another person disappeared and then another, and then, suddenly, people began vanishing in large numbers.'

'Which people?' the Grandmother nearest her asked.

Acorna told her.

'Hmmm,' was the only reply.

Thariinye said, 'So we were wondering, Wise Ones, if you know anything about Vhiliinyar that might explain what's causing this problem. Since you have been around longer than anyone else, we thought you might remember something that will help us find our friends. Anything you can remember would be useful, even dating as far back as the time of the Friends.'

'We're not *that* old, sonny,' a Grandfather informed him. 'And if we were wise enough to know all about it, we'd have been wise enough to warn you to avoid it, wouldn't we? Vanishings on Vhiliinyar . . . I've never heard of such a thing, myself.'

'Oh,' Thariinye said, with a wink at Acorna. 'Then Maarni must have been wrong when she said how knowledgeable of ancient history the Ancestors are. How sad. I'm sure that, whatever has become of her, she'll be understanding if you don't know enough to help.'

The old Grandfather gave a snort and a very indecorous laugh and one of the Grandmothers, a rather plump one, nuzzled Thariinye's cheek with her horn. 'Isn't that the cutest thing you ever saw? The little dear is trying to manipulate us.'

'Aren't you the clever one, though?' cooed another Grandmother.

Thariinye ducked his head boyishly at being caught out. But Acorna said, 'I don't see how we can be said to be manipulating you. We've told you already we need your help. And Maarni *is* among the missing, though it's true we don't know what she's thinking. But she certainly found a lot of worth in the stories you told her, and that's

105

part of what gave us the idea of coming to you in case you know something that might help.'

'Maarni is that nice girl who likes those tall tales you tell her, Hree,' the plump Grandmother said to the Grandfather.

'Oh, yes, she's a polite girl. Always brings the most delicious flowers she grows herself when she comes for stories. I'm sorry she's missing. Wish I *could* think of something to help. Which of my stories did she tell you?' he asked.

'The one about the waterfall was the first one,' Acorna said. 'That was awfully interesting. It certainly shed some light on the characters of the Friends. I had no idea they ever thought of the Ancestors in *that* sort of way.'

'Well, of course they did, silly girl. Otherwise, how do you suppose your kind came to be?'

'Haarilii, don't scandalize the poor girl. Of course it took more than that, sweetheart, there was a lot of scientific tinkering involved in getting from us and them to you. We were alien lifeforms to each other initially, after all.'

'She also mentioned – after we found an artifact – that there were once another kind of Linyaari – *sii*-Linyaari, I believe she said. They lived in the oceans. She told us that they'd been gone for some time, that they vanished one day long ago.'

'Is that what she said?' one of the Grand-mothers asked in a brisk disapproving voice. 'Some things she wasn't supposed to repeat.'

'Really?' Acorna asked. 'Why not?'

Thariinye asked eagerly, 'Was it something maybe to do with breeding?'

'Thariinye, do not be rude!' Acorna told him. It

wasn't that she thought there was anything one shouldn't speak of regarding breeding. It was just that it seemed to be all Thariinye was thinking about. That wasn't exactly the case – Acorna thought he was just hoping the topic the Ancestors expounded on first would be the one he found most interesting.

She was rather surprised therefore when one of the Grandmothers said, 'How did you guess?'

Before he could answer a Grandfather continued, 'It's not about breeding in a recreational kind of way, sonny, I know what *you're* thinking. It's about the scientific kind of breeding, which supposedly takes the strengths of two species and combines them to make what should be an even stronger species. It requires some fiddling by those who are directing the process. That's how the Friends took themselves and us and came up with you younglings. But it's also how they came up with the *sii*-Linyaari.'

'How can that be?' Acorna asked, though she could think of several reasons how it *might* be.

'The way I heard it,' the plump Grandmother said confidentially, 'it's because the Friends were *not* all alike. Some were one kind and some were another.'

'I'm sure they meant nothing *bad* by it, creating those strange creatures,' said a very old Grandfather. 'They were just trying different forms out. They did that, my grandsire said. Always tinkering.'

'Aye,' said a very old Grandmother wisely. 'My Grandam hinted that the Friends had many different appearances – that even the same person took many seemings sometimes. She never came right out and said shapeshifter, but she did say – and she had actually met them, mind you – that we were not the *first* people they took to themselves and blended with. That they had done it elsewhere, with other races. Vhiliinyar was only one of the planets they had inhabited throughout their long history.'

'But you're not supposed to repeat that,' the plump Grandmother told them. 'It would upset people.'

'Yes,' Acorna said, finding herself a little stunned by the information, 'I can well imagine. That would explain the existence of the *sii*-Linyaari, I suppose, but what about their disappearance?'

'Tell us again what happened back on Vhiliinyar,' another Grandmother said, cocking her ears forward to show that she was listening most intently to Acorna.

'Well – except for our friends going missing, nothing, really, which is what was so odd,' Acorna told her. 'You would think, given our telepathic powers, that if something was about to capture our people or make them vanish as it did, even if the ground swallowed them up or some unseen bird of prey swooped away with them, at least one of them would have cried out for help. But no one remaining reports hearing anything like that, through their minds or their ears. The missing people were just *gone*.'

'And you're sure it's not those bug things?' asked a Grandfather with a narrow-eyed half-snort toward the sky.

'No, Grandfather. If it had been the Khleevi carrying them off, Aari would have known. He senses them, you know. Besides, the Khleevi were never good at hiding their presence or at any sort of subtlety, for that matter. Khleevi like their victims to scream, and to prolong the screaming as long as possible. They depended on terror as their primary tactic. It is what they feed on. Why would they do something so puzzling that no one can figure out whether to be afraid or not? It would serve no good purpose for them.'

'What I'd like to know is, if something on Vhiliinyar made our folk disappear, did it make Khleevi disappear, too?' declared a Grandmother. 'And if it did, why didn't it disappear all of them? Preferably before they made such a big mess of our planets.'

'You know, I'm beginning to remember something,' the eldest Grandmother said. 'I was talking with Grandam once about our natures. You remember don't you, Hraaya, the old stories of how fierce and smart and courageous our Terran forebears were? How the only way they survived was to be so wily and dangerous that the men of Terra could not capture them without trickery?'

'Ho, yes, who can forget? It's part of who we are.'

'Yes,' she said. 'But it's not part of who *they* are, these younglings. The Friends, I remember Grandam saying, did not believe in fighting or killing, even when extremely provoked.' She paused, ate a mouthful of grass, and chewed thoughtfully. 'And *I* remember asking, well then, how did they deal with people who wanted to

109

hurt them – maybe hurt their younglings? And she said, oh, they didn't do anything violent, but the aggressors disappeared. I wish such a thing worked on the Khleevi. It is certain those bugs were nasty enough to deserve to disappear. Perhaps your answer lies there, child. You did say you thought it might be something from the Ancients.'

Acorna let her breath out in a deep sigh. Progress, at last. She began munching on a grass stem herself. So, once upon a time the Friends had caused aggressors to disappear. Interesting maybe, a little, but she still didn't know how the Friends had caused it, or why it didn't work on the Khleevi when they invaded Vhiliinyar, or why the long-gone Friends would cause people who were not aggressors, but their own descendants, to disappear now.

Thariinye, reading her, said aloud, 'Well, I think, if it is the Friends come back to haunt us, that these disappearances are a mistake. I bet they wouldn't have let it happen if they were still around – I mean, the Friends took off a long time ago, didn't they? So – if they left something there that started grabbing people – it probably just didn't recognize us.'

Acorna looked at her young male friend, who was speaking matter-of-factly and – as usual – without troubling to engage many of his higher intellectual functions, as if he had suddenly manifested genius. Which, in a way, he had.

'Excuse me, Khornya,' said the Attendant in the lime and fuchsia silks, approaching from behind, 'Thariinye, we must ask you to retire for now and

110

leave the Ancestors to their own company. So much stimulation, especially in the wake of the disaster that recently overtook us and the enormous output of energy required to restore the Ancestral Meadows, drains their stamina and vitality. Do you see how translucent their horns are becoming, just from conversation, without even the strain of healing?'

'Nonsense, Granddaughter, I'm as spry as I ever was!' insisted the Grandmother who seemed to be this woman's special charge. But the woman stroked Grandmother's nose and cheeks and kissed her between the eyes and said, 'Yes, but I can't keep up with you. And Khornya and Thariinye have had a long journey. If you are not tired, they probably are.'

'Ah, yes,' the oldest Grandfather said. 'They don't make younglings like they used to.'

Acorna smiled at the remark, one so appropriate to the conversation they'd just been having.

The Attendant in lime and fuchsia, whose name was Imaara, led Acorna and Thariinye to a pavilion and showed them where they could lay their sleeping mats. 'You know, you might wish to consult the Ancestors' library,' she said.

'But I thought that the destruction of our planetary records by the Khleevi was total, that nothing remained of the files—' Acorna began.

Imaara said, 'Oh, I don't mean any of the Linyaari records here on narhii-Vhiliinyar. I mean the Ancestral ones we Attendants use as our handbook, training manual, journal, history, chronicle, what have you. These are personal records, not part of the planetary system of pooled

111

knowledge. The main Linyaari archive was destroyed during the attack, but not our work. Our original materials are always carefully protected, and new material is divided among us. It is a continuously growing work, you see, as parts of it are still under construction.'

'Really?' Acorna asked.

'Oh, yes, it is a careful record of our Ancestors' preferences, habits, histories, and perhaps most important for your cause, for, of course, I couldn't help but overhear – it's my job to do so, in fact – all of the Ancestors' utterances. We have historical notes dating all the way back to the time when the Linyaari first began attending the Ancestors.'

Thariinye yawned but Acorna told the Attendant that, yes, indeed, it sounded like something that would be helpful in clarifying some of the more enigmatic remarks the Old Ones had made. 'Could you show me those records now?'

'It's getting very late,' Imaara said.

'I understand, but we have missing people to find and we have no idea how much danger they may be in. The very restoration of Vhiliinyar may depend upon what we find here.'

'Perhaps, but you must rest sometime. The oldest documents in our archive are very fragile. We would not want you to make a mistake that would damage them through exhaustion-induced clumsiness. Also, they should be studied in natural light. Artificial light can cause deterioration of the pigments. Be calm, little sister. This thing will take what time it takes. One learns the ways of time, living among the Ancestors.'

The Attendant's words sounded very wise and

important and all that, but Acorna still had difficulty suppressing impatience as she lowered
herself to her sleeping mat. Didn't they understand how urgent this was? She was prepared to
fume all night about it. It niggled her for perhaps
a nanosecond before exhaustion caught up with
her and she fell into a deep sleep.

SEVEN

Imaara woke Acorna and Thariinye before first light.

(Come. It is time to read.)

She stilled Acorna's questions and Thariinye's grumblings with a swift thought and led them around the lake and across the meadows, to a cleft in the hill. As they approached, Acorna noticed that windows had been carved into the hillside at three different levels, and when they entered the cave concealed by a few recently grown trees, she began to understand why the time was so important.

The sun had been rising as they walked to the cavern. As they stepped foot inside it, the first rays of the morning blazed a trail across the floor of the cavern and lit the chamber as if they were outdoors.

The walls of the cavern were covered with glowing paintings in what looked like new pigments. 'Hey, they've fixed this up nicely,' Thariinye said. 'Decorations and everything.'

But one of the symbols depicted there had captured Acorna's attention. She lagged behind Imaara's brisk steps to examine it. 'Look, it's the same one we saw on the *sii*-Linyaari artifact.'

Imaara returned to look at what had caught her guest's attention. 'Oh, those are the copies of the paintings we made from the walls of the original cave on Vhiliinyar.'

'Original cave?'

'Yes, where we first kept the Ancestral archives. That cave had been used in that manner for many years, the Ancestors said, before our people became adept at the written word. The early Ancestors used to make pictographs, though I believe many of the earliest images were drawn instead by the Friends and may be their form of the written word. Our language and writing systems are descended from theirs, but are not the same, as our vocal chords and hands could not form all the same sounds and characters as theirs. These paintings would have been lost after the Khleevi attack on Vhiliinyar, except that the Ancestors have rather long memories, good visual memories at that, and we were able to piece together the graphs from their recollections after we were forced to leave our home so precipitately. We did bring most of the written archives with us, though – some were irreparably damaged in the haste of the transfer, but most survived. Come, I'll show you.'

She led them to an upper level, a circular room lined with fine crystals. The sun snaking into the chamber from the strategically placed window bounced off of these and caused the floor to shimmer with rainbows. Imaara drew forth some storage boxes and scooted them to the middle of the floor. A long low table with a bench on either side made a place to sit and study the contents or to add to them.

Before Imaara left, Acorna said, 'This original cave on Vhiliinyar, Imaara, where was it located?'

'Near the great waterfall, the Vriiniia Watiir, in a cliff near the sea. It was a very secret place and hard to reach if you didn't know how. The key to entering it was passed down by generations of Attendants. And – by the way, Khornya, Thariinye, these records you see today are secret as well. They are for the Attendant class of Linyaari, shared only among ourselves, and kept shrouded from general knowledge by our life-bonded words to maintain silence. I trust our privacy will remain inviolate? You may act upon anything you learn here, but not reveal the source of your knowledge. I show you this place now only at the direct orders of the Ancestors.'

'I heard no such suggestion,' Thariinye said with surprise.

She smiled. 'Even the most favored of the Linyaari people do not share the most intimate confidences of our Ancestors. Good thing for them it is, too. Most of them concern the state of the Ancestral digestive system. But a few are of more interest to others—' she waved her hand indicating the records, and nodded as Acorna raised the lid of the storage container and extracted a few ornate wooden binders containing several sheets of what looked like processed leaf and grass material blanched and pressed, held together with long dark purple fibers from the *lilaala* vine.

The writing was crude and faded. 'These must

be the oldest surviving records of our people,' Acorna said, handling the leaves gently and with reverence, and feeling uneasy with the crumbling texture of the edges between her fingers.

'They are,' Imaara said. 'It is believed that these are the records made by the first Attendant, who was in fact the biological son of this Ancestor here,' she pointed to a word that could have been a name. 'The Attendant, who never names himself, we call Hrunvrun, the firstborn, and his records form the basis for the training of all future Attendants.'

Thariinye looked at Imaara and then at the paper. 'I had no idea your craft had such a lineage, Lady.'

She blinked at him and Acorna heard her thought, (What is it that you suppose people who work with Ancestors would have, young man? Short-term thinking? Like, perhaps, yours?) With that, she turned and left them with the documents.

Acorna, though she was very good with languages and translations, found the faded ancient script daunting and nearly indecipherable. After all, though she had spoken a few baby words in Linyaari, the first language she had learned as a child was Galactic Standard. She still had to concentrate to be as fluent in her native Linyaari as the rest of her race.

And though Thariinye was a native speaker, he was not particularly analytical in his language skills. Despite his attempts, he was not much help in deciphering the scrolls. The LAANYE was, Acorna's hopes to the contrary, not a lot of help

117

either. It could scan the written words of a culture, but these words were faded in places and written in multiple hands. Also, most of the documents were too fragile for her to dare to use it upon them. The little device worked much better with spoken words than written ones, especially ancient written ones.

Acorna sent a message to Imaara, (I realize these documents are secret, but could we have permission to make copies of some of them for linguistic analysis?)

(Oh no,) Imaara replied. (I'm afraid not. The content of the documents must not leave the library or be shown to anyone else who is not an Attendant.)

(Then could you spare someone to translate them for us?) Acorna asked. (We are having great difficulty understanding the contents. And time is very important in this matter, as I said. The problem is both a personal one and also one that affects every living being in our society – Linyaari and Ancestor alike. The terraforming project on Vhiliinyar is on hold because of the missing people from the survey team. Many of my friends and relatives have vanished without explanation. We must get back to Vhiliinyar and try to find them before we can move forward to reclaim our home planet.)

(A moment,) Imaara thought.

In a few minutes an Ancestor spoke, very formally compared to the conversational tones of yesterday, to Acorna's and Thariinye's minds.

(You have seen the Attendants' library. That is enough. Go. Return to Vhiliinyar and do what you must. We have helped all we can for now. Perhaps later we'll be able to help more.)

'They're dismissing us?' Thariinye asked. 'Just like that? I don't believe it! I had no idea this was a quiz, did you?'

Acorna shook her head, as perplexed as he was. 'No, I didn't. Perhaps for now it's better not to read too much into what the Grandfather said. It seems to me the Ancestors are often quite literal, which makes them hard to understand. You've had more practice at it than I have. But we're clearly not wanted here, and nothing we've seen is going to help us without a translator fluent in the ancient language. Time is not standing still. If Captain Becker is ready, we should return now to MOO, relay what we've discovered, and go back to Vhiliinyar.'

'So we can disappear, too?' Thariinye asked. 'I don't know, Khornya. Don't you have more of a plan than that?'

'You don't have to go with me,' she told him. 'You could even stay here on narhii-Vhiliinyar. After all, you have your family and friends to consider.'

'Whereas yours have vanished, first lost in our wars and now snatched from Vhiliinyar during the survey. Yes, yes, you make me feel *so* much better. Of course I'll go with you. Aari would not forgive me for letting you go unprotected,' he added, puffing out his chest a bit and adding a strut to his walk.

'That's very kind,' she said with a perfectly straight face. 'We will mark ourselves, of course, with all sorts of tracers. Hafiz will wire us up so

119

we resemble Mac. We will not return to Vhiliinyar until we can be found by other means than telepathy,' she told him. 'We'll have personal locators, olfactory and visual indicators, and anything else anyone can think of. I promise, we will be *very* hard to lose.'

EIGHT

'You're taking Mac,' Becker told her on the way back to MOO. 'No argument. I can't send the *Condor*'s computer, but now that Mac's finished upgrading himself, he's smarter than Buck.' Buck was what Becker called the *Condor*'s computer.

As they approached the Moon of Opportunity, Mac approached the bridge. His gait was curiously off balance and he held his head at a strange angle. As he tromped down the metal grid leading from the crew and main cargo bays to the bridge, Thariinye asked, 'What's wrong with him?'

And then they saw that there was now what appeared to be the long end of an exceptionally large screw coming out of Mac's forehead.

Becker groaned and buried his head in his hands. Acorna read his mind. He was suppressing a very obvious and bad pun.

'Is that a joke?' Thariinye demanded of Mac, pointing at the metal horn.

'Androids do not joke, Thariinye,' Mac said. 'I have modified my cranium in an attempt to assimilate myself to your culture. If your people object, as Khornya has told Captain Becker, to the presence of non-Linyaari on your troubled home-world, then I seek to become more Linyaari. Also, while my horn cannot heal, it is excellent for prying and tearing and boring into things and could be used to hold the supports of collapsing substructures together in an emergency. Also, if I spin it in reverse, it can extract things. I have attachments for it concealed in my abdominal wall. Do you wish to see?'

Becker's eyes were running with water. He kept blowing his nose noisily on his sleeve. Acorna could see he was struggling to keep from dissolving in laughter. His valiant battle was so convulsive he couldn't seem to catch his breath.

'Captain!' Acorna said, and thumped him on the back. She'd try her horn next, if she had to, but she had no idea if it worked on someone who was threatening to die laughing.

'I'm s-sorry, P-Princess. But you gotta love that guy. And you *gotta* take him! Oh, Lord, his horn has handy dandy attachments! I love him. I really do love him.'

Mac smiled a broad, if unaccustomed, smile. He'd been working on his facial expressions.

Thariinye, still a bit worried after watching Becker's reaction that his race had been insulted, changed the subject. 'Speaking of love, Captain Becker, I have not heard you mention Nadhari Kando on either leg of the voyage. How is she?'

Becker shrugged. 'Energetic as ever, probably. I dunno. Haven't seen much of her lately.'

Acorna was immediately concerned. She had thought the two of them happily mated, and surely these things turned out well for *some* people, even if her own love life was – she wouldn't consider that now, not until she could do more about it. With Aari among the missing, it hurt too much to think about. Instead she said, 'Oh, Captain, have you had a falling out?'

'Not really, nothing like that exactly, Princess. No, don't look so worried. Salvage consultants don't have lifemates the way you people do. Neither do lady-commando-warrior-security-chief-honchos. The truth is – well,' he looked a little bashful and slightly shame-faced. 'She took a shine to the new commander of the Federation outpost.'

'She is unfaithful?' Thariinye asked. 'Really? The females I know are all extremely faithful.' He said the last somewhat regretfully, which was understandable. He was very good at flattering members of the opposite sex. Since he was a very attractive, articulate, and virile young male of excellent family, and since the Linyaari mated for life, the ladies took him at his word, which was in Thariinye's case not, unlike the words of the Ancestors, to be taken literally. Especially in matters concerning sex.

'I wouldn't put it that way exactly. Nadhari let me know what was going on. Pretty loudly. She got all ticked off just because I was enjoying the dolmathes Andina fixed for me. These warrior ladies really have bad tempers, you know. Though they're awfully flexible, they can be kind of – lumpy – off the training room floor. Not cuddly, much. Actually, Nadhari took the incident pretty well. For her. It only took Kaarlye a touch of his horn, and my arm and head healed right up. Nadhari even said she was sorry, afterward. But she still spends all her off-duty time with that soldier boy.'

Acorna sighed. Apparently Nadhari was not the only one who had made other mating arrangements. Becker did not appear to be distraught, though, simply cautious.

Thariinye was fascinated. 'Does it not injure your honor to be thrown over for another male like that, Captain?'

Becker looked as if he wanted to protest, then grinned wryly. 'Not as much as it would have injured the rest of me to be thrown the way Nadhari would have liked to. Her finer sensibilities and fondness for me plus my great personal charisma kept her from doing worse. Frankly, son, between you and me, I was getting worn out. I was still real flattered at how much she cared, but I was getting exhausted. That's how Andina and I got to be – uh – close. She noticed how puny and thin I was becoming, and she decided I needed feeding up. She suggested ways to get rust out of my hull, too, and clean up some of the cargo. Her company owns the cleaning concession for MOO, you know, and all of the cleaning products Hafiz intends to peddle to people in this little corner of the universe.'

'Impressive,' Thariinye said. 'Though not as impressive as Commander Kando, I must say.'

'Go ahead and say what you like. You know what Nadhari told me the last time we were together? She said she found me restful. *Restful!* That's not the kind of thing a man likes to hear from an exciting female. But I gotta tell you. I find

Andina restful, and it's pretty nice not to be constantly sparring with someone.'

'Andina suggested the shape and purpose of several of my horn attachments,' Mac said with what passed in him for enthusiasm. 'The scraper-sander and dicing attachments were entirely her idea, and she helped modify some of the others as well.'

Becker looked at Mac again as he spoke and burst out in helpless laughter once again. 'So she helped you cook this up, did she? I don't suppose you have an attachment that will help you with the gardening?'

'Oh, yes,' Mac said. 'I have an excellent one for weed pulling, though it is somewhat awkward to use without further bodily modifications.' He demonstrated by assuming the weed-pulling-with-the-horn position, which required him to all but stand on his head.

'Yeah, I can see that,' Becker said. 'Somehow I don't think that's going to catch on with the Linyaari. But it's a good try.'

Acorna said thoughtfully, 'You know, Captain, I think perhaps it is a good idea to take Mac. So far as we know, everyone who has disappeared is a Linyaari. It may be for lack of a better target. But despite Mac's courteous attempt to assimilate himself to our race, if whatever is taking our people wishes to take Linyaari specifically, per-haps it will ignore Mac and allow him to witness the disappearance of—'

'Us?' Thariinye asked. 'That's reassuring, Khornya.'

'Perhaps not, but it's not unlikely either,' she

said in a matter-of-fact voice. 'And Mac could be very hard to stop if he decided to rescue us.'

'I would,' Mac said earnestly. He turned to Acorna and said in an almost flawless imitation of her Linyaari accent, 'I take it then, Khornya, that you now accept me as part of the rescue team?'

She smiled at his use of the Linyaari pronunciation of her name. 'I doubt we could do it without you,' she told him.

It took several precious hours to convince the Council that Mac should be included in the roster of the search and recovery team, and it took almost as long to convince them that Acorna, Thariinye, and the cat should be the other members of the team.

Had Liriili still been *viizaar*, it would have taken longer still. However, with many of the Council members, including the *aagroni* and Neeva, missing, only five were present to make the decision. Their concerns were more for the team's safety than anything else. That was why they were concerned that Acorna should participate, even though they acknowledged her losses – of Neeva and Aari and his family – gave her a strong motivation to solve the problem. Once they convinced the Council that the controls they proposed to safeguard themselves were as stringent as possible, the Council was more amenable to allowing them to proceed.

Another persuasive argument was that fewer, rather than more, people on Vhiliinyar's surface, backed up by intensive air surveillance, was not only the most cost-effective method to proceed, but also probably the most effective method of locating the lost ones, and the least likely to result in more personnel losses. They acquiesced to Acorna's plan.

The Council's approval of the addition of Mac to the team, however, was not made thanks to logic alone. Nor was it made because they considered him a device instead of a person. The Council, which could have found Mac's 'modifications' insulting, instead were touched by the inventiveness of the android's attempts to blend into their society, and his earnest desire to help them. His horn impressed them so much that one of the senior Council members joked that Mac would next have to modify his hair follicles to make his short sandy brush cut grow out long, curly, and silver as befit a star-clad Linyaari. Mac promised to give it his full attention as soon as the current mission was successfully completed.

Once the Council was won over, it was just a question of getting the equipment Acorna wanted supplied by House Harakamian. It was a lot like a gambling game Hafiz had taught her as a child – a shell game. It involved multiple ships, each a bit farther out from Vhiliinyar. A large ship would monitor the surveillance ship and Acorna's party from the depths of space. A smaller surveillance ship would enter close orbit around the planet, ready to send down help to those on the surface at a moment's notice, though it would return to the mother ship as needed for refueling or necessary maintenance. Between the two ships, there would never be a moment when Acorna and her friends would be out of contact with those monitoring them. While in orbit, the smaller ship would monitor the team's every word and breath as well as all of the many other signals transmitted by the sensors Acorna, Thariinye, Mac, and RK wore. The cat's sensors were embedded in a special collar which Becker and Acorna had buckled around RK's neck with some trepidation, despite Acorna's best attempts to communicate its function to the cat. However, for once the cat didn't object, and seemed to rather admire himself in the ornate neckpiece.

Becker fussed during all of the preparations. Acorna and the others could hear him muttering to himself all the way down to Vhiliinyar's surface as they began their mission, only seven days, Vhiliinyar time, since Aari, Maati, Yiitir, and Maarni disappeared.

He was afraid that his friends would vanish, no matter how careful they were.

Acorna did not have the heart to tell him that it was her fear, too – and perhaps the heart of her plan.

NINE

'You sure you can track them, Nadhari?' Becker's voice boomed across the com links as the *Condor*, on MOO, spoke to the surveillance vessel commanded remotely by Nadhari Kando.

'Becker, you are like a mother hen with one chick. Every possible sense and emanation has a sensor attached to it. The landing party members are lit up like Christmas trees.'

'Getting pretty folksy there, Nadhari. What, your new boyfriend used to be a farmboy on Rushima or something?'

'That is none of your business, Jonas. Neither is this mission, from here on out.'

'I'm sorry, Nadhari. You know I only noodge because I care.' Becker sounded truly contrite. Acorna could just imagine the sort of face he would be making to – well, there was no one for him to make a face to aboard the *Condor* now. Aari and Maati were gone, and she, Thariinye, Mac, and RK were in the flitter headed for the site of the great waterfall.

Thariinye disagreed with her chosen target area.

'I want to save Maati and Aari as much as you

do, Khornya, but more people disappeared from the site of the laboratory, and other places. Shouldn't we start there?'

'We are more familiar with the terrain in that sector,' Acorna reminded him. 'Besides, there's something else I want to check out.' She flew past the place where she had last seen Aari and the others. The plants swayed gently in the wind, green and inviting unless you knew their true nature. 'The waterfall was near the sea, right?'

'Yes,' Thariinye said, with exaggerated patience.

'And Imaara said that somewhere between the fall and the sea was the old cave where the archives were kept. If it still exists, I'd like Mac to have a look at the walls.'

'Too bad that when Aari and Maati disappeared, they took that black coral thing with them,' Thariinye said. 'Mac could have looked at that and probably reconstructed the whole language of the *sii*-Linyaari. If only we'd thought to take him to Vhiliinyar to see the Ancestors with us. Of course, the Ancestors probably wouldn't have talked to us if he'd been with us. Still—'

Acorna, ignoring him, was tuned in to the mineral content of the areas beneath them. 'That seems a likely spot,' she said. 'I'm getting a sense of – hollowness, and of limestone there. A good place for a seashore cave.'

She set the flitter down and the four of them disembarked and walked cautiously forward, the two males following Acorna, while RK stalked ahead of them, his bushy black-streaked gray tail lashing. He was armed not only with sensors but also with plenty of repellent for the carnivorous plants. He seemed to think he was immune to attack.

Thariinye, much less cocky now that they were on the ground, furtively examined himself now and then, inspecting his feet or arms, to see if he was vanishing yet.

Mac simply took in the devastated landscape, impassively storing what he saw as data.

Acorna's steps across Vhiliinyar's surface were tentative at first, then as they moved closer to the place she had sensed from the flitter, grew more confident. Until she literally came up against a stone wall. At that point she stopped, staring at the rock as if willing it to go away, because she knew it shouldn't be there. She turned to Thariinye and Mac. They shrugged. Thariinye scratched his head and Mac looked as if he was trying to calculate the rock's density and how much thrust it would take him to burst through it.

RK came up with an immediate and much simpler solution. Without waiting for the rest of the party, he sprayed the wall. Then he walked over to one side of it, and rounded a corner that had been concealed by the shadow from an over-hang. He stood just beyond their sight, except for the tip of his tail, which he kept flipping as if to signal them in case they were so dense they hadn't figured out where he was.

The cat was right. There was an opening in the rock, one that seemed to lead downward almost immediately. But it was heavily choked with rocks, mud, broken bits of Khleevi scat, and other debris. It hardly looked passable.

'Of course, with mountains and cliffs leveled and waterfalls and seas buried in muck, we could hardly expect the cave entrance to be in any shape to use,' Thariinye said glumly. 'Besides, the cave must be buried so deep that it's impossible to get to – that is, if the whole thing hasn't caved in.'

Acorna said, 'The fact that there is still some sort of an opening at this level indicates to me there's a good chance that the cave hasn't filled in. I certainly didn't get a sense of it being filled in when I read the elements in the substrata here. But that's beside the point. Getting through to see what shape that cave is in is our problem right now.'

'*Not* a problem, Khornya,' Mac said. He had strapped a pack to his back when they left the flitter, and now he shrugged out of the straps and plowed through the contents, extracting pick and shovel attachments that locked into his hands. 'Stand back,' he advised, and attacked the blocked passage.

RK bolted and jumped to the top of Thariinye's head, holding on with all his claws as rock and mud began flying from the hollow in the rock he had so proudly discovered. Acorna didn't need to be telepathic to read the cat's mind.

'*This* is the treatment I get for showing those stupid people the way?' he was clearly thinking indignantly.

Thariinye was clearly yelling, though he couldn't be heard over all the noise Mac was making. Acorna extricated the cat from Thariinye's scalp as gently as possible, which wasn't very. A liberal application of horn-healing was necessary for all parties concerned except the cat, who retreated a considerable distance from the android-made avalanche and sat down to wash.

Thariinye was still in a bad mood, even after his scratches were healed. He nodded toward the storm of debris flying from beyond the rock. 'What the Khleevi didn't destroy, that android will if he keeps this up. What good will it do him to uncover the cave if he builds a mountain in front of it?'

But just then Mac reappeared, pulled something else out of his pack that turned out to be a collapsible wheeled carrier. He filled it with a load of debris.

'There,' Acorna said to Thariinye. 'He's thought of that. Mac, we can haul that away for you.'

Mac looked puzzled. 'But what would I do while you were doing so? Until I am further in, Khornya, the immediate area surrounding my excavation will be dangerous for organic life-forms. I will be quick. I promise.'

So he trundled off with a load of rocks and dirt and fragmented Khleevi scat, dumped it, then returned to reattach his pick and shovel, which he had removed to wield the wheelbarrow.

'Won't you wear your batteries out or something?' Thariinye asked.

But Mac had already returned to his digging and Thariinye's remark was lost in the thud, chink, crunch, hiss of the shoveling of dirt, the breaking of rock, and the tossing of both onto the growing pile beyond the cave. In a very short time

Mac was so far in the tunnel he was creating that Acorna and Thariinye could remove piles of debris without being hit by the flurry of flying gunk generated by Mac's current efforts.

As Thariinye loaded up his first cartful, Acorna said, 'Stay close enough for me to see you, and I'll do the same. I don't want us to go too far when we're spreading this stuff around, lest one of us disappear without the other noticing. I think if we just keep a path clear to the entrance it will do for now. The Khleevi left such a mess that our little contribution here does not matter. Uncle Hafiz can pretty things up when he terraforms.'

Thariinye was more than willing to go along with this plan, always being one to maximize results and minimize work, if possible. Even working so close to the cave entrance, soon enough he was tired, his white face and silver mane brown and black striped with dirt and sweat, and his breath in short supply. But, like Acorna, he kept at the job. He was not the most industrious of males, but he was not about to let a female outwork him, either.

RK supervised his human companions as they worked, and now and then entered the cave to check on Mac's progress. He had apparently forgiven the android, deciding that the attack of the flying landscape was not personal nor was it aimed exclusively at Makahomian Temple Cats.

During the entire procedure, their communication and monitoring channels were kept open so that the surveillance ship could hear and observe everything that went on. The ship had long-range scanners and was able to watch them as they went about their tasks, so it was not necessary to speak to them directly all the time to keep them posted on what they were doing, though periodically Acorna or Thariinye would direct a comment or a question to the ship's personnel.

When the sun set, they kept working, using miners' lights attached to their helmets. Loading dirt and rock by hand into the wheelbarrow by the erratically bobbing glow of her lantern, Acorna imagined herself in the place of one of the child miners she had rescued from Kezdet. She thought how hard their lives must have been as they did this backbreaking work day after heart wrenchingly weary day, with no more light than she had, far underground, punished if they slackened their pace even for a moment. When she thought of Maganos Moonbase, which she had helped Delszaki Li, her old mentor, transform from a useless moon into an educational and vocational school for the former child slaves they had rescued, it made her feel less burdened by her present task.

Thinking of the Moonbase brought her friends and family to mind. She would find Aari, Maati, Neeva, and the others. She would. She *would*. And they would be fine. *Just fine.* Nothing bad would have happened to them. *Nothing at all.* They only needed her to come and get them. Any other circumstance was unthinkable.

(Hold on. We're coming. I'm coming. Can you hear me, Aari *yaazi*, Maati, Mother-sister Neeva?)

She was so busy hauling dirt and concentrating on not panicking over her missing loved ones

135

that she didn't notice that the incredible noise of excavation had stopped or hear Mac speak to her until he tapped her on the shoulder.

'I believe,' he said, 'that I have reached the entrance of the cave you spoke of. The entrance was not so badly blocked as we had feared it might be, nor the cave so damaged. There is writing on the walls that you will wish to see. I've used my laser attachment to solidify strips of the walls for support and stabilization – and yes, Khornya, mindful of your instructions regarding the petroglyphs and the artifacts, I ascertained that none were contained in the material I fused before I did so. But as we lack any other sort of material with which to shore up the walls, the fusing was necessary to prevent further cave-ins. I have no ambition to be flattened in this adventure, nor to see you so afflicted.'

'We understand, Mac. Thank you,' Acorna said. She was already inside the cave as she said this, picking her way forward on the rubble-strewn floor. The passage led steadily, even steeply at times, downward, for an amazing length considering that Mac had been doing all of the clearing by 'hand.'

'This job was one in which one of those picturesque little railroad devices would have improved my efficiency, and our journey,' Mac remarked, practically in her ear, startling Acorna into stopping, which stopped Mac, cramming Thariinye, who was behind him, between the android and the steeply descending path.

Acorna wondered if RK had come with them and looked around for him. Becker would never forgive her if the *Condor*'s first mate was the first of their party to disappear.

Her lamp caught two gold coins hovering above Thariinye's head, further back and higher up on the path, and then there was a streak of fur, a graze of claws, and the cat landed on the path in front of her. With an impatient glance backward, RK began stalking his way down the tunnel.

Acorna smiled. 'The cat is playing the canary,' she told the other two.

'He doesn't look as if he is,' Thariinye observed. 'He is not making chirping noises or trying to flap his paws.'

Mac said, 'I believe Khornya is referring to a barbaric mining custom from antiquity, in which the miners took a small caged bird with them down into the mines. If there was a leak of toxic gas, the bird would die first, and its death would warn the miners that the shaft was unsafe and they must leave immediately.'

As if he understood every word Mac had said, RK suddenly stopped, turned to Acorna and gave a kittenish mew, then put his paws on her knees, clearly asking to be lifted. She picked him up and he settled around her shoulders. A natural born leader he might be, he seemed to say as he licked his fur into place, but while he was willing to assume equal risks with his team, he was not about to risk one hair of his precious pelt just so they could run off and leave him. He would ride for this portion of the journey, and hang on tight to his transport. Acorna winced a little as the cat's claws sank into her neck.

The light beams from their helmet lamps cast

shadows on the jagged walls, moving crazily as they picked their way through the passage to the cave. The shadows cast by that light made the rescue team look like a party of rubberized marionettes jerking along on invisible strings as they descended. It was an eerie journey.

All but Mac jumped when the com link came to life, and the surveillance ship's captain, one Yaniriin, spoke into their ears.

'Khornya, Thariinye, and Maak,' he said. 'We just had a sighting of something interesting near the laboratory camp. The source looks like a single person. We're sending down another flitter to check it out.'

'That sounds like good news, Yaniriin,' Acorna said a bit shakily, torn by hope. 'Maybe one of our lost ones has returned. Please keep us posted as you check it out. We are now inside the passage to the cave we were seeking. Do you need us to return to the surface and meet the new flitter at the lab site?'

'I see no reason for that, Khornya. But keep listening to us as you work. Depending on what we discover, we may need you later. And keep us informed of what you discover, as well.'

'Of course,' she said. 'But there's not a great deal to say yet. We haven't reached our destination.'

'What are you looking for?'

She hedged. The importance of this cave and the existence of petroglyphs made by the earliest Ancestral Attendants were a secret she had promised the Ancestors and their Attendants she would keep. But she didn't need to identify

138

exactly what she was looking for to justify her actions.

'Someone at base camp talked about hearing underground rumblings when the *aagroni* went missing,' she answered. 'I decided it might be worth looking for underground installations, either left behind by the Khleevi or by our own people, to see if they could have something to do with these disappearances.'

'With all due respect, that sounds like a waste of time to me,' Yaniriin said. 'Shouldn't you back-track to all the places where the lost ones were last seen instead?'

'We will do that as well, eventually,' Acorna assured him. 'But we are hoping to find a key here as to why the disappearances occurred. Besides, if you are right, and we backtrack to where our friends disappeared, it seems to me that I stand a great risk of losing my new team members as well as the previously missing survey members. And, although if we vanish that would probably tell *me* what became of the others, it would hardly enlighten the rest of you. I hope to find the reasons for these disappearances, and thus find the missing survey personnel, without getting lost myself.'

'With the sensors, you could probably be traced, if you went missing.'

'Yes, that is the hope. But, until we test that theory, we have no certainty, do we?' she said. 'Just find a bit more patience in your heart, Captain. The information I seek here could be very valuable.'

'Very well,' he said. 'You must forgive me,

Khornya. Aarlii, who disappeared with three others from the *Siiaaryi Maartri*, is my firstborn.'

'I'm sorry to hear that, Yaniriin. I share your grief. Perhaps you don't know, but my lifemate and his kin-sister, his parents, my mother-sister, and my former crewmates from the *Balakiire* are also among the missing. Be assured that I will do everything I can to find them all as quickly as possible.'

The conversation, overheard by at least fifty people of three different races and spanning the vastness of space, seemed oddly intimate, down here in the dark where she, Mac, and Thariinye moved slowly between the narrow, rough-hewn walls of the newly opened passage.

'Here!' Mac said suddenly, pointing to a spot just within the pool of light cast by Acorna's head-lamp. 'The cave entrance is here!'

'We have found what we were seeking, Yaniriin,' she said. 'I will now explore it.'

'Continue communication, please,' he said. 'I want a full report, and—'

As she stepped out of the rough passage and into the wide opening that had been the cave's mouth, her com unit failed. The indicator light on her shipsuit went dull and lifeless, and her receiver was silent despite repeated attempts to hail the surveillance ship.

'Thariinye, please tell Yaniriin I have had an equipment malfunction,' she said, but Thariinye did not appear to hear her until he had joined her and Mac in the cave's entrance.

'That's funny,' he said. 'My com unit is dead.'

'How odd.' Acorna decided a small test was in

order. Signaling Thariinye to stay put, she stepped out of the cave once more. Her com link activated with the words, '– silence. We've lost—'

'Yaniriin, this is Khornya. This cave has some sort of barrier to our com units. I am not sure how or why. Perhaps the mechanism causing this is part of the answer we seek – the reason why our friends and family are missing. Therefore, I feel it is essential to continue exploring, despite the communication difficulties. We will not be able to maintain contact with you while we are here. However, one of our party will remain outside the cave entrance as long as possible to maintain visual contact with the others, and transmit our report to you.'

'That sounds very risky, Khornya. Perhaps you should return to your flitter and rethink your plan.'

'Negative, Yaniriin. But we will take no longer than necessary in gathering the data we need. That's the best I can promise. I am going to step back inside the cave now, but please expect contact to be resumed within sixty seconds by myself or one of my compatriots.'

'I read you, Khornya, but I still don't care for—'

His last word was cut off as Acorna stepped back inside the cave entrance.

TEN

During the journey to Vhiliinyar, Mac had been studying the few entries Acorna and Thariinye had been able to make in the LAANYE from the Ancestors' records, and now he and Thariinye were eagerly checking these entries against the very faint and faded scratchings on the cave walls. The first glyphs they saw were much damaged by the rock that had fallen against them during the cave-ins, but as they retreated farther into the cave, the damage to the paintings was less.

'We have a problem,' Acorna told her team members. 'This chamber blocks our transmissions to the surveillance ship quite thoroughly. One of us needs to stay out in the tunnel, maintaining contact with the ship and visual contact with the team in the cave.'

'That's no problem,' Thariinye said, straightening up at once. 'I'll be glad to stay outside. I think I've given Maak enough clues that he can decipher these scribblings – excuse me, ancient glyphs – readily enough. You can assist him as well as I can now.'

'That's very gracious of you,' Acorna said, suppressing a smile. 'If there's any news about who that person found wandering near the base camp is, please duck in and tell us, will you?'

'Oh, certainly,' he said, and with what seemed to Acorna to be a sigh of relief, he stepped outside the chamber and into the tunnel, where he stood facing them, his mouth moving as he spoke into the com unit.

'Thank you, Khornya,' Mac said. 'It will be easier to concentrate without needing to pay attention to Thariinye as he regales me with stories about various young females of his close personal acquaintance.'

Acorna laughed for the first time in several days and squatted down beside Mac, her hand stroking RK's back as he strolled back and forth between them. The cat's fur bristled slightly at the nape, just to let whatever there was at large that might hurt them know that he was prepared. If necessary, he could puff himself up to three times his normal size. That should throw a good scare into anything unwise enough to accost himself or his companions.

The work began to go very quickly, with Mac moving more swiftly than Acorna could along the walls, recording the drawings and translating the writings, until he was out of her sight. Soon she had to duck out for a moment to tell Thariinye she needed to move farther back in the cave to keep Mac in visual range. 'I'll be able to hear you if you pop your head in now and then and call for us,' she said. 'We'll call back. If we fail to respond, please signal the surveillance ship and relate the problem, then come and see what is wrong.'

143

Thariinye looked up from the com unit, into which he had been alternately babbling and listening appreciatively, and waved her on. 'Yes, oh, yes, Miliira, I remember her, Vriin. Saucy little – she's your lifemate now, you say? Well – er – congratulations. I always liked that girl.'

Acorna shook her head and returned to the cavern.

'I assume this is all making sense to you now, Mac?' she asked.

'Oh, yes, Khornya. The writings are not difficult to translate, being mainly pictorial, and in a base language that strongly resembles modern Linyaari, in which I am fluent, except that these early Ancestors of yours were very poor spellers, and are inconsistent in their symbology for certain concepts. This makes these glyphs harder to understand than they would otherwise be. But I believe I now understand what these walls have to tell us.'

'Is there anything you've read so far that you feel might be helpful in our current situation?' she asked.

'Not so far. The communications are mostly about where the best pasture is to be found, and the various indispositions of your ancestral race and cures for them, dietary preferences, that sort of thing.'

'Is there anything about the Ancestral Friends?' she asked. 'Do you know enough now that you might be able to scan the remaining glyphs and see if you can pick up a mention of them, or of these caves, or of the shield we're encountering – or of any sort of weapon?'

'I will try that, Khornya,' Mac said, and began to scan the walls even more rapidly until he said, 'Aha!' in a highly dramatic manner, his finger pointing in the air as he said so. 'Here they are, mentioned several times. It says . . .'

'You're both out of visual contact,' Thariinye called out rather crossly. 'Are you quite all right?'

'Yes, Thariinye, we're fine,' Acorna called. 'But we're going to be here for a bit. Check on us, say, every five minutes.'

'Oh, very well,' he said, as if he had more pressing matters to attend to.

Mac meanwhile was moving deeper into the cave. The cave wound much further back, but presently they came upon a carved staircase leading upward, as it had in the Ancestral Attendants' library on narhii-Vhiliinyar. The glyphs spiraled up with the staircase so they followed them to the upper room.

'It is odd. The mentions are more frequent as the entries appear to increase in age and crudity, Khornya,' he told her. 'Here! This one. It says, "Here I set down the stories of the Ancients as told to me by my own four-legged ancestors, whom I serve. I have long wondered at the difference between our mother people, the four-footed and finned ones with the healing horns and rather primitive minds, and our father people, the technologically advanced and sophisticated ones who call themselves simply our Friends.

' "Across time and space they came to rescue us and . . . " '

'Khornya? Mac?' Thariinye's voice called from the cavern room beneath them.

'We're here, Thariinye,' Acorna answered.

'Yaniriin wants us to return to the flitter and go to the base camp. The person they saw wandering around is Liriili.'

'Oh.' Acorna sighed. She had so hoped it would be someone else. Anyone else, in fact. 'We'll be there as soon as we can, but I believe that, having put so much effort into it, we should finish here first,' Acorna said. 'After all our hard work, I would like to hear what these walls have to say, even if it delays the pleasure of our reunion with Liriili.'

RK looked up at her and meowed loudly. He, at least, liked the former *viizaar*.

'But tell me what you know about her re-appearance. I would like to know how she is. Where was she? What happened to her? Does she know where the others being held?'

Thariinye said, 'I'll get back to you on that, Khornya.'

'You didn't ask?' Acorna said, stunned.

'Not yet,' Thariinye said. 'But I will do so now.' Silence again.

'Sometimes I worry about that boy.' Turning back to Mac, she said, 'Go back, Mac. That first line, what was it?'

He repeated it.

'Across *time* and space,' she said. 'I wonder . . . Of course, some time differences are inherent in space travel. It may mean nothing.'

Thariinye's voice cut through the silence around them. 'Liriili says that what happened to her was that she got lost. She left the flitter for a moment to go look for food. But the laboratory structure was not where she remembered it being. When she turned back to the flitter, it was not there either. She wandered around the area of the base camp growing more and more confused, she thinks for many days. Then suddenly she was facing the laboratory structure again, only it was deserted. She says she saw no one else between the time she left the com unit and the time she was rescued. Yaniriin wants to know if we wish to speak to her before she is evacuated to the surveillance vessel. Personally, since she has so little to say about her time away, *I* have no wish to speak with her.'

'Hmmm,' Acorna mused. 'Her *time* away.'

Mac looked up and saw her twisting a lock of her mane around her finger thoughtfully, chewing slightly on her lower lip with an abstracted look on her face.

'Khornya? What shall I tell them?'

'Tell them to ask her – oh, never mind. I think I should do this myself. I hate to break this off here, but I have some questions I think may shed some light on our predicament. Ask them to wait before evacuating her. I would like to ask her some specific questions there where she was lost and rescued.'

'Do you think she was abducted by aliens and returned to the same place?' Thariinye asked.

'Invisible aliens? The same ones who took the others? The ones that never showed up on our sensors? It seems Liriili never saw an alien. Surely they wouldn't have gone to all that trouble to grab

147

her just to return her to us without even intro-
ducing themselves. I find the alien theory
doubtful, Thariinye, don't you?'

'Yes, I suppose so.'

Mac said, 'Khornya, do you wish me to remain
and continue the translation?'

She sighed. 'No, Mac, I might need you.
Besides, given all that has happened, I don't like
being out of touch with any member of my team
for any reason. We will come back and finish this.
The cave has been here since the first Linyaari
waited on the first Ancestor. It survived all during
our history and even made it through the Khleevi
attack when almost nothing else did. I am sure the
opening will be here when we can return and
continue our investigations.'

They rejoined Thariinye outside the main
room's entrance, checked in with the surveillance
ship, and began the steep trek back up the tunnel.
RK chose to ride around Thariinye's neck as the
tall male led the way back to the surface. Acorna
made use of the time to be briefed by the ship's
captain, though he could tell her little more than
Thariinye had already.

'Liriili is complaining that she was deserted
and left to starve for days and now you are keeping her from returning to civilization, Khornya,'
Yaniriin said. 'I have explained the situation to
her, and the flitter crew have opened their minds
to her, but she still seems to feel it is all a plot of
some sort.'

'It sounds as if she has suffered no ill effects
from her ordeal then, Yaniriin, and is still very

much herself,' Acorna said. The path they were following was very steep, and at times she had to use both hands as well as her feet to keep herself upright during the ascent. She was thankful for the distraction. Somehow, Liriili always managed to try her patience. Even rescuing the former *viizaar* ran true to form. 'Tell Liriili that we are moving as quickly as we can. Quicker than is comfortable, even.'

That was certainly true. In their haste, Thariinye kept kicking rocks back into her face, and as she drew level with him, RK's tail tickled her nose. Mac was so close behind his 'horn' prodded her in the back occasionally.

It was very hot in the tunnel, and close.

She spoke slowly, pausing for breath between her words, 'We must regain the surface and then there is a little bit of a hike to the flitter. Then perhaps another two hours' ride to the base camp? Try to get Liriili to complain more rather than less while she waits for me, Yaniriin. It should not be difficult. Perhaps she will remember something she endured that she has not yet mentioned that will give us clues to the whereabouts of the others.'

'Very well,' Yaniriin said. She could hear the reluctance in his voice as he contemplated spending more time than he had to listening to Liriili.

Acorna said, 'Bear in mind, Captain, that once she is evacuated from the planet's surface you will not be hearing her complaints vicariously, but on your own bridge, and she will be standing right next to you as she delivers them. Every moment we delay postpones that scenario.'

'Oh – yes. I suppose there is that,' he said, sounding somewhat abashed.

The team continued its upward journey until they were near the tunnel mouth when Yaniriin suddenly said, 'Wait! There is something, someone, moving near your flitter. Let me zoom in for a closer look.'

'Someone Linyaari?' Acorna asked, breathless because of more than the climb now. Could Aari or one of the others have come back, too? Perhaps whatever had taken the research teams was now releasing all of them. 'Can you tell who it is?'

'Not yet. Unlike yourselves, this being is not carpeted with an array of sensors. Let me look more closely. How odd . . . The being is not Linyaari. No horn. But it is very large—'

'Two feet? Four feet? More?' Thariinye asked.

'Hard to tell. Something seems to be draped over its lower portions, but I would guess four. It is very bulky. From what we can see, it could be an animal of what your human friends call the ursine species, Khornya, the sort that is heavily furred and may stand on two legs or four.'

'A bear? On Vhiliinyar?' Mac shook his head, grazed Acorna's shoulder and stepped a steep step backward, only just catching himself against the wall and preventing himself from falling. 'Highly unlikely.'

'Until we have sent the flitter to investigate it and determine its intent, perhaps you should stay in the cavern,' Yaniriin suggested.

'I would like to see what it is,' Acorna said.

'If it is harmful, you might regret that decision,' Yaniriin said. 'Wait for the flitter to come get you after we have investigated.'

'Becker *said* we should have brought weapons,' she murmured.

'That would not have been permitted,' Yaniriin said most severely. 'It does not appear to be Khleevi, from what we can see, at least. But that does not mean it will not take a bite out of you.'

In the time since Acorna had met the first emissaries of her people – her Aunt Neeva, Thariinye, and the other crew members of the *Balakiire* – even the most sheltered Linyaari had become more aware of the universe around them. Some of them even realized that the Khleevi were not the only hostile lifeforms they might have to contend with. When Neeva and her ship had first come to Kezdet, the Linyaari had believed beings were either *Linyaari* or *Khleevi* – good, like their own species, or horrible and alien like the invaders who had destroyed Vhiliinyar. Now Yaniriin was acknowledging that this being near the rescue team's flitter could be an enemy, even if it was not Khleevi.

'I am armed,' Mac told Acorna. 'I did not deliberately bring weapons onto your world, but devices which can be used as weapons are a part of my physiology. I assure you we are well protected.'

'Against some things, perhaps,' Yaniriin said, overhearing this. 'But it would be better if we could determine what this being is, contain it, isolate it, and find out its intent before it meets three Linyaari on foot.'

The com unit went silent for a moment and Acorna heard an odd noise from behind her. She looked back to see Mac wiping his eye, though it was perfectly dry.

'Is something bothering your vision, Mac?' she asked.

'I weep internally for joy, Khornya. Did you hear? The captain said three Linyaari. I am considered one of you now.'

'Don't expect Liriili to be so broad-minded,' Thariinye said. 'I don't suppose it would hurt anything if we just stepped outside the entrance, just a little, to cool off and get a breath of air while we wait for the flitter to inspect our new friend and then come and get us.'

Acorna had to agree. It was unlikely that whatever was prowling around their flitter would be able to see them at the cave entrance. And though Mac and the cat seemed spry as ever, she and Thariinye were both hot, tired, and sick of tasting the dust of the tunnel.

They stepped cautiously outside and each uncorked a water bottle and had a long swallow.

Mac ran a maintenance check on himself.

RK sat on the ground at their feet, made an L of his back legs, and washed himself along the lower belly and tail.

'What are you doing? Get back inside the cave!' Yaniriin barked suddenly. 'It's coming toward you, whatever it is, and – wait, there's another one.'

ELEVEN

'Where?' Thariinye asked, scanning the landscape. 'I don't see a thing!'

'Never mind, just conceal yourselves!' Yaniriin ordered.

Acorna had already ducked back just inside the tunnel. While Thariinye was talking into his com unit, she glimpsed, over his shoulder, two large heavy hairy beings running toward them, brandishing long sticks with points on the ends – spears. Spears?

One of them was covered on the top with matted red fur, and on the bottom with matted brown fur. The other's top fur was black to midway down the trunk, then mottled gray. They ran very swiftly for such ungainly looking beings but Acorna decided they were roughly humanoid – after all, they seemed to be able to use rudimentary tools.

As they drew closer she saw their eyes from under their shag of hair. They looked wild, ferocious, definitely hostile, and they were fixed on Thariinye and the mouth of the cave.

Thariinye had frozen.

Acorna rushed out, grabbed his arm, and

pulled him back inside the cave passage. And abruptly, she herself was pulled further back into the cave so suddenly that she fell over backwards.

'I am sorry, Khornya, and I shall be sorry to lose the esteem of your people, but I believe these beings mean us harm. Run back into the cave and keep running. I will cover your flank.'

Mac snapped out his pick attachment from one arm. In the other he held his laser. She untangled herself from Thariinye, who had also fallen, and rose to her feet, pulling him with her. Though she would never wish to leave a friend to danger in order to protect herself, what Mac said made excellent sense. Two such obviously primitive beings would be no match for Mac. Not that he was alone. A bristling, snarling RK, larger than Acorna had ever seen him, blocked out the twilight from between Mac's legs with bushels of enraged fur.

She was reassured when she saw that instead of confronting the beings directly, Mac had backed into the cavern, seeking the best place in which to make a stand. He was clearly going to use caution and good sense in his defense of them. RK looked up at Mac in astonishment then abandoned his battle stance and hightailed it back to Acorna and Thariinye. Acorna could almost hear the cat think that he could protect them as easily from back here as from up front with an android who wouldn't feel anything if that long pointy thing got stuck in him.

The hairy monsters suddenly filled the entrance to the cave, while Mac, some yards back, said, 'I caution you not to come nearer. We are peaceful beings but my hands are lethal weapons and I will use them to defend my companions if necessary.'

RK turned and growled and fluffed again.

'Also,' Mac said, as the hairy monsters laughed, seemingly at the lameness of his warning, 'there is a cat of great fierceness.'

In answer to this the shaggy red-topped monster thrust his spear at Mac, who broke it off while burning the spear from the hand of the other monster with his laser attachment.

That was all Acorna saw, for just then Thariinye grabbed her hand and all but dragged her off her feet, pulling her down deeper into the tunnel toward the cave's mouth.

And then they were running, panting, running, running, sweat pouring off them, running deeper and deeper, the passage walls swirling crazily in the tilting light from their headlamps.

Behind them, very distantly, horrible roars and growls interspersed with occasional erudite exclamations from Mac, such as 'I see that your hirsute condition functions as something of a shield for entrapping the weapons of your foes! Let us see if it can capture a laser beam! Aha! Take that,' echoed off the walls of the tunnel.

Really, it seemed to Acorna that there was no need to retreat quite so far, but Thariinye's thoughts roiled with the beat of his footfalls.

(He who fights and runs away will live and love another day; he who fights and runs away will live . . .)

Obviously Thariinye had spent too much time pouring over the hard copy books of aphorisms

155

among the literary litter aboard Becker's *Condor*.

Had Mac appeared to be actually endangered by the hairy louts attacking them, Acorna would have returned immediately to help him. The cat already appeared to have done so, which worried her. Fierce as Makahomian Temple Cats might be, they were flesh and blood, whereas Mac's own anatomy was much more complex and not very organic.

But even RK's feline battle cries faded in the distance as Thariinye pulled her swiftly along, past all of the area where Mac had translated runes, then down a corridor that branched into another corridor. At the second branch she gave a mental bellow that stopped Thariinye in his tracks.

(*Whoa!*) she said. (This is a good way to get us thoroughly lost.)

'Oh, Mac will find us,' Thariinye replied breezily.

'That is true – if he doesn't get pulverized. Which is another reason that we should not proceed any farther. We should be close enough to help Mac if he or RK need it.'

Just then they heard a terrible bellow and a rumble, clatters and thumps and rattles of rocks and earth falling.

A cloud of dust billowed toward them and Acorna charged for it. This time it was Thariinye dragging along behind *her*.

She tore back through the cave corridors as quickly as she could, but from what she could see through the clouds of dust, the place where daylight had once poured into the passage from the tunnel's entrance was now shrouded in total darkness except for the light cast by the lamps she and Thariinye wore on their foreheads. And then, through the dust and debris, another feeble light wobbled toward them, growing brighter as it came.

'Mac! Are you alright?' she called.

'Yes, Khornya, but the cat has sustained an injury and unfortunately my horn, while quite useful in other ways, lacks the healing capabilities of your own. He is quite a brave cat. One of the beasts attempted to decapitate me with a large sword, which would not, of course, have killed me, but would have seriously disabled me long enough for the monsters to reach you. RK distracted the monster by jumping onto its head and raking it with his claws. He is bleeding rather badly and I did not wish to continue the battle when my comrade in arms needed your help. So I collapsed a small portion of the tunnel on the monsters, between them and us. That should slow them down until the flitter arrives.'

Acorna dropped Thariinye's hand and ran forward to meet Mac, whose shipsuit was torn into so many tatters that it made him look almost as shaggy as his recent opponents. RK looked up at her and meowed once, and dropped his head back onto Mac's arm. Acorna bent her head and tried to search through the cat's fur for the wounds, but the dust was so thick she could see very little and besides, she was afraid of what all this dust was doing to all of them. The haze was far beyond the scope of the usual sorts of airborne pollutants Linyaari horns were so good at cleansing. She walked backward in front of Mac as they descended to the cave entrance, touching as much of RK as she could with her horn, while trying not to accidentally gouge Mac.

After a few seconds of this, RK roused himself, grabbed her horn with both hands and licked it, then wriggled free of Mac and trotted down to Thariinye, where he proceeded to wash again.

'A mighty warrior,' Mac said admiringly. 'He fought bravely, and with no technological attachments to help him.'

Thariinye knelt down and scratched RK's head, until his hand met with a swipe of claws. 'Oh, the cat has attachments, and though I wouldn't exactly call them technological, they are effective,' he told Mac, rubbing his horn over his new wounds.

All of them quickly moved further back into the cave, as far away from the choking clouds of dust as they could easily get, to where Thariinye's and Acorna's horns could purify the air more quickly.

'You know, Mac, you really frightened Khornya,' Thariinye said. 'She taught me how to fly without the benefit of a spacecraft, making a glider of me as she towed me in her wake coming to save you.'

'I apologize for frightening you with the cave-in,' Mac said. 'But I knew the elders did not want me to kill the monsters, yet the monsters were quite persistent. It was a dilemma. I do not read minds, but after a few moments, I could understand their words, which were a very antiquated form of one of the early Terran languages, a forerunner of Standard Galactic. Oddly, they seemed to think you were the monsters, and were thinking mostly basic thoughts such as "Kill, kill, kill the beasts" back and forth to encourage each other, and laughing as they did so, reminding me in their own rough-hewn way somewhat of my former owner, Kisla Manjari. I landed several blows with the flat of my pick on their heads, but they were impervious. I doubt the cave-in will damage them, but it will provide us with protection for the moment, and I can dig us out soon enough when the flitter arrives with help.'

'Famous last words,' Acorna muttered.

'Excuse me?' Thariinye said.

'Nothing, just something my uncles used to say about planning things in times of danger—'

Two bellows, some more crashing and rumbling, a great deal more clatter and rattle, and a lot more dust belching into the cave followed.

Neither the Linyaari nor Mac coughed, but the cat ran back into the cave. Without a word, the others followed him.

As the fluff of tail disappeared around the corner Thariinye and Acorna had not taken, Acorna called, 'RK, it's all right. We're coming. But slow down or you'll be lost and we'll never find you.'

RK peered around the corner, his tail lashing impatiently, as if to say, 'Fine with me. You people are nothing but a lot of trouble,' which seemed remarkably ungrateful considering that they had just healed his undoubtedly otherwise mortal wounds.

But then, cats were not fabled in song and story

159

for their undying gratitude. Acorna winced at her own apt pun and joined the cat in the corridor he had chosen. Thariinye and Mac joined her, with Mac lagging behind as rearguard while the others tried to outdistance the dust.

'Stop!' Mac said. 'I can scan the images on these walls into my processor very quickly, but not *this* quickly.'

'Are you still suspended from a high place on *that*?' Thariinye asked, literally translating a slang phrase he had picked up from Becker. 'Those things are making a fine mess out of your cave-in. For all we know, they may be moving enough rock to get through to us right now.'

'Judging from what we have seen, I would say that is quite likely,' Acorna said. 'I feel it is best for us to go as far from them as possible at the moment. We might be able to lose them here in these caves, making further violence unnecessary. Besides, RK is having a difficult time breathing in all this dust. Further in and away from the worst of the haze, Thariinye and I can control the air quality much faster with our horns.'

'Very well,' Mac said, and his tone surprised Acorna. The usually genial and cooperative android was almost grumbling. 'But this data is extremely interesting and it is, after all, why we came here.'

'True,' Acorna said, 'and it is most commendable of you to show such dedication to your task. And, at some more convenient time, we will resume our work. However, I think that, rather than doing what we came here to do, our skills and lights would be put to better use for the moment looking for an alternative way *out* of here.'

'These are superior lanterns with a very long life,' Thariinye said.

'And I can always recharge them from my own cells,' Mac pointed out.

'And who is going to recharge you when you run out of energy?' Acorna asked. 'Though I realize how unlikely such an event is,' she added when Mac protested. 'How long has it been since our conversation with the captain, Thariinye?'

Mac answered. 'Approximately half an hour, Kezdet time, Khornya.'

'Not long enough,' she said. 'Stay here. I'll be back in a moment.'

'Where are you going?' Thariinye asked.

'Back to the tunnel to tell Yaniriin of what happened and what we are doing. I will also mark the way we came to this place, then we can keep marking as we go. That way we can find our way back, as soon as it is feasible. Or, once our people get past the monsters at the entrance and the cave-in, they can find us.'

But when she reached the main cavern room, she found that the rocks from the cave-ins caused by their hairy friends outside had tumbled down the tunnel and choked half the room as well as the entrance. Now they were well and truly trapped until Mac had time to dig through the rock again. And it looked like this time the job would be a lot more difficult. It appeared her instincts were right – it might be easier to seek another way out of here than to tackle that rock fall a second time. Furthermore, her com unit worked no better

161

inside the cavern than it had before. The survey ship personnel would be very worried about them. Still, matters were not desperate. The blockage kept the monsters at bay for the moment. And Yaniriin knew they were inside the tunnel somewhere. In time, people would come to search for them if they did not find another way out.

On to the next matter. How to mark their passage? Even if no rescuers arrived, such markings would help her own party retrace their steps when it became necessary. She had no ball of yarn, no bread crumbs, no chalk. The sensors in their shipsuits did not work in here. Or did they? Perhaps they simply did not work outside the cave to detect what was inside and vice versa. They might work very well inside the cave itself. It was a good idea, and she would test it as soon as she rejoined the others. Nevertheless, she and her friends must be able to count on something more tangible to retrace their steps. Equipment that had failed once for no apparent reason could do so again. Of course, it was possible that Mac had already stored in his database the entire sequence of runes from one room to another, and so the whole exercise was unnecessary. But if Mac became separated from them, they needed a fall-back position.

So what could she use to mark their paths? Something effective ... Something easy to use ... Something more basic ... Something there was a ready supply of ... And here it was all around her: rocks.

She filled her pockets and hands with them and

began laying them in fours, one for each of them. She placed each pile six paces apart, the distance between herself and the end of her lantern beam. That way, they could always see the next pile of rocks. And, even if the lantern was dead, they should be able to find the rock piles by pacing.

She handled each pebble before piling it with the others, so it would be marked with the scent of her hands, which quickly grew rough and chafed under the unaccustomed work. When that happened, she used her horn to heal them, and continued laying a path of rock cairns until Thariinye tapped her on the shoulder.

TWELVE

Acorna looked up from her passage-marking to see three expectant faces – Mac's, Thariinye's, and RK's where he lay draped across Thariinye's shoulders.

'We're on our own for now,' she told them. 'That cave is half full of rubble from the cave-in, and it will be tough getting into the passage. So I'm marking a trail. You two might want to fill your own pockets with rocks while we've got such a nice supply of them. I've already marked this far. I'll go back for another load now.'

Her friends agreed with her. While they loaded up with rocks, Mac also continued his work on the cave drawings, which he certainly had the time to pursue now. The flitter was only an hour away, according to Mac's calculations.

'Well, then,' Thariinye said, 'actually, all this effort is unnecessary. We could just wait to be rescued. Those monsters aren't likely to find us through the mess they made. The ship will have warned the flitter and Yaniriin has undoubtedly sent properly equipped reinforcements to help capture our guests.'

'True,' Acorna said, 'but I still believe we

should continue our own efforts here. The survey ship might decide we were killed in the cave-in. Or there may be some problem up on the surface with digging us out that we're unaware of. For example, what if there are a *lot* more of those hairy things running about the planet? Besides, we came here to explore. Why don't we do it? I agree with Mac – he should return to deciphering runes. And I'd like to see if my mineral sense can tell me more about the geological origins of this place, and look for another way out.'

'Even if there was another exit at one time, there's probably not now,' Thariinye advised. 'After all, the main entrance was buried pretty deep.'

He looked dejected, and rather frightened. Thariinye was not a coward, no matter how cautiously he had behaved recently. She had seen him charge Khleevi when his friends were in danger. But he was not one to court death unnecessarily – especially when no one interesting was around to be impressed.

So she gave a smile and a little shrug and turned toward the hidden mysteries of the unexplored cavern, saying, 'You have a point. On the other hand, the recent upheavals we've witnessed and those caused by the Khleevi when they were here may have exposed something that was less accessible in the days when the Attendants used this place. Who knows what we might discover? We might even be heroes! Look on it as an adventure.'

Thariinye perked right up.

Mac's pace, as he tried to translate and record

the runes all around them, was much slower than the one they'd have used if the situation was truly desperate, but Acorna was in no real hurry. They continued for a little while in this way. She, too, needed to concentrate as she mapped out the geology of the rock around them.

Thariinye, however, suddenly felt the need to reassure her. 'We'll be fine, Khornya, you'll see. They'll be here for us in no time. Why, I'll bet the ship dispatched extra flitters which have netted those beasts in cross tractor beams and are hauling them aboard a craft specially rigged as a jail. Where do you suppose those hairy things were from anyway? I've never seen anything like them.'

'Mac says the language is ancient Terran,' she replied, not really paying attention. The walls just ahead bore runes that were much older and more faintly etched than any they'd seen before, and beyond them the cavern walls appeared to be bare. 'So perhaps they are from some devolved space colony.'

'Full of beings who don't know how to comb their hair or use lasers but are capable of space travel?' Thariinye argued. 'Unlikely, Khornya. Really! Use your head!'

'That's what I'm trying to do,' she said, and turned him gently back the way they had come. 'Perhaps your skills would best be utilized helping Mac with his translations. You are the only one of us to whom Linyaari is your first and native tongue, after all.'

When he was gone, she felt pressure against her leg and saw that RK had remained to keep her company. Quietly. She smiled at the cat.

She opened her mind and put her hands upon the walls of the cavern, walking them one over the other as she paced the length of the corridor, not forgetting to leave her little stone quartets as she paced. When she had finished with the wall on one side of the corridor, she followed it back down the other, breathing as deeply and steadily as she could. The mineral composition was what came first and most easily to her. Limestone with veins of quartz and copper, basalt and deposits of ametrine and azurite.

Gradually, she could feel what was beyond them, just a bit at first, and then, more deeply.

Stone, stone, stone, sand and . . . water! Moving, surging water, waves and knots and fathoms of it, deep, very deep, beneath her feet.

To one side dirt and stone, the granite of a fallen mountainside.

The other side was what she had hoped to find – lighter, thinner, air on the other side intermixed with other things she could tell much less about, though there was stone there . . . Her sensory impressions were being clouded by emotional ones. Disappointment . . . no . . . something deeper . . . disillusionment . . . repugnance . . . and a longing . . . A longing for what, Acorna wondered. Love? Nurture? The emotion felt like a child wanting its mother. In fact, it reminded her somewhat of the impressions she had received so strongly, if not always consciously, from the child slaves on Kezdet, the orphans of war victims torn from their burning and bombed homes and the arms of their dead parents to be forced into the lowest and most degrading sorts of labor. Unlike Kezdet, there was no actual fear involved in the strand of emotion. Not here. But there was anger. A lot of it. What was that about?

She increased her concentration, deepened her breathing, and stared ahead of her. Suddenly, the corridor flooded with light.

Along the walls where the runes had been, holos sprung into life – images, stories, vids, and vignettes of all sorts enacted themselves in a continuous loop down the corridors. She started to call Thariinye and Mac to see, and as she did so, the walls grew dark and cold again, glyphs scarred and no longer vibrant with tales of life as it had played out here.

Slowly she coaxed the images back again, reaching out with her thoughts and emotions. She kept walking, in her excitement forgetting to lay down stones to trace her path, forgetting about the landslide, about her companions, forgetting everything but the panorama around her and her need to get to the beginning, to the very beginning, so she could begin to understand what she saw.

But when she reached the source of the flowing river of narrative, it appeared to cascade from the ceiling at the dead end of a tunnel. Walking closer, she saw that the end wasn't dead after all. Stone steps were carved in the walls, embellished with the glyphs and runes forming the riverbed of the torrent of tales. And above the steps was a more prosaic symbol, a sign as clear to her as any she had ever seen on Kezdet.

'EXIT,' it said.

THIRTEEN

RK found Acorna as she started climbing the steps. The crisp sturdiness of them disappeared, along with the EXIT sign and the visual story stream, as the cat took a solid swipe at her leg and yowled for attention.

She stumbled as she reached down to protect her leg and her hand connected with a familiar set of claws. The steps were in the past, as were the runes she had seen so clearly, and the story that had gushed through her and that seemed to have deserted her now. Stones clattered under her feet, rolling away and causing her to slide down a rubble-filled incline.

She struggled to remember what she had seen in the runes, the story that had been flying past her on the walls.

We the Linyaari, made people of the Hosts, do now see it as our only course and duty to assume the role of caretakers of our Ancestors, those whose horns we bear. Them will we keep safe and sacred from exploitation, from degradation, from suffering of all kinds, while we build our own society.

The thread of the story fled her more quickly than it came, carrying its messages away as the sea carried messages written on the sand. She couldn't bring it back, couldn't pull it up in her mind to look at it, to hear the words that had sung in her cells just moments before.

Now something else was singing, far less melodiously if no less meaningfully. Yowls and caterwauls filled the cavern and she felt something brush against her, but she was loath to return to the present. She wanted to catch those last few words, memorize them before they could drain away, look for the clues she sought in them. She knew that somewhere within them, within this place, lay the secret of the disappearances of her lover, her aunt, her friends. But the clues contained in the words fell away from her like a planet's face falling from view when a vessel launched into space.

She slipped, her feet flying out from under her, and connected with something that tumbled down the sliding stones with her.

The something was RK, of course, and he didn't like being ignored and then tumbled down a small rockslide. The cat rushed into action the moment they stopped moving.

He would get her attention, oh, yes, he *would*! However could such a normally sentient being as Acorna suddenly lose her senses so far as to disregard *his* presence? He would have to give her the old treatment. He snagged her with a claw and darted out of the way before she could catch him to make him stop, then zapped her again from the opposite direction to the one she faced. He kept her attention until she was once more thoroughly in the ruined tunnel.

He was still at it when she snatched her leg away from the reach of his claws and said, taking a deep breath, 'Thank you, RK. I'm glad you found me, but that'll be enough of that for now.' She tried to pull herself up from the place where she had been. The information she had gained in her trance, she knew, was useful, fascinating, and maybe even invaluable for their mission, but the feelings accompanying it were so sad. So very sad.

She flicked a tear from her eye with the tip of her finger and tried again to remember it all, but simply couldn't. Was she crying because of what she had seen? Or was she just thinking of Aari and wanting him back? Somehow she didn't *think* the feelings that she was now at the mercy of related directly to the disappearances of her friends, but how could she be sure when she couldn't recall clearly what she had seen?

She felt something in her hand – she still held the last four rocks she had been ready to mark her path with when the walls began to flow. 'Hmm. I fell down on the job I see, RK. Guess I'm lucky you came along. Well, that was strange. I hope the others can find us.'

It was not an issue she had to worry about long. RK's yowling had attracted plenty of attention, and soon Thariinye and Mac thudded up to them, the light of their lamps bobbing in the dark like some kind of crazed fairies flying before them.

'Khornya, you're bleeding,' Thariinye observed. 'A lot.'

'Oh, yes. So I am.' She gave RK a look that caused him to wash rapidly as if to remove any of her blood from his claws and show that his conscience was clean. He had, after all, only been thinking of her. Well, her and maybe a nice juicy mouse, but none of those tasty little creatures were scampering around these halls.

'Why did RK attack you, Khornya?' Mac asked, picking up on the byplay between Linyaari girl and Cat, thereby displaying more sensitivity than Thariinye had shown.

'To pull me back into this world,' she said with a sigh, and held her fingers out to RK to show that she bore no malice. He licked his paw, licked her fingers, and returned to the paw, all to show her he had no hard feelings either.

'Were you somewhere else?' Thariinye asked, and the tone of his voice told her that he had not seen the river of images she'd seen.

She sent him a thought picture of it, and although she still couldn't exactly sort out one part of the story from the next, or recall any details, she felt it rushing over him as it had her. He stood reeling for a moment looking as if she had hit him on the horn with a hammer.

'Whee-ee! Is *that* what it means!' he exclaimed. 'Did you get anything like that, Mac? Oh, sorry, forgot you aren't telepathic.' To Acorna, he said, 'I'm amazed that I didn't pick that up while it was happening to you. I wonder why?'

She considered the question carefully, and her answer more so.

Some Linyaari – Neeva, for instance, or Aari, or Grandam certainly – would have picked up immediately on the unusual surge of psychic energy in an enclosed space such as this. Apparently the cat had perceived it, and he wasn't even Linyaari. But it was probably unkind to point that out to Thariinye, so she said truthfully, 'I wasn't sending. I was concentrating very deeply on receiving mineral impressions from our surroundings. I certainly wasn't expecting what came and wasn't prepared for it and it was, as you saw, very ... preoccupying. If you had tried to find me with your thoughts, you surely would have become as enmeshed as I was in the images.'

'Perhaps,' he said. 'I am very strong-willed and not as suggestible as females are apt to be. I would have picked up on it, I'm sure, but probably not been as overtaken by it as you seem to have been.'

RK looked up at Acorna, laid one ear flat and twitched his brow whiskers as if to ask, 'Should I scratch him for you?'

She looked back at the cynical expression on the broad-striped furry face and laughed. The cat reminded her remarkably of Becker.

It would probably be good for Thariinye if she argued with him. Maati – she felt a sudden pang and an accompanying sense of urgency – Maati would certainly have done so.

'Perhaps we could compare what you learned during your paranormal experience with my translations, Khornya,' Mac suggested.

'Absolutely,' she agreed. 'But first, I think one of the things I learned is that there is, or at least there once was, some sort of door there up near the ceiling. I was trying to reach it when RK – er – arrived.'

'Excellent,' Thariinye said. 'Since it is near the ceiling, perhaps it will lead to ascending passages that may bring us back to the surface – with any luck at some distance from the monsters.' He brightened. 'Or perhaps by now our people have apprehended them and they will no longer be a problem.'

Acorna pointed to the pile of rubble on which she had been standing. They could all see that there were definitely slots in the wall above the pile of stone, which had evidently been a landing of some sort, where steps or a ladder had been attached. At her signal, Mac gave her a boost that raised her high enough to reach the fourth, and most complete, indentation, from which she could easily reach the ceiling.

Feeling around the walls and overhead, she dislodged cobwebs and dirt that descended on Mac and Thariinye. Mac stood unmoving beneath her while dirt gathered in his upraised eye sockets, nose, and mouth, but Thariinye sputtered. He brushed at himself so vigorously that he brushed the light from his head, where it dangled for a moment from his horn before falling to the cave floor and shattering. RK had removed himself a safe distance before anything fell. He stirred only to walk over to Thariinye's light and dab at it with a paw, as if testing a snake or a mouse for signs of life.

Acorna's long, clever fingers found the hair-wide outline of a rectangle that might have been an opening, but nothing she did could deepen or widen the tiny irregularity in the ceiling's fabric.

She shook her head and motioned to Mac to let her down.

'Be very careful that my horn does you no injury as you dismount,' he said.

'I will,' she said, jumping lightly to the floor. 'And now we must trade places. I think your horn is our ticket out of here. Now *you* hop onto *my* shoulders.'

'I am considerably heavier than you may think,' he told her. 'It will take both you and Thariinye to support my weight.'

RK flipped his tail and looked away. Clearly the android could not depend on *him* for support.

Mac did not overestimate his weight. Even with both of them supporting him, it was difficult to elevate him to the necessary height. When at last he stood with a foot on each of their shoulders to distribute his weight evenly, he was still too heavy for either of them to bear it for any length of time. Finally, he stepped back onto the tops of their packs so that both of their shoulders and their backs supported his weight. In that way, they managed to support him long enough for him to explore the area using all of his varied sensors. Once he had mapped the opening's perimeter, he said, 'You may wish to duck your heads during this portion of my mission,' and craned his neck so that his horn touched the crack in the ceiling.

His horn's drill attachment began to hum, and dirt sifted down, but after only a moment he stopped. 'I am unable to move my head with enough freedom to trace the opening with my drill.'

'Can't you unscrew it?' Thariinye asked.

'My head? Yes, I could, but that would detach it from my central nervous system, which contains the controls and power for the drill. The same problem applies to the horn. Besides which, it appears to me that this fissure, while it indeed indicates the opening Khornya professes it to be, has been in some manner sealed shut.'

'You could try your laser. That would probably open even a seal,' Acorna suggested.

'Oh, very well,' he said with un-androidlike peevishness. 'But I wished to make use of my horn. Its capabilities have not yet been field tested, and this seemed to me to be an excellent opportunity.'

'You shouldn't have dropped all that dust in his nose, Khornya,' Thariinye said. 'I think you made him blow a chip.'

'Maybe. But before I gave voice to that thought I would remember that from where he is standing he can squash you easily.'

'You are right,' Thariinye said. 'Mac, you can wield the laser from down here. If you would jump down please, before we are each several inches shorter?'

'Very well,' Mac said, 'but, while injury is possible, I doubt that it would cause significant compression in your bodies. The scenario you have outlined is extremely unlikely.'

'You aren't the one standing here with an android pressing you into a pulp. Now, you *can* use your laser on that doorway or whatever it is from down here just as well, can't you?' Thariinye asked.

'Yes, I have the template recorded so I can target it easily,' Mac replied, and hopped down, sending chips flying from the stones paving the floor of the cavern.

Stones paving the floor of the cavern?

'Caverns don't usually have floors,' Acorna said, kneeling to inspect the damage as Mac wielded his laser.

'Nor doors in their ceilings,' Mac said, restoring the laser to its hiding place and flipping the pick attachment out into his hand. 'And doors that are meant to be opened generally are not sealed.'

This gave her a moment of pause. Why *had* the door been sealed? Was there something harmful above? But she had felt no fear in that morass of emotion that had come to her through the walls. Grief, yes, but not the same sort of grief she was so familiar with in Aari's makeup. 'It was sealed long ago,' Acorna said reasonably. 'It cannot have been sealed to keep *us* in or out after all this time. Use caution, but open it.'

Mac gave a short nod of understanding and backed up a little distance, as they all did. With a slight flick of one finger he caused his pick to grow a handle. It extended far enough that he was able to sling the point of the pick into the rectangle on the ceiling. It did not give when he pulled, but as soon as he jerked the pick back, the sealed door creaked slowly open.

Mac flipped the pick back up so it caught the upper edge of the exposed ceiling.

He glanced at Acorna. 'I believe Captain Becker has indicated that it is courteous to allow ladies to precede one through a doorway, Khornya.'

Acorna looked up into the darkness, her lamp's beam swallowed before it reached the top of the hole.

'I suppose I could go first, but may I begin by

standing on your shoulders again, Mac?' she asked.

'Or,' he countered, grabbing the pick with his other hand, and walking himself up the wall until his feet were even with the ceiling, 'we could try this.'

'Now what?' Thariinye asked.

'Now I release my hand from the pick, and do a flip that will insert my lower body into the space beyond the hole. Then I haul the pick up, reattach my hand, and lower the pick to pull the two of you up behind me,' he said. He no longer sounded peevish. Now he sounded smug.

Apparently RK thought so, too. With a light and graceful feline leap he launched himself from the floor to the small of the android's back, then delicately put first one paw, then the other, on the top of the hole, sniffed, meowed, and jumped up, the slightly twitching tip of his brushy tail the last they saw of him for a second. Then suddenly his eyes and teeth appeared in the opening once more, looking down at them as if from a tree.

'Hmmm,' Acorna said. 'I wonder if someone has been reading to RK from *Alice in Wonderland*.'

'What?'

'It's a book,' Acorna said, as Mac performed the inhumanly flexible maneuver he had outlined and thrust the pick down for them to latch onto. 'And I think RK may be borrowing from its pages.' Above them, the cat vanished into the dark, its grin last of all.

FOURTEEN

Getting Liriili into the flitter had been hard enough, but getting her to shut up and allow the pilot to deliver her to the ship was proving to be tedious in the extreme.

'I demand to be taken back to the Council on narhii-Vhiliinyar immediately,' Liriili declared with as much hauteur as if she were not only still *viizaar* of that planet, but also High Commanding Queen of the Universe, had there been such a title.

'Madame, we have explained to you—' Yaniriin began, but to no avail. He was fortunate enough to have escaped previous encounters with Liriili, but he had heard stories, and from what he could hear, they were all true.

'Again, I demand to return to my old world and be presented to the Council. I have endured an ordeal beyond belief and my story must be told. I alone—'

'If you are going to say that you alone have experienced what you've been through, lady, I doubt that,' Yaniriin interrupted *her* this time. 'You disappeared, sure, but so have a third of the people we sent to scout Vhiliinyar for rehabilitation.'

179

'Yes, I noticed that,' she said loftily. 'I turned my back for only a moment and when I looked, the laboratory and all of its staff had vanished. I notice, of course, that someone has slyly put the building back now, but where is the *aagroni*? I thought he had too much pride to stoop to such cheap tricks.'

Yaniriin said carefully, 'The *aagroni* has vanished along with the others, lady, and is still missing. But he was there when you vanished, and he was there for days afterwards. Did you not see him where you went when you disappeared?'

'I would hardly be complaining of his behavior if I had, would I?' she said.

In between fielding her remarks, Yaniriin was speaking with Lady Khornya and her companions in the search mission. He was almost relieved when Khornya told him she wished for him to keep Liriili on the site so she could interview her. It kept her out of his ship for however long it took for the interview to be concluded.

If he thought Liriili would be pleased by this decision, he was informed of his mistake at once.

'I, who have been deprived of food, water, and the company of my peers for lo these many days and nights while I shivered on this desolate Khleevi-ravaged place, fearing who-knows-what horrors to be visited on me, am to wait on the pleasure of that chit of a girl?'

'Lady Khornya hopes that if she interviews you here, Madame, she will gain clues to where you have been and where the others might be. It is her mission—'

'It has been her mission from the very beginning to undermine my authority, and now she wishes to endanger my life with her dallying? And you, a man responsible for commanding a starship, permit this?'

He hadn't known what to say to this, and had consulted with Nadhari Kando, asking if perhaps Khornya's wishes *should* be disregarded. Liriili, who no doubt *was* still suffering from exposure – certainly, from what the shuttle crew who treated her initially said, she *was* dehydrated and rather thinner than before. Should she be taken straight back to MOO?

Commander Kando was emphatic that Khornya's instructions be followed, however – a fact which he was about to relay to Liriili when the first of the monsters was spotted by the ship's scanners.

He immediately dispatched two other shuttles, but the craft which could reach the team quickest was the one already on the planet's surface. That, of course, was the same one being monopolized by Liriili's dramatization of her own experience, and by her general disagreeableness.

'It seems you will get your wish after all, Madame,' Yaniriin informed her. 'The recon and rescue team is in peril and the shuttle must be dispatched to its assistance.'

'What sort of peril?'

'A monster, or wait – make that monsters – seem bent on attacking – oh, no, they are under attack now!'

'Khleevi? That stupid girl said she had

destroyed the Khleevi. Oh, I told the Council how untrustworthy she was, and here they are back again.'

'No, ma'am, not Khleevi.'

'You needn't think I am going to allow you to put me in the path of those Khleevi again for *her* convenience,' Liriili said with increasing shrillness. 'She'd like that, if they killed me—'

'Vilii Hazaar Miirl?' Yaniriin addressed the shuttle captain directly.

'Aye, sir?'

'You will proceed to those coordinates. If Lady Liriili wishes to leave the planet's surface, she may accompany you. If not, leave her there and a later shuttle may find time to transport her when the crisis is over.'

'Aye, sir.'

'You are *not* leaving me behind?' Liriili cried, aghast.

'Not if you cease and desist all verbal communication and load yourself aboard immediately, Madame. Otherwise, leaving you behind is exactly what we *will* do,' the captain said with satisfaction so profound that it was no doubt uncharitable and unbecoming in an officer of the Linyaari space fleet.

Liriili opened her mouth but Vilii Hazaar Miirl, who had initially entertained *kind* feelings for the castaway, as well as compassion for her plight, started to shut the shuttle door in her face. Miirl was actually hoping Liriili would utter just one more word, but the former *viizaar* pulled herself together, haughtily opened the door, boarded, and dumped herself into one of the seats, her mouth clamped into a hard thin line. She didn't bother to shield her thoughts at all, but with a nod from Miirl, the crew chief shoved a horn helmet over Liriili's horn, muffling her outraged ruminations. 'For your safety, lady,' the chief said with deliberately officious crispness.

While it did not take the shuttle nearly as long to reach the coordinates Yaniriin dictated as it would have taken a flitter, a great deal happened while they were en route.

Yaniriin kept Miirl and her crew apprised of what the ship's sophisticated long-range visual scanners were showing.

'The beasts are shaggy, covered with what appears to be coarse fur or hair. Their movements indicated bewilderment initially, but that has turned to aggression. One attempted to board the flitter, but when it was unable to do so, it attacked the craft with a weapon of some sort.

'Oh! Wait! Here comes the second creature, joining the first one. They appear to be allies, and do not attack each other, which is perhaps unfortunate for us. The second one is also attempting to board the flitter. No. Perhaps it was sniffing the craft, for now it is less tall, as if it has hunched over. Now it is slowly proceeding along the route taken by Khornya and her team to the place where they dug the tunnel leading to the cave.'

Silence interrupted these reports, while Yaniriin communicated with Khornya, Thariinye, and their android and *pahaantiyir* associates.

Suddenly Yaniriin said, 'Oh, no. The team has emerged from the tunnel. Now it appears that the monsters have seen them, and they are attacking!

Have you a sturdy net aboard your craft, Vilii Hazaar Miirl?'

'Aye, sir,' she answered. 'And there's a very strong tractor beam on this craft, too – it is one of House Harakamian's, used for construction, and capable of moving heavy ground equipment, I understand.'

'Excellent. Khornya and her friends will have need of that. If you can increase your speed at all, please do so.'

'Unfortunately, this sort of craft isn't actually built for speed, sir, but we will do the best we can,' Miirl promised. 'Perhaps if we offloaded extra personnel?'

'Nice try, Miirl, but I'm afraid I cannot condone abandoning your passenger for that reason.'

'It was worth a try, sir,' Miirl responded.

Liriili couldn't hear her over the craft's drive and, with the horn helmet on, couldn't really read her well either.

After a few moments of breathless silence, Yaniriin said, 'Oh, to be there now! Thariinye and Khornya have taken shelter inside the cave but their companion, Maak, has elected to guard their rear. The scanners can just make him out, standing at the entrance to the tunnel while the hairy monsters charge him, their sticks pointing at him! He counters mightily and one of the monsters pulls from his body what seems to be another weapon. He is attempting to remove Maak's head. What is this? Some small beast – it must be the *pahaantiyir*-like *khaat* they call Riidkii – has flown onto the monster's head. At any rate, the scanners show Maak has not diminished in height, so he seems to have kept his head. Now Riidkii has fallen and now he is not there – oh, neither is Maak. He has lifted the *khaat* and is carrying him deeper into the tunnel, but the monsters follow. What is this? Our scanners detect a laser. A great explosion! Oh my, the tunnel is collapsing. But only on the monsters. What a relief. We can still see the sensors on Maak and Riidkii all the way down the tunnel, going very fast and – there are Khornya's sensors, and Thariinye's. Now they are all back inside the cave and we can no longer see them. You will be relieved to know that the lifeforce sensor for Riidkii improved in strength once Khornya met them, so whatever wounds the *khaat* sustained were healed.'

'We are coming within visual range of the flitter now, Yaniriin,' Miirl told him.

'Very well then – ahhh! Perhaps there will be no need. There was just another explosion; did you get a visual on it? Can you transmit anything closer than what we are currently receiving?'

'Yes, Captain, I am sorry to report that it appears that the entire tunnel has just collapsed but – there is movement. There's our quarry! They have escaped being crushed in the tunnel collapse! Both of them. Oh, by my horn, how ugly they are! Disgusting!'

The crew chief told her, 'I've just released the net, Vilii Hazaar.'

'Excellent, chief, stand by. We're coming into tractor range now. There they are, clear as the horn on your head, Yaniriin. They are shaking their manes and have begun to toss the rocks from the tunnel's entrance aside, as if they are desperate to reach Khornya and her team. They are in range . . .'

'Deploy tractor beam when ready, Miirl,' Yaniriin said.

'Got them!' Miirl said as the two huge shaggy figures were jerked off their feet along with the boulders they held in their hands and pulled horizontally through the air until they were dragged into the steel cargo net, which closed around them and their rocks.

'Excellent! Haul them aboard and return to the ship so that we may properly incarcerate and perhaps interrogate them, should they be sentient. See if you can pick up their speech patterns, if they have any intelligible ones, on your LAANYEs.'

'But what about Khornya's team, Yaniriin?' Miirl asked. 'They are buried!'

'Other shuttles are on their way.' After another silence, he resumed speaking, 'Nadhari Kando has sent to MOO for earth-moving and digging machinery to be brought by Linyaari crews to the surface of the planet. The Council has given permission for Captain Jonas Becker, the great friend of Lady Khornya, to bring his salvage ship *Condor* to the surface as well.'

'Is that not highly irregular?'

'He has been on our planet before. He was the one who rescued Aari the Survivor. Also, the valiant Riidkii and Maak are crew members aboard his ship.'

'Ahhh, well, the Council's decision is understandable then. We are now loading the monsters

– oh, oh, quickly, the masks. The smell of them is not to be believed, Yaniriin. Have your crew don masks before opening the air locks when we come aboard. And have sufficient personnel standing by to purify the air as soon as possible.'

'That's affirmative, Miirl.'

The shuttle flew back to the mother ship with Liriili and the captives. Meanwhile, the other two shuttles Yaniriin had dispatched earlier landed near the tunnel.

Before the crew from the first shuttle could disembark, the other shuttle immediately vanished – crew, ship, and all – right in front of their horrified eyes.

FIFTEEN

The miners' lanterns did not cast enough light to see very far, but Acorna knew at once that although she and her companions were not yet above ground, they were out of the cave. Wherever they were, it was spacious, and the air was, if not especially fragrant or heady, oxygen rich and clean without the need for horn purification. And the floor was smoothly surfaced, laid out by sentient hands.

Nevertheless, the space smelled slightly musty and felt derelict.

'Hello-o!' she called. 'Aari, Maati, Neeva? Are any of you here?' She found she was expecting not an answer but an echo. She got neither. Her voice sank into the darkness in the same way the sound of her footfalls and those of her companions died on contact with the pavement.

However, since she had no actual idea where she was, continuing this journey seemed as good a way as any to begin searching for the lost ones, since she also had no idea where *they* were. She sent out mental feelers, but could not honestly say that there was any response to them.

The beam of her light and Mac's stopped a few

feet from their faces, where a mound of earth sloped upward, extending past the boundaries of the light. In three places it bore deep, even gouges about four feet long and a half a foot deep.

'Khornya, look, we are at the base of a mountain!' Thariinye said. 'And it is indented just as the wall was down below. Fortunately, the incline is less perpendicular.'

'I suppose we'd better climb it, then?'

'Why?' Thariinye asked.

Mac and Acorna said in unison, 'Because it is there!' Mac had uploaded the same books she'd read aboard Becker's ship, one of which included the famous words spoken by George Leigh Mallory, when asked why he wished to climb a mountain called Everest on Old Terra.

Acorna remembered the words because they sounded very much like the things Becker had quoted his adoptive father, Theophilus, as saying. The saying also reminded her of her own adoptive fathers, Calum, Gill, and Rafik, and she felt a surge of longing to see them.

Would she ever again see any of the people she loved, those who had disappeared, or those from whom she had now become separated?

But then, realistically, a person could ask herself that question every time she took a space voyage anywhere – or any time she stepped away from the people she cared for, even momentarily.

She sighed and began the climb. As mountains went, it was more of a foothill. In fact, she had been in spaceports with taller gantries. In *fact*, she realized, as her feet met flat, even flooring once more at the top of the climb – 'This isn't a mountain. It's another staircase. The cavern must have been the basement level of some great structure – maybe it's where the Ancestral Hosts and Ancestors lived when they first came here. Though this level doesn't seem to have access to the outdoors, the upper levels must have. The Ancestors would need that.'

As she climbed, she realized that the sounds of their breathing were gradually being augmented by another, more subtle sound. She stopped, holding her breath, and motioned for the others to do the same.

Hisss. Slap slap. A receding susurration as soft as the sound of a silken gown moving across skin.

'I think that's the sound of the sea,' she said.

'What sea?' Thariinye asked, his face tense in the light of her lamp as he strained to hear. 'The seas were all destroyed by the Khleevi. No, it's probably some giant carnivorous mutant cave rat dragging its tail back and forth on the floor as it comes to eat us.'

'Why, Thariinye!' Acorna said, smiling at his grim joke.

'What?'

'How – colorful,' she said.

'I heard what you were thinking!' he chided. 'You were thinking *"I didn't know he had that much imagination."* And you're right, I don't have. Never have had. But the way things have been going since we arrived, it doesn't take much to realize that any strange sound can hardly be something normal and pleasant. It must surely be some new disaster.'

RK had been flitting merrily in and out of the

light of their lanterns, chasing his own shadow.

Suddenly he gave a small 'Yow!'

Light appeared from nowhere, blinding them as it pierced their dark-accustomed eyes, flooding them with a painful brilliance.

'What?' Thariinye yelled, his nerves well and truly on edge by now.

Acorna's eyes readjusted, and she saw the cat sitting by a long white wall, patting it with his paw, blinking at it rapidly with eyes that were all iris, the thin slit of pupil undetectable at this distance. 'There doesn't seem to be anyone here but us, but I believe we've found civilization,' she said.

The light was not actually as bright as it had seemed at first. It would have been called 'atmospheric' in certain upscale eating establishments. Because of the wall-wide area it covered, it sufficed to illuminate the corridor, but did not provide enough light that one could see colors clearly.

Still, it showed that they stood in the corridor of a building at least the size of Uncle Hafiz's grand ballroom in his principal palace, or the spaceport on Maganos Moonbase, or one of the Amalgamated Mining Corporation office buildings she had visited with Calum, Gill, and Rafik. On the street side of the corridor, the central-most of several portals still stood, supported by two ornate columns. Four other portals had broken and allowed the wide awnings above the doors to collapse into them.

'I don't believe anyone is here,' Thariinye whispered.

'No, but the illumination system in the walls still works,' Acorna said, struggling for a normal tone herself. 'At least that one did. If there are others that also work, we should be able to find our way around here pretty well.' She walked over to the wall opposite the one RK had touched and laid her hand upon it. It brightened the light in the corridor, and revealed more clearly that there were five additional arched doorways on the inner wall. All of these still contained sets of double doors carved with characters similar to those in the glyphs in the cavern.

Making his eyes wide and gesturing with his brows toward the nearest inner door, Thariinye indicated that he didn't see why Acorna didn't try it.

She gave a little huff of impatience and pushed the nearest door, which slowly creaked open at her touch.

'I believe I have some lubricant in my left ankle which could take care of that problem,' Mac offered in a sensibly normal voice.

'I'd hang on to it. I doubt you have enough for every door in here,' Thariinye told him, his voice still subdued.

(Afraid the giant carnivorous mutant cave rats will hear you?) Acorna teased. (Because they're a little late. We were in the cave for hours and they didn't even show a tail tip.)

(It's lucky we had RK with us is all I have to say,) Thariinye answered.

The psychic byplay concealed the trepidation they all felt on entering the ancient room. The light from the corridor penetrated the interior for no more than the sweep of a ball gown's skirt. Acorna backed up, took a deep breath, stuck out her hand, and the wall she touched responded by lighting one side of the room.

The chamber was not as vast as she had thought it might be from the corridor. Unfurnished and empty, the glowing walls decorated with a few paintings and symbols were its only salient feature.

'What do these things say, Mac?' Thariinye asked.

'I have no idea,' Mac said.

'After all that translating?'

'These are not in the same language,' Mac replied. 'Certainly there are similarities, but it will take a great deal more input to be sure I am translating them accurately.'

Acorna examined the placement of the words on the walls and above the doorway. She let out her breath and felt the emptiness of disappointment replace it. 'I doubt they say anything vitally important. I recognize that one over there from my earlier adventure,' she said, pointing to a door. 'It says EXIT. My guess is that other words near the entryways are also directional, telling where different rooms in the building are and their functions. These,' she spread her hand and waved it above some smaller notices at other points in the room, 'probably say things like "please refrain from loud talking" and "kindly do not run with scissors within this building."'

'Why would they run with scissors?' Thariinye asked. 'And what *is* a scissors anyway?'

'An old Terran edged implement for cutting,

made obsolete by hand-held lasers. That was just an example. But I have seen signs like this in many civilizations as I traveled with my foster family – I'm almost sure, given the locations, the signs are the administrative kind of stuff put in big buildings to keep large numbers of people under control.'

'How do you know they needed to control large numbers of people here?' Thariinye asked.

'Well, they'd hardly have needed such a big building if they didn't have lots of people in the area sometimes, would they?' she replied, wondering why Thariinye didn't use his head. Did he think it was put there as an ornament?

'That's true,' he admitted.

After all the trouble they had taken to get here, this place was a big letdown. Even though it was kind of eerie, deserted as it was, it was so ordinary. Perhaps their friends were here somewhere, but there didn't seem to be anyone around. The silence of the place, and the profound feeling that there had been no life here for a very long time, discouraged the searchers.

Acorna sent out a mental call, and Thariinye did the same. She broadcasted so loudly her head hurt with the effort, but felt nothing in return. Thariinye shook his head and rubbed it. Same results.

Still, she couldn't shake the feeling that this place had *something* to do with her missing friends. Perhaps putting the structure in context with its surrounding would help. 'Rather than take the time to have Mac translate all of these, I think we should look around and get the lay of the land, examine some of the other structures and see if there is any clue here to what this place is, who lived here, and if it has anything to do with what's been happening to our rescue teams.'

The others agreed to this, and they left the building through the doorway between the two columns Acorna had noticed earlier. Along the broad street were many other buildings of size, though none as large as the one from which they had come. Most of these were fronted with columns too, or arched entryways, all of which appeared to be fairly open. Acorna looked for glass or some other barrier but found nothing, neither did she find frames in which such materials would have been contained.

But touching exterior walls caused them to light up, and by touching every wall they passed, the team found they could see as well as on a moonlit night on narhii-Vhiliinyar.

They entered none of the buildings at first, but walked down the street until they came to a side street. This one sloped downhill to another street. The building they had just come from had a further level that appeared to open out onto the lower street as well. So did some of the others.

Mac used his sensors to search for lifeforms in the buildings as they passed, while Acorna and Thariinye broadcast calls for their people. They stared into the gloom of the hollow-eyed buildings, lighting the walls that would light.

'Have you noticed that none of these seem to be dwellings?' Acorna asked Thariinye. 'If there are no meadows, no gardens, where did people eat? Excrete?' She evaluated the area around her again. 'Of course, we're assuming that Linyaari lived here, along with the Hosts. And we don't know what sort of lifeforms exactly the Hosts were. But surely they needed to prepare food somehow and dispose of waste. They must have rested. And yet we have found no facilities for any of those functions.'

Rounding a corner where the street sloped downward, they all stopped and stared for a moment at the broad expanse of water fanning out from a long shoreline at the foot of the hill.

'Perhaps they used the sea for all of those activities,' Mac suggested, and continued walking, the other two trailing in his wake.

Meanwhile, RK ranged on either side of them, running up and down the street and twisting circles around them, darting off down the side streets, deliberately jumping onto the walls and up onto things to touch the walls of upper stories. He was having a grand time. Acorna let him enjoy himself. There didn't seem to be anything that could harm him here in this deserted town.

Thariinye was clearly fascinated by the place. He sometimes walked backwards to view the city behind them, sometimes swiveled his head, scanning the streets around them, and sometimes stared out at the wide water.

'Kubiilikaan!' he announced at last. 'This must be it! The great city told of in the Elder songs, the city by the sea, the one where the Hosts lived when they brought our Ancestors to live with them.'

'Well, I suppose that explains why it doesn't seem to be very Linyaari-like, and why the writing is in an unfamiliar language. Still – except for being subterranean, of course, it looks so ordinary,' Acorna said.

'Well, after seeing the needle-spires of the Iraani, hearing the Singing Stones of Skarness, even seeing the bubble worlds people construct as temporary bases, what *wouldn't* seem ordinary to you? I mean to say, have you really *listened* to the songs and stories of our people?' Thariinye asked. 'Except for a bit of poetry here and there, they actually tell of very little we haven't seen, and grander, on other worlds in other ports,' he pointed out. 'Sad, that, really.'

'But think how wonderful it is to be walking the very streets of the original place that the main pavilion city of narhii-Vhiliinyar was named for,' Acorna said, wonderingly. 'A city so old it was assumed to be legendary or lost forever.' The difference between the two places was astounding. This city, though far more ancient than anything on the second Linyaari homeworld, had obviously been built and run with considerable technology.

As they drew nearer to the edge of the water, they saw down on one end of the shore the husks of several spacecraft and gantries, along with the domed buildings of a large spaceport. It occurred to her that the spacecraft were the first transportation they had encountered.

Acorna indicated the underground sea. 'Here's your mutant cave rat, Thariinye. It was the noise of the sea, as I thought all along!'

But Mac contradicted her, politely. 'My auditory sensors detect very little sound coming from that body of water, Khornya. It is relatively still, with no tide at this time.'

She strained her ears toward the water and realized Mac was correct. The sea was silent. In fact, she had not heard the small mysterious noise since first entering the building from the cavern.

'I find this very odd,' Mac said, holding out his hand with a little instrument he had caused to materialize from somewhere on his versatile body. 'I can see, and you can see that there *is* a sea, and *now* my detectors are also showing that there is indeed the sea we see before us.'

'We can see that,' Thariinye said. 'What's your point?'

'They did not show this body of water when we were above ground,' Mac replied.

'Nor did our ship's, nor those of any of the other ships, including Becker's,' Acorna told him. 'I suspect the same thing that blocked our transmissions to the survey ships once we entered the cave may be responsible for concealing all of this from the ship's sensors. This place may be in disrepair, but it has some sort of shielding devices that are working miraculously well to conceal its presence and contents.'

The shields hadn't protected the city from everything, though, she thought. Besides the damage to many of the buildings, there was one more very obvious breach in the defenses.

The street they were walking disappeared abruptly into water, which was lapping against the outer walls of a row of buildings that did not appear to have been built as waterfront property. Indeed, the doors of many of the nearest structures were awash in water, which entered halfway up their doorframes.

Farther out, lurking under a few feet of water, were the tops of other buildings. Debris that looked like it might have come from the timbers of docks floated on the water.

But most impressive, even in the very dim glow emanating from the buildings a block away, was what was actually *in* the water.

Far out into the bay an island of debris rose to the shadowy heights, blocking the view of the waters and opposite shore beyond.

'The ceiling has caved in a little there,' Acorna said, pointing. 'It must have been well built to have sustained that much damage and not completely collapsed.'

Thariinye's nostrils twitched till he pinched them shut with his fingers. 'Nothing's quite as revolting as the stench of Khleevi scat. I wonder that we didn't smell that before the salt water.'

'I did,' Mac told him. 'Or rather, my olfactory senses detected it. But its range is relatively limited and the scat is in its solidified and less pungent stage. The salt water occupies a much larger area and salination has increased as the years have passed. It has essentially pickled the scat in brine.'

'Eeewww, lovely,' Thariinye said. 'Now there is a thought. I hope for their own sake there are none of those *sii*-Linyaari still in the water. Though I'd like to meet one. They must be very graceful and they sound so – exotic. Like aliens, only, more like us – possibly, we could cross-breed, don't you think?'

'I doubt that you would find anything that has been in that water sexually appealing, Thariinye,' Mac said. 'Even if something living remained. And my scanners show that nothing living has dwelled there for a very long time.' He asked suddenly, 'How do the songs and stories of your people say that this city came to be underground and underwater?'

'They don't say,' Thariinye told him. 'But they talk of verdant fields and towering spires and skies – yes, skies of aubergine, skies of amethyst, skies of indigo setting the twin jewels of Our Star and the Consort.' His voice rose to dramatic heights as he pronounced these words, then sank back to normal. 'So, yes, it must have been above ground when these stories and songs were written, I'd say.'

'I wonder how far below the surface we are,' Acorna said. She looked away from the sea, up the labyrinth of buildings, some shorter, some so tall she could not see the tops of them in the limited light. And she began to realize there must be a reason for that. 'I want to climb to the top floor of one of these buildings,' she told her companions. 'Mac, could you climb up in another? And Thariinye?'

'Why?' Thariinye asked. 'I like it here.'

'Unless you like it well enough to remain here until we starve to death, we need to explore some more. I'd like to learn what we came here for.'

'How do we know it's here to learn?'

'We don't, of course, but where else would it be? We have ships and flitters in the air, and we thoroughly explored the solar system around

Vhiliinyar before the survey team even landed. None of those ships saw anything out of the ordinary. We know whatever it was that took our people did not come from there. Besides, all of the disappearances have been from the planet's surface. Then there's the shielding around the caverns and this city that blocks our sensors. I believe, if we look, we might find something that will help us find our friends who disappeared.' She desperately wished that it was Thariinye who had disappeared and Aari who was by her side now – Aari and Maati both. Even the little girl would have been a better companion on a mission like this one than Thariinye. 'So the answer, it seems to me, is somewhere right here. Maybe even here in this buried city.'

'I heard what you thought!' he said. 'You think I'm useless! I'm not that bad. Maati will tell you that when we find her. I can certainly be counted on to do what's necessary – if I know what it is. Maati and I survived plenty of adventures on our voyage together. She quite depends on me, or I certainly wouldn't be here risking my neck and the rest of me on this mission. And Aari thinks highly of my abilities, too.'

'I will think highly of them as well,' Acorna said, 'if we get Aari and Maati back to tell us what a great help you are. But in the meantime, for me to think highly of you, you need to climb highly in one of those buildings – one so tall we can't see the top of it. I want to know what is on the ceiling of this place. Maybe we can even find a way out.'

'Oh, well, why didn't you say so?' he asked.

The three of them each found one of the buildings that scraped what passed for a sky in this underworld and climbed to its top. Acorna re-entered the building from which they had entered the underground city.

Just inside the doorway, she broadcast again. This time, maybe it was because she was alone, or maybe because she wanted to so desperately, she thought she felt a query in return, just her name, 'Khornya?'

But then RK looked up quizzically and said, 'Rryow?' and she thought what she heard must have been the cat's reply.

She wanted so badly for it to be Aari, she thought with a surge of loneliness and worry for her lifemate that she had been suppressing during the whole adventure. Instead of concentrating on missing him, she had tackled each task she thought might bring him closer. But now, for a moment, she felt the weight of the worry that he would never return, that having found her life-mate, she had lost him again so suddenly. Worse than that, she worried that he needed her, that perhaps he was hurt and calling her name, longing for her to come and heal him, that he was facing an enemy they should be fighting together. Of course she was anxious for the fate of Neeva, of Maati and the others as well, but she ached for Aari.

RK rubbed against her, breaking her concentration, and she patted him, then continued as she had done before, putting one foot in front of the other.

Fortunately for both of her feet, and the rest of

her as well, the upper floors of this building had staircases that were in much better repair than the one they'd faced on the lower level, and the walls lit sufficiently well to allow her to see all the way up on each level. RK was with her, making his presence felt in the usual way, dashing ahead, then jumping back down to land on her shoulders or in her arms if she stretched them out to catch him.

Once she reached the top of the last staircase in the building she stopped to catch her breath, then began exploring. By leaning out a broad window she could touch one of the outer walls of the building. It lit. In its gentle light she could see that there was a balcony all around this story. When she walked out on the balcony and looked down, she saw the streets of the city below where the walls still glowed from her team's passing.

A block away, another building lit from top to bottom and Mac's voice crackled to life on the com unit, which worked perfectly well among the three of them, even if they could hear nothing from the other Linyaari survey team members outside of the cave. 'Khornya,' the android said, 'I can see you from here! I trust your rise in this world was uneventful?'

'It was.'

'Mine, too,' Thariinye said. As he spoke, another building a block away, its position triangulating with hers and Mac's, lit all the way to the top story. Like three large candles, the buildings illuminated the area around them, including the sky, which rested upon their rooftops, and the rooftops of other buildings of the same stature.

'Would you look at that! They made columns of their skyscrapers!' Acorna cried. 'The buildings do not just scrape the sky. These columns hold up the sky.'

SIXTEEN

Yaniriin and Vilii Hazaar Miirl surveyed the prisoners with distaste born not from their smell, which was rapidly dispersed, thanks to the horns of the Linyaari crew, nor even their appearance, though that was frankly disgusting, composed as it was of layers of filth, matted hair, caked blood, dirt, and skin, where they could see it, that was a carapace of dirt. The creatures' eyes were deeply shadowed by swags of hair mats, and their speech for the most part consisted of shouts and grunts and threatening noises. But the Linyaari reserved the bulk of their disgust for themselves. What actually disgusted the Linyaari most was the concept of having to hold anything prisoner at all.

'Have you been able to read them?' Yaniriin asked Miirl.

'I confess I haven't had any desire to,' she admitted. 'Surely these stinking, oafish louts can have nothing to do with the subtle, quiet disappearances of our people?'

'Maak indicated that their language appeared to be some form of Terran,' Yaniriin said. 'Perhaps when Captain Becker arrives in the *Condor*, he will help us communicate with them in their own tongue.'

'Maak did indicate that the form of the Terran language they spoke was extremely primitive,' Miirl said doubtfully. 'Becker seems to be an advanced representative of the species.'

Nadhari Kando put in a comment from her command station on MOO. 'Trust me,' she said. 'That's no problem. Becker can be very primitive when he wishes.'

'I heard that,' Becker said over the com unit. 'Give me a minute and I'll be there to prove you wrong.'

Since Becker was once more crewless, he chose to land the *Condor* on Vhiliinyar near the remaining shuttle, the one that had *not* instantly disappeared. He flew his own current shuttle, a sweet little Linyaari egg he had salvaged from the wreckage of one of the larger ships destroyed by the Khleevi attacks, to the surveillance ship. He would donate the shuttle back to the Linyaari if they wanted it, especially if he couldn't talk Hafiz into *buying* it back for them. But just now it made quick work of getting him where he wanted to go.

When he boarded the surveillance ship and was shown the prisoners he said, 'Hol-eee hermitage, boys and girls, how can I tell anything about these fellas, if they are fellas? One or both could even be female for all we can tell – can't see their eyes, much less anything else important down lower. Their mouths are all covered up with hair so I can't even lip-read if I need to. These guys need a shave and a haircut worse than any life-form I ever saw in all my born days! Not to mention a bath. Don't you guys have a beauty operator on board this ship?'

They looked baffled and he said finally, 'Well, okay, then, I'll do the honors but first I just want one of you to make sure I won't get cooties or rabies or anything from touching these two. And I'm gonna need some tools, and some space to work in.'

Finally, while Becker stalked off, muttering to himself about how a man had to do a job himself if he wanted it done right, Yaniriin did as Becker asked, he purified whatever he could reach with his horn, making sure to keep well away from the teeth or the ragged claws that protruded from the fingers of these creatures. Yaniriin noted that their prisoners' hands were shaped more like Becker's than like his own.

'And me without my chain saw,' Becker muttered to himself when he returned. He brought forth some metal shears from the leather-wrapped tool kit he'd had in his egg-shuttle. 'I sure hope you've got these guys fully secured,' he said, as he stepped into the enclosure with them.

'I think some soap and water will be in order pretty quick, Cap'n,' he told Yaniriin as he started chopping off great hunks and clots and mats of felted hair that piled up at his feet, despite the prisoners' anguished protests.

The creatures were bound tightly in the net and could not struggle very hard, but the net itself made Becker's work difficult, as he could not get underneath it to work freely on his subjects. He had to make do as best he could, inserting his shears in between the webbing of the net and taking off a lock of hair here, a matted string of hair there.

He and the Linyaari loosened the nets just a bit, and as Becker pulled the captives' wrists free of the hair, human and animal, covering them, he bound them securely with a couple of Red Bracelet restraints that he'd picked up along the way in his travels. The prisoners weren't going any place now. They were disarmed, tied up, and in a space ship. These were definitely not high-tech warriors. It wasn't going to be easy for them to escape.

As he finally began to make headway in his shearing, Becker saw that they only had a few teeth between them and those were all rotten, and that their skin was covered with injuries. 'No wonder they're so damned mean,' he said. 'These guys must be in a world of hurt with those chop-pers and all these sores. I think I'm going to need a little Linyaari help here. Could somebody get a horn over here and heal these boys?' Several Linyaari stepped forward and laid their horns on the prisoners, who were unappreciative.

As Becker worked, he hummed to himself, a little tune he had learned on Kezdet as a child laborer, a lullaby some of the older children sang to the younger. His singing had a noticeable effect on the captives, who must at any rate have been tired from their fighting. They stopped strug-gling. In fact, eventually they seemed to find all these attentions soothing, maybe even reassuring, and they soon fell asleep.

'Will you look at that?' he asked the Linyaari.

'Two little lambies counting sheep while I'm shearing them.'

As the hair mats piled up on the floor, human features emerged from beneath the overgrown beards, mustaches, and hair. Once the hairy outer layer was gone, it was clear that these were two young humanoid men, who had not been in very good shape, wearing animal skins over shredded clothing and pieces of metal armor, much rusted and dented. In some places they had had scars from where their armor had rubbed them raw. In others, their skin had healed right over the foreign material. And they had more than their share of old battle wounds, some healed, some still healing. The injuries eased even as Becker watched, thanks to the efforts of the Linyaari healers.

Miirl smiled a soft, close-mouthed smile that reminded him, not too strangely, of Acorna when she was amused. 'I believe that is why your suggestion that we apply our horns to these fellows was a good one. The relief from the discomfort of their vermin and sores has allowed them to rest peacefully. Their teeth will take a little additional work to reconstruct, but the decay has been arrested. Their dispositions may be much improved as well, when they awaken, though one cannot predict that sort of thing.'

'Well, that's the best I can do for them for now,' Becker told Miirl, Yaniriin, and the crew. 'I haven't got all day. Still have to dig Acorna and the boys out of the tunnel, and the cat. Who knows what the oxygen supply is like down there . . .' He slapped the newly bald, fully disarmed, cleaned, healed, and bound warriors each once lightly on the cheeks and said, 'So come on, you sleeping beauties. Wake up and smell the tea!'

They instantly bolted awake, growling, but he smiled at them in a friendly way and said, 'Okay, boys, let's have it. We'd like to hear your life story, but names, ranks, and serial numbers will do for starters. If you want, you can save the rest till we get to the flaming-bamboo-under-the-fingernails portion of our conversation.'

'They do not understand,' Miirl said.

'Obviously. Didn't expect them to. This calls for a more basic approach.' He tapped himself on the chest, 'Me. Becker.' And pointed to them, 'You?'

'Wat,' said the (formerly) red-haired one.

'Wat,' said the (formerly) dark-haired one.

'What?' asked Becker.

'Their names,' Miirl said, with Acorna-like gentleness that got Becker's attention. 'They are doing as you asked and telling you their names. Both are named Wat.'

'How'd you know that? I thought you needed me to translate – oh, I get it. You read them, huh?'

She nodded. 'Their intention is clear. They are feeling much better. They are now trying to communicate with their new manservant, which is how they see you, since you are quite clearly not their mother.'

'We'll just change *that* little notion,' Becker said, turning back to them. 'Okay, you crewcut canaries, you speak Terran, I speak Terran, we should be able to come up with some kind of understanding but I need you to *sing*.'

Both began babbling at once. As they talked,

their voices rather nasal in a singsong rhythm that went up and down and up and down, with a few familiar words interspersed, Becker grinned.

'Oh, please do not frighten them by baring your teeth so, Captain,' Miirl said.

'I'm not scaring *them*, honey. Being scared of teeth is a Linyaari thing. I don't believe it, but these guys are a cross between Beowulf and Chaucer! I'm pretty sure they're gabbing at us in Old English. I'm not exactly fluent in it, but the old man – my Dad, I mean – and I used to play around with and read some of the epic sagas to each other when the salvage business was slow – real slow. This'll be a piece of cake for you. You already have a lot of the words in the LAANYE, but it probably doesn't recognize them on account of the accents. Now that they are cooperating, once you get the right mix in your translation, you'll figure it out in no time flat. You guys are geniuses. Go on, try a question yourself. You'll do better than me. I can't read minds and you can. Besides, I can't hang around here chewing the fat with these guys all day long. I have to go dig out my pals.'

'Very well, Captain Becker, we will try,' Yaniriin said. 'But please stay to monitor our initial efforts and instruct us on how to improve them, before you return to your vital mission.'

'Sure thing, Cap'n, but make it snappy, will you? I've already lost a lot of time already – and Acorna, my feline first mate, and that other kid might be in real trouble. Mac can take care of himself, but I'm gonna have a few choice things to say when I catch up to him about letting the kiddies get into trouble.'

'We will not waste your time, Captain. Miirl,' Yaniriin said, 'would you like to try questioning these beings? You seem to have established an affinity with them already.'

'Just finishing adjustments on the LAANYE here, Captain. Oh, yes, I believe I have a couple of simple phrases in their tongue.

'Velcommen,' she said to the captives in an impeccable up and down nasal singsong that seemed to trip lightly from her Linyaari tongue. 'Who are you? What do you want?'

They replied in a gabble so fast that even Becker couldn't understand them, but Miirl gasped and stepped back a pace.

'What did they say?'

'They said they were something called liege men of what I gather is a sort of warlord named Bjorn. They tell me they came to hunt the four-legged unicorns and kill them to take them back to their master for the good their horns will do him. They want to kill our Ancestors!'

The two Wats were now leering and poking at each other.

Miirl looked horrified. 'They say their master was particularly eager to get the horns when he sent them because he had just become lifemates with a very much younger lady named Ingeborg the Buxom, and our horns – or the horns of the four-leggeds – are believed to restore manhood.'

The men began shouting and pointing with their bound hands and trying to stomp their bound feet, sounding very commanding. 'They say they have been wandering many years in their quest – that they had their hands on some of the four-legged unicorns when, all of a sudden, they fell into a deep sleep. When they awakened, the unicorns awoke, too, and bounded away – into a countryside these men had never seen before. But they recognize us as the descendants of the unicorns they hunted. They say that, now that they have us in their power, they demand our immediate and unconditional surrender.'

Becker laughed. 'I'm starting to like these guys.'

SEVENTEEN

Maati's strongest concern about her recent change of venue was the discovery that having a big brother along for the ride was definitely a mixed blessing. He was being very bossy over events nobody could change, nobody had planned, and nobody knew what to do about. Not even him – whatever he thought. He gave more silly orders than Liriili.

Yiitir and Maarni, on the other hand, were a lot of fun.

It had all begun when she, Aari, and the older couple had been standing looking at the *sii*-Linyaari artifact. All of a sudden, they were facing a bright river tumbling from the distant mountainhead, framed by tree-covered hills just ahead of them. Turning, they beheld a wide open sea with a white sand beach on their side of the river. On the opposite bank stood a great city. It was a big improvement over the Khleevi-wrecked landscape they'd just been looking at. She had thought Aari would say, 'Let's explore.' But instead he got all huffy and cautious. And, after they couldn't contact any of the other Linyaari survey teams, much less Acorna, he'd said, 'We must interact with others as little as possible. We should keep to ourselves until we know what's going on.'

'I hate to disagree with you, young fellow,' Yiitir had pointed out, 'but if we keep to ourselves, we're unlikely to *learn* what's going on.'

'Oh, look,' Maarni said. *'Piiro!* I haven't been out on the water since way before we left Vhiliinyar and there are two *piiro* sitting right there empty, just waiting for passengers.'

'I'm very hot and weary,' Yiitir said. 'A little row and a bit of a swim would be lovely. How about you, Maati? What do you think?'

'She doesn't swim,' Aari said.

'How do you know?' she asked indignantly. 'You've been in my life again less than a *ghaanyi* and already you're an expert on what Maati can and can't do? It so happens I – I can learn. You'll teach me, won't you, Yiitir?'

'Oh, I'm very bad at teaching anything other than my own specialty, I fear, but Maarni is a good teacher and a good swimmer. She taught all of our younglings before we left Vhiliinyar, and many of her students, too.'

'Have you people forgotten about all the others who have disappeared? That we are on a serious mission here, and cannot contact a single member of the survey team? We have no idea what has caused us to come to this place, or where this place is.'

'I'd say that was rather obvious,' Yiitir said. 'We have disappeared, too. Far from being killed or chased by monsters, we now find ourselves in a very nice place, which I guess to be Vhiliinyar of several thousand *ghaanyi* ago. If I am correct, that

215

would be the original Kubiilikaan over there, the home of the Ancestral Hosts.'

'Yiitir! I just saw one! I'm sure I did! A *sii*-Linyaari!' Maarni was jumping up and down like an excited child. 'Oh, let's go try to talk to them!'

'You don't know their language,' Aari pointed out.

'We *are* telepathic,' Yiitir reminded him. 'And we share ancestors on at least one side, according to what we know of them.'

'It's an opportunity not to be missed,' Maarni said, tugging at her lifemate's hand. Maati found herself dancing along beside them while Aari stood scowling.

She didn't really understand his attitude at all. It wasn't like there was any danger. If Yiitir was right about where – no, when, they were – the Khleevi were an unthinkably long time in the future.

(Come on, Aari,) she pleaded. (It'll be an adventure! Come with us. There's nothing to be afraid of.)

(You don't understand, Youngling. You haven't been trained. All of this has just been thrust upon you. What we do and say now could change history beyond our imagining. No one will have told you about the space-time continuum and why you must be careful –)

(Not to meet yourself coming and going?) she replied scornfully. (Oh, we had all that before I left school. Grandam made sure I had progressive tutors. I learned all about that stuff and Grandam and I talked about it some, too. You know what she said?)

(You're about to tell me, I take it,) his thought came through huffy and impatient.

(Grandam said that if people go back and change history, then that's sort of like birth and death, isn't it? It's just fate. It's what happens. And maybe it's for the best. Maybe history should be changed. Besides, what else can we do but relax and explore? Can you get us back to where we were?)

(No, but I can stay put and hope that our friends will be able to find us.)

(They sure were not able to find anybody else that was lost! We are stuck here. Why can't we look around? Grandam would say we should take advantage of the situation if we can't change it.)

(I can't imagine her saying something so simplistic and irresponsible,) Aari said.

That made Maati so mad she didn't even try to conceal it. (She was *not* irresponsible! She was the most grown-up Linyaari of anybody ever but she wasn't always looking for bad in everything like you do. You want to talk about irresponsible? Who was it who couldn't even get himself and our brother to the ship in time to be evacuated? I would have had the benefit of your attitudes and teachings a long time ago if you had just been on time for take-off! Instead I got Grandam to bring me up, while our parents went off looking for you and Laarye. And you know what? I'm glad! Grandam was wise, not full of gloomy old scary stories about making it so your future self is never born. What do we know about the future or anything else? Our life is wherever we are at the time, isn't it? Well, isn't it?)

She had been sending so fast and so furiously that she didn't notice until she ran down that he had grown very still, very sad.

'Oh, Aari, brother, I am so sorry!' she said, running over to try to catch his hand and make up with him. But she had gone too far. He hated her now. He wasn't sending hate, but he *was* pulling away from her as if she had some sort of horrible contagious disease.

'No, no, you might be right. Go along with Yiitir and Maarni. I will wait here and tell anyone who finds us where you are.'

And so she did. Maybe when he'd sat on the beach by himself long enough, he'd realize he was being silly and come and join them.

And she caught his thought, not actually intended for her to hear, (She is still young enough to think that things always come out all right, that your friends always find you, and that nothing very bad will happen.)

Maati felt an answering flutter of unease. Of course, she *had* been through a lot of bad things, but basically her brother was right. There were usually a lot of good people around to help her out of whatever predicament she was in. Though, in her secret heart, so far, she still sort of preferred the Khleevi to Liriili. Their attacks at least were less personal.

'The youngest gets to push off!' Yiitir commanded cheerily, as he stood in the bow of the little boat and struck a pose worthy of the admiral of some great navy. Maarni was rummaging in the pack she had had with her when they were – transferred? Shifted? Transported?

The folklorist came up with a LAANYE and a small notebook and *stiil*. Very low tech, but still light and handy and it did the job of writing.

Maati rolled up the cuffs of her shipsuit and waded in, pushing the little *piiro* into the water and jumping aboard afterwards with such enthusiasm that the boat wallowed precariously. Yiitir flailed around and sat down abruptly. Maarni laughed. Then Yiitir handed Maati a paddle and kept one for himself, and together they paddled the *piiro* out into the water.

They saw some other boats, including some very large ones, out on the water, and people were moving around on them – a few were Linyaari, but most were another sort of person, rather like Becker and Uncle Hafiz but longer and slimmer. Their movements were very graceful, she thought, and there was something Linyaari-ish about them, although they had no horns and she couldn't see their hands and feet very well. Their hair resembled that of the humans Maati had met, too.

'Can we go talk to them?' Maati asked. 'It would be wonderful to finally meet one of the Friends, don't you think?'

Yiitir said, 'There'll be time enough for that if our situation can't be sorted out. But I think we should merely listen for the moment. Aari was right, you know. We mustn't disrupt things by letting on where we're from and what we're doing here unless it becomes a matter of life or death for us.'

'As if we knew what we were doing here!' Maati said. 'You know, if we have been brought back in time, who do you think brought us here? They did! The Friends. Somehow or other. So they could send us back.'

'There is a flaw in your logic, you know,' Yiitir pointed out.

'What? It seems sensible to me,' she said.

'The Friends were all long gone by the time we were born. They couldn't have brought us here deliberately. Not us specifically, at any rate. They didn't know we existed.'

'Well, yes, but even if they didn't aim for us specifically they must know how our coming here happened.'

'Why?' Maarni asked. 'Perhaps we're here as the result of something the Khleevi left behind on Vhiliinyar.'

'Can't be,' Maati said with an impudent grin.

'Why not?'

'Nothing has tried to eat us yet.'

'A valid point,' Yiitir agreed. 'She has you there, my dear.'

'Still, I do not think communicating our plight is a good idea. We might be as big a surprise to them as they are to us.'

'I suppose – oh, *look*!' Maarni cried as something flashed from the water with a brilliant dazzle of blue-green and a spume of spray. Just for a moment Maati had seen it – a horn among wet strands of long greenish hair.

She was about to dive overboard after it when Maarni put a firm hand on her shoulder. The elder Linyaari sent out a mental message, broadcasting very loudly. (Please come to see us here on our *piiro*. We understand that our races are related.

We would like to know you better.)

They waited, paddling placidly in the lake, which had little rainbows of color floating on the waters from some kind of strange substance that Maati had never seen before on the lakes or seas of narhii-Vhiliinyar. It smelt funny, too, she thought, wrinkling her nose – nasty stuff. But it wasn't the water she was interested in, but what was in it. Maarni sent out her plea again, reassuring the *sii*-Linyaari she meant them no harm, but simply wanted to hear their stories and songs, wanted to meet them.

Meanwhile, they kept paddling out to a small island. Over on the far side of it, they rested their arms, floating gently and admiring the birds flying by, the way the suns gilded the shore with a tawny sunset, and the mildness of the air.

As soon as they were on the other side of the island, their *piiro* was surrounded by turbulence in the form of streaks racing through the water toward them.

And then they, too, were in the water. Maati gulped and splashed and sank beneath the waves, in spite of her best efforts to stay afloat. She was going to drown here in this strange world.

It seemed Aari was right.

EIGHTEEN

From the vantage point of their three skyscraper towers, Acorna, Thariinye, and Mac saw that in many places, despite its reinforcement, the sky *had* fallen. Huge triangles of the ceiling's fabric, a substance Acorna guessed to be similar to that used in Linyaari space vessels, bulged with debris covering whole smashed city blocks.

All she could see of the sea from the vantage point was the part washing over the lower city and the debris column in the middle. But she got a vaster and more shadowy impression of the landward side. Ranging outward from where she stood, as far as her eyes could see, were outline beyond outline beyond outline of buildings stretching endlessly into the darkness. How could she and her friends ever explore all of this?

There were hundreds of buildings as tall as the ones they climbed, though not all were as large in circumference, and not all had survived the depredations of time and Khleevi in the world above. Whole blocks of the city lay buried under earth, trees, and Khleevi scat. Other buildings, less sturdy than the columns, lay in pieces, shaken by the earthquakes that had so disrupted the surface, Acorna guessed. It was very difficult to see too far by the mere glow of the building walls.

(Aari? Where are you, *yaazi*?) she called again, disheartened by the distance yet to be covered, the buildings to be explored, the length and breadth of the city.

(Khornya!) A cry came, its intensity stunning her. Though the volume was faint, the sound of her name was a desperate plea for help.

(Aari!) she cried, but received no answer. (Aari?) Silence.

She called again and again, until her mind ached and she heard another call, not Aari.

(Khornya?) This was from Thariinye, and uncharacteristically timid.

(I heard him, Thariinye, I did! And he sounded terrified,) she said.

'She heard Aari,' Thariinye told Mac. 'You must have imagined the tone, Khornya. Aari would not be terrified, no matter what. He is very brave.'

She ignored that, but insisted, 'I heard what I heard and he's here somewhere. They all must be.'

'I didn't hear him. Perhaps it's your building.'

'I doubt it, but it's a theory. Look, from here I can see that there's actually another floor above the one you're standing on – Mac's, too. Can you see the same thing on my building? If so, I think we should go to see what's there.'

It was true. Whereas the story on which each of them stood was the last one at the top of the stairs, surrounded, at its perimeter, by something of an open porch with columns on all sides, the very top

223

floor on Mac's building and Thariinye's appeared quite solid.

'Yes, your structure contains another layer as well, Khornya,' Mac said.

Continuing to cast a mental broadcast as loudly and as far as she could, heedless that it could be picked up by whatever unseen enemy had spirited away the other Linyaari, she clicked across the stone tiles and touched the inner wall.

And found herself looking down onto a huge dark globe that encompassed the center of the building. The inner wall was transparent.

'It's like one of those ancient lighthouses in Becker's pirate books!' she said to the others. 'See if you have one. If we can light them, we'll be able to see more of the city, have a better chance of finding our people.'

As she spoke she found the single door giving access to the globe. Opening it, she entered.

A narrow circle of floor was separated from the globe by a railing, but she found, leaning forward, that she could easily touch the globe with her hand. Unlike the walls, it failed to light up, and for a fleeting second she was disappointed.

It appeared to be held aloft by columns of something that moved slightly, even in the gloomy light cast by the walls, something quicksilver with a shine to it. The ancestor to the interior streams of the Linyaari pavilions, she decided.

Circling the globe, she saw no controls of any sort. Then, in one place, there was a small narrow extension to the walkway, leading to the globe. When she set foot on it, it jiggled. Then she saw a tiny point on the globe's vastness, just at the end of the extension. She also noticed that there were loops in the ground level of the railing, and realized that she was meant not to walk on the extension, but to lie down upon it, hooking her feet into the railing. She found that by doing this, her horn was in the proper position to touch the globe.

Breathlessly, she craned her neck just a tiny bit and made the touch, then shut her eyes tightly, expecting a blinding light. However, the person who had dreamed this up no doubt had a healthy respect for his or her own vision, for the globe merely shimmered, then glowed, then glittered at various spots, growing a bit brighter. It did all of this without increasing in temperature either on its surface or in the room surrounding it. Acorna was easily able to return to the outer portion of the building before the light blossomed into a small brilliant sun. It lit the ceiling in the area for two blocks beyond the building with the violet and rose hues of dawn.

'Behold the dawn!' Thariinye bellowed in her ear via the com link. 'I have one, too!'

And from beyond the transparent partition an answering brightness met that of her own globe.

'Mine does not work,' Mac said and Acorna heard disappointment in the android's voice.

'Did you find the little walkway and the contact point?' Thariinye asked.

'Yes, but it does not care for my horn modification. Perhaps the alloy from which I constructed it is inappropriate to the function.'

'Hmmm,' Thariinye said. 'Or it could be that the tip of your horn is the wrong size or shape.

Maybe we should do a little filing when we return to the surface.'

Mac sounded brighter. 'An excellent idea. Actually, I have an array of files along my spine if you . . .'

'Gentlemen!' Acorna stopped them.

'Yes?' they both said.

'Look!'

Once more standing on the outer balcony, she beheld the city in much, if not all, of its glory.

'I can't see the end of it!' Thariinye cried. 'Where are the grasslands and meadows? But, oh! Now! With color! How beautiful! And how huge! Oh, Khornya, we will never find them here!'

Now they could truly appreciate the glory and the magnitude of this underground city and what it had once been, as well as assess the damage that had been done to it.

Where the globe's illumination flooded the street, the buildings danced and seemed to change shapes as the walls bulged and buckled, melted and grew, doming, spiraling, flattening, expanding, contracting, a living breathing panorama of color and light. Soft natural colors brightened to vivid, darkened to jewel tones, shifted to alien light modes that Acorna had never seen before – pattern and form shifted.

(What an exhausting place to live!) Thariinye thought. (No wonder we saw no sleeping dwellings here. No one could sleep with all that going on.)

(Impressive,) Acorna agreed. (But it brings us no closer than we were before to finding Aari and Maati and the others.)

(True, and Maati's just a little girl! A youngling! She was so proud of being star-clad, Khornya. So proud of finally hearing thoughts. Quite annoying really. Thinks she knows more than I do – or anyone else. I wish I could find her right now so I could tell her how irritating she can be.)

(She'll be with Aari, and the elders,) Acorna told him, (and Kaarlye and Miiri are missing, too. So if they've all been taken or sent to the same place, she'll have more family around her than either of us do right now.)

(Of course she will,) Thariinye said, his thought-image one of RK quickly shoveling dirt over a recent production. (I'm not worried or anything, just appalled at how inconsiderate the little scamp is, disappearing when we need her help.)

But the thought-picture of RK reminded Acorna that she hadn't seen the cat for some time.

'Has anybody seen RK recently?' she said into her com link.

An assortment of negatives came back to her from the others in her party.

'Oh, no,' she said. 'Now RK might be missing, too!'

'We must find him then!' Mac said. 'Captain Becker will be most aggrieved with us if we lose his first mate.'

(Half the Linyaari population missing and now we have to worry about RK,) Thariinye grumbled internally, just loudly enough for Acorna to hear.

But he and Mac joined her swiftly, and helped her hunt the area around the globe and the rest of the floor of the building besides.

She stopped them with, 'I've called the cat until

227

my throat hurts, and sent him urgent mental messages as well. It's no good. If RK is here, he is ignoring all calls.'

Mac responded sensibly, 'It has been, by my calculations, fully twelve hours since the cat last slept. Cats require a great deal of sleep, and my observations of RK lead me to believe that he is very feline in that regard. I suspect we shall find him curled up somewhere warm, snoring.'

'A good point,' Acorna said. 'Then let us continue looking for him.'

They searched every floor of the massive building, all along the glowing walls and the inner chambers to the ground floor, without success. Acorna began to think the cat had wandered back outside, in which case he would only be found when he wished to be.

She looked out into the street. Perhaps he was merely curled up by the door, waiting for her to finish. It wouldn't be the first time he'd bowed out of some activity the cat felt was boring to take a nice nap. But he wasn't sitting by the door. Then, as her thoughts and her footsteps stilled, she heard something. 'Listen,' she said.

'What?'

'There it is again. That sound I thought was the sea.'

'Yes!' Mac said. 'I hear it now, too. And purring. I hear purring. It is coming from below.' He indicated the level beneath the street, the one leading to the cave.

They slipped and slid back down the steep incline they had climbed to reach the ground floor. The glow from the wall of the upper story was dim down here. This was not a place they had seen clearly before, since, upon coming out of the cavern, they had had no idea that they were in a place where walls glowed. Now, however, Thariinye walked over and touched a wall, and this lowermost floor was illuminated.

RK lay near the inside wall, purring. As they approached him, lighting the wall, he looked up and mewed as innocently as a kitten. He'd been caught napping, but he wasn't the least embarrassed. As he stood up and stretched it appeared he had not a care in the world.

'Now *why* do you suppose he chose this spot for his nap?' Thariinye asked.

Acorna bent to pet the cat. When she touched the wall next to RK, she straightened up at once. 'Because this wall is warmer than the rest. And it's vibrating. We haven't examined this floor thoroughly, but do you know, I could swear there is some sort of humming coming from whatever is inside this level.'

'We will investigate it,' Thariinye said.

Acorna was already trying the door nearest the cat, but to her surprise, it was locked firmly, as nothing else they had seen in this city had been.

Mac stepped forward, his laser at the ready. 'Allow me,' he said.

But as soon as the laser cut the lock, a piercing siren split the air along with a loud voice clearly commanding them to do something, but speaking in a language none of them understood.

RK, upset by this rude disturbance of his rest, bolted for the hole into the cavern and jumped down into it.

No one paid him the slightest attention. Instead they entered the room that had been locked.

Once they illuminated its walls, they beheld no ordinary meeting room, but a vast chamber taking up the entire interior of the huge building. At its core, something silvery and metallic-looking spun inside a transparent cylinder. The walls here bore glyphs, too, but these changed constantly.

'This entire wall is a screen,' Thariinye said, walking along and watching the numbers change. They did not appear to be made of light, but seemed painted on the walls like the other glyphs, and yet they morphed at even intervals, reflecting new data that had no meaning for any of the team.

'There will be controls somewhere,' Mac said knowledgeably, searching along the walls. 'Something is generating this whirling and this changing of data on the wall glyphs.'

'Perhaps the instrument panel is in the floor,' Acorna said when Mac's survey produced no results. 'You know, this might be the control room for the lighting, especially the globes on the top floors. We didn't hear it or feel anything when we came through before because we hadn't yet activated any lights.'

'I do not think so, Khornya,' Mac told her. 'The lights, for all their power and sophisticated design, are relatively simple mechanisms. They would not require so much data as we are seeing here. I will try to translate some of this writing.'

She had wandered to the far side of the silvery column and now saw that in addition to writing, the wall contained a huge map. It was not merely a flat wall map, but a globe, and she could see, just barely, that it revolved slowly.

'Thariinye,' she said. 'Look at this. Do you recognize any of the features here?'

'No,' he said, and then it turned very slightly and he said, 'wait, yes, I do! This is Vhiliinyar. See, here's the gravesite and here's the cave where Aari hid and – look, there is a little dot of light there, do you see?'

'Yes, oh, but now it's gone.'

'Everything here is in a state of constant flux,' Mac said, with appreciation but also with some frustration. 'It is very difficult to accumulate data when it is changing faster than I can record it.'

Acorna drew closer to the map, and touched a point of light. A glimmer of understanding stung her finger like a crackle of static electricity. 'That is Fiirki,' she said. 'That's exactly where he disappeared. The light *must* stand for him. Thariinye! Mac! Come closer! I've found something! This map – it locates some of our people.'

'Where they were before they were lost, or now?' Thariinye asked.

'Hmm, I don't know. What would you say, looking at this?'

'I'd say it is history,' Thariinye said dismissively. 'There might have been another Fiirki in the old days. You see here? There's the seashore and the Vriiniia Watiir, over here the mountain ranges are where they belong. This is old Vhiliinyar, not Vhiliinyar as it is today.'

She sighed and leaned a bit heavily on the map with her palm. It disappeared, and reappeared, changed. This time the features Thariinye pointed out were missing, as was the light that stood for Fiirki. But there was another cluster of the tiny lights, one of them purple, the others white, except for two larger lights, one the size of a pin's head instead of its tip, the other the circumference of the pupil of an eye. The first of these was pale aqua, the second dark pink.

Nearby was a linear representation of the blocked tunnel and the cavern.

'Look at this!' she cried and Mac and Thariinye did so, very excited.

'That's the surface as it is today,' Thariinye said. 'The big lights are probably the shuttles Yaniriin was talking about. I wonder if this map shows this hidden city and maybe who is down here? It would help us locate the others.'

Acorna placed her hand on the map again, to see if it would change. It did. And it showed three small lights in the center of the map, and another, somewhat smaller and silvery in color, to one side. But what dominated the map was the depiction of the silvery column in the center of this room – and its branches spreading all over the city, superimposed on the other structures but concentrated at the top of the buildings that served as supports for the ceiling.

'Fascinating,' Mac said.

'This thing has tentacles?' Thariinye said, casting a wary eye on the column swirling up the center of the chamber.

'A conduit pattern might be more accurate,' Mac said. 'I believe it is a representation of energy flows in the lighting system. Touch the map again and see what it does. Touch it on the lake.'

Acorna obliged and the map shifted dramatically. This time it showed the features of the lake's surface again, except that the waterfall was not there as it had been in the previous image. Instead there was a flowing river, dots of blue-green light in a much vaster body of water than the current lake, and four small white pins of light among the blue-green lights. Some boat-shaped things were drawn in with several lights attached to each, these a mixture of white and gold.

'I believe that the white lights are Linyaari,' Acorna said. 'I wonder – could those aqua ones, that seem to be in the water, be the *sii*-Linyaari?'

Thariinye said, 'I think you are setting too much store by this thing. The topography for this map isn't right. The lake is much too big and there is no river where that one is – hasn't been as long as anyone seems to recall – and the waterfall is not there. This isn't a real place.'

'Not now,' Acorna said. 'But maybe it was once. I begin to think we don't need to look for a where for finding our people. We need to look for a when.'

She triggered the map again, and again, and again, and always she came up with a different picture. Finally one appeared where the vortex of the silver whirl showed, and its branches as they would appear if they could be seen through the surface of the planet as it currently was. Except that they were all broken up, and even as she watched, bits of the silver stuff blobbed off and bounced away from the main branch.

'I wonder if those silver bits symbolize something that is energy or organic in nature,' Acorna mused.

'I would say energy,' Mac replied, eyeing the column.

'I think I had better take a look in that topmost story of the building I was in,' she said, tracing the path of the silvery line from where it began to slightly up and out. 'I didn't explore thoroughly there because I noticed that RK was missing. But I think it might be wise to take a good look there now.'

'I will accompany you,' Mac said. 'Perhaps if we find anything I may be of assistance in determining what it is.'

'Don't think you two can leave *me* down here,' Thariinye said. 'I find that thing extremely unsettling and refuse to be left alone with it.'

But before they set foot outside the chamber, RK pounced back into view and from below a familiar gravelly voice called, 'Hellooo-o! Becker here! Come out, come out, wherever you are!'

NINETEEN

When confronted with the short, hairy creature who was the first being he met on his way into the city, Aari forgot his diplomat's training, remembered Becker's vids, and said, 'Take me to your leader.'

Actually, it wasn't so much that he forgot his training as that he liked some of the new ways he had learned recently. The demand, voiced by both protagonist earthlings and protagonist and antagonist 'aliens' had a nice ring to it, Aari thought. It was forthright and honest. Unlike his recent dealings with his little sister.

But Maati would have been angrier with him than she already was if she had known he intended to do this. He had, from the first moment he had deduced where they were, every intention of causing disruption to the space-time continuum. He simply wanted to do it alone. One person would cause less disruption than four, he reasoned, especially if that person was well aware of the dangers. Besides, Khleevi capture had made Aari far less trusting than he once was. Until he knew exactly when they were and what the beings in charge were like, he preferred that his sister and the two elders paddle around safely in the water looking for mythical *sii*-Linyaari.

The creature peered at him from under fronds of eyebrows and said, quite clearly, 'Your accent is peculiar. You're one of the new batch, aren't you?'

'New batch of what?'

'Youngsters. Although you're pretty old for a youngster. Shouldn't you be – shorter?'

'I was,' Aari said ruefully, referring to his twisted and broken spine after the Khleevi had finished with him. 'I didn't care for it, so I grew.'

The creature cackled and slapped himself on his thighs – at least, Aari was assuming it was a male. The creature looked mostly humanoid, it walked on two feet, it had two arms, rather long, and two eyes, deep set under the frondish brows, and two large ears with points at both tip and lobe.

'Can you tell me where and when I am?' Aari inquired.

'Where and when you—? Oh, I see, you're one of the batch that didn't get done properly. How'd you get way out here, child? You should be back at the palace, learning from your elders, or getting your head reprogrammed or whatever it is they're doing to fix the ones who don't come out right.'

'Come out right?' Aari asked.

'Like you. For instance, you didn't get the Gift, did you? All of us got it, and all the unicorns, but some of the youngsters haven't had it at all. Like you.'

'Gift?' Aari repeated cautiously.

'Telepathy. I've been trying to read you, so that I know where to take you, but I cannot figure you out. I can't read you.'

'Oh,' Aari said, keeping his mind as carefully blank as he had been doing, as he had learned to do with the Khleevi. Among his people, when one wanted to be understood and helped the first thing one did was open up one's mind. He had learned the hard way that there are many circumstances in which that was not a good idea. So he would let this creature think he was a not very bright child, as long as it did what was asked. 'I did say where I wanted to be taken,' Aari told him courteously but perhaps a little obstinately, as if he were indeed stupid. 'I wish to be taken to your leader.'

'So you did, so you did, and so I shall, so I shall.'

Soon they were walking uphill, and now Aari noticed that the Host's legs were really a lot longer than they had seemed to be at first, and that the Host himself was taller. As tall as Aari was, in fact.

As they strode up the hill into the central part of the city, Aari tried to take in his surroundings, but even while he was watching, they kept changing. Buildings shifted from shape to shape, from color to color, and the skyline continually altered so that sometimes a tall cone-shaped spire was in one place, sometimes in another, or a modest low round dome shape in hot pink suddenly acquired a spiral onion dome with purple and lavender jewels and enamels.

Vertigo was setting in, and Aari couldn't help showing his bafflement.

237

His guide laughed, a low rolling chuckle. 'You are *much* younger than you look, son. This,' he waved a broad and horned hand to indicate the city, 'is your home. The changing is all smoke and mirrors of course, a trick of light.'

Aari said nothing. He felt he couldn't speak without revealing himself.

His escort, the hairy fellow, not so short now as he once was, Aari was sure of it, led him up a moving ramp leading into the ground floor of a towering column whose top seemed to be in the sky.

It changed into a pyramid as they entered, with hieroglyphics dancing on the outer walls. All around them beings in a wide variety of shapes and sizes went about their business. Many were tall and thin, and almost as pale as he was, but without horns. But the majority of the creatures displayed a fantastic diversity of appearance. Their hair came in all the colors of a laser-flashed rainbow, as did their clothing. Their skins, too, ran the gamut of every imaginable shade from pale to deepest blue-black, and some were even multicolored, splattered in various patterns. Some were hairy and squat; some massive. Some wore clothing; some were so covered in fur or hair that it was impossible to tell if they were clad – if they were, their garments were covered. Among those beings on two legs ran various four-legged sorts of creatures. Birds nested on the tops of the buildings and didn't seem to mind that the structures' tops bobbed up and down like the tails of the four-legged, RK-like creatures that bounced importantly through the throngs.

No one took the least notice of Aari and his guide, but as they entered the building and descended via another moving ramp, glowing walls displayed in sequence pictures of meadows, forests, storms, blue skies, and calm seas. Aari tore his eyes away from these and found those of his host locked firmly upon him.

'You're not from around here, are you, son?'

Aari realized almost immediately the problem with demanding to be taken to the leader of a species heretofore unknown to you. Which was, once your demand was met, and you were taken to the leader, you found yourself among a great many followers as well.

Looking around at the many pairs of eyes drilling into him as if they could visually vivisect him, Aari suddenly recalled the way the vids where someone was taken to a leader usually unfolded. Once the alien was presented to the leader, the followers waited for the leader's signal to pounce upon the intruder and administer whatever treatment was given to miscreants. Such treatments, as he recalled, were invariably unpleasant.

His guide ushered Aari into a large room with walls filled with images and words that moved, melted, and reformed like everything else he'd seen in this city thus far. As they entered, at a look from the guide, several people stopped what they were doing and realigned themselves so they stood between Aari and the door.

In the center of the room a large swirling silvery column ascended toward the ceiling.

'Highmagister HaGurdy,' Aari's guide said. 'I

met this being on the road from the sea. I took him for one of the new batch at first.'

'How could you?' A small slender woman with hair like flames and snow and eyes like the lushest grasses asked in a voice as musical as the Singing Stones of Skarness. 'He is much too mature. The others are children.'

'Then it came to me that perhaps he was one of the batch living in the sea, that he of all of them had successfully mutated into the desired form . . .'

'Highly unlikely,' Highmagister HaGurdy said. 'Do you think we didn't test them all before releasing them to the waters?'

'But as I spent time with him, though I could read no one thought clearly, it became evident to me that he had seen nothing here before. He is not one of us, nor is he one of our chosen Guests or Offspring.'

Highmagister HaGurdy walked toward Aari. Like his guide, she grew nearer his height as she drew nigh him. Her scent, which was basically one of wildflowers and musk, had an unpleasant overlay of chemicals. Although she was clad in a gown of velvety deep blue, it was incongruously covered by the same white laboratory jacket sported by the other occupants of the room.

Aari tipped his horn to the lady respectfully. 'I beg to differ with my guide, Hiimaagii,' he said, the limitations of his Linyaari tongue not allowing him to speak more of her title than that. 'I believe that I am one of your offspring, but many generations removed from now. I have become lost in

240

time and I come to ask you to return me to my own time.'

He deliberately suppressed thoughts of his friends. He would tell this formidable female of them when he knew if she could be trusted. In all of the stories the Ancestors told, the Friends, the Hosts, were benevolent and helpful and there was no reason to mistrust or fear them.

But he knew all too well that reality could be somewhat different than stories.

'Now how can that be?' she asked. 'Certainly you appear to be exactly what we are working toward in our current creations. Except for your somewhat misshapen horn, you are all that we hope our new batch will be when they are grown, but they will not reach physical maturity for thrice a twelvemonth.' She looked at Aari and he felt as if more than his mind was being expertly probed. 'And you, my lad, are well past that age, and no youth. You know, based on the evidence before me, I am tempted to believe your wild claim.'

But her incredulity was no greater than his when he realized that if all the stories were true, this slender and beautiful female before him was his ancient ancestress on the un-horned two-legged side. How could she be his many times Grandmother, though?

A small smile played across her lips and her contours grew softer and broader, her cheeks plumper, and her hair tucked itself into a braid, the snow overtaking all but a hint of the flame of it. The meadows of her eyes were undimmed, however. 'Is this guise more appropriate to your way of thinking, Great Grandson?' she asked Aari. She had clearly read his thought, even though he had tried to suppress it.

'It *is* less distracting,' he replied.

Dimples morphed into her cheeks and she gave him a Grandmotherly smile.

'So when do you come to us from? And how have you come to be here?' she asked. 'And where are your companions?'

'When? I take it then, you truly believe I have traveled from the future . . . And what companions are you talking about?'

'Surely you did not come alone from the future. I see hints of those who accompanied you in your mind. And why, if you don't mind my asking, did you come at all? We, of course, travel to many times and places in the space-time continuum, but you are the first unauthorized visitor we have ever received from another time. At least, I assume no one here sent for him?' She sent the question around the room and all of the other people shook their heads and declared that they had nothing to do with his appearance. 'Besides, if we had sent for you, you would have arrived in this room. How did you happen to arrive elsewhere on this world? Or at all, for that matter?'

'Yes, how?' the others asked and now that he looked at them, they appeared a bit older than he thought at first, all were grayer, and had kindly aspects to their faces. Though they were not Linyaari faces, still, they now had something of the Linyaari about them. Something from the two-legged, unhorned side. They gathered around chattering questions at him and asking for facts of physics to explain his journey. How could he explain to them what he didn't understand himself? But he was about to relate everything that had happened to him on his journey here when the lady took his arm in hers, and one wall of the room opened to yet another, more interior chamber. 'Never mind all that for now. He has come to us at the right time. He is no larval being, but a full-grown male in his prime, and the prototype for our descendant species. Great Grandson, if you will just lie on that table there, we need to take a few samples.'

They surrounded him and their kindly aspects were revealed for the lies they were. They all grew monstrous eyes and pincers, looking exactly like Khleevi to him as they forced him onto the table. They ignored his protests and struggling, except when the Highmagister *tsked*, *tsked* him, saying, 'We cannot hurt you – at least not permanently. The other side of the family can immediately heal any small hurts you might feel, you know . . .'

But it wasn't the hurt or lack of it that made him struggle under their hands. In fact, it wasn't who they were or where he was that concerned him now. After his experiences at the hands of the Khleevi, he simply could not stand being strapped to a metal table again. Not for any reason. His mind was no longer his own, and he fought harder than he could ever remember fighting anything. And somewhere, from far away, he heard the only comforting sound he could imagine, maybe the last comforting sound he would ever hear. His beloved lifemate crying, 'Aari!'

'Khornya!' he bellowed, with all of his voices, physical and mental. That cry alone and then all was blackness.

TWENTY

'Oh, Captain Becker!' Acorna cried. 'Thank goodness you have come! Our Ancestral Hosts have this machine here, and I believe it allows time travel. Help me fix it so that I can fetch our people back, please. I believe they have become lost in time.'

'Is that what is going on?' Becker asked. 'No problem. We'll have 'er fixed in a jiffy.'

'What is a jiffy?' Thariinye inquired.

'Another time thing,' Becker said. In an aside to Acorna, he said, 'Why don't you let *him* fetch your lost ones back, Princess? You're handy to have around and he'd be no great loss.'

'I heard that,' Thariinye said, with a curious combination of indignation *and* dignity. 'And I think it highly premature to start talking about who is useful and who is not until we have determined how this device works and how best to retrieve our missing friends.'

'I have a few hypotheses, based on the data at hand,' Mac said. He was applying pressure to the map rapidly and repeatedly and storing the data it presented as it changed.

'You'd better be careful there, buddy, you

could maybe break that thing,' Becker cautioned. 'It's an antique. In fact – wheehee, would you look at this place! This would be some very high class salvage.' He saw Thariinye's horrified look and Acorna's rather stricken one of disappointment in his attitude toward her people's ancient secrets and said quickly, 'Just kidding, guys. Honest.'

'I hope so, Captain. Right now we need to concentrate on how to use this machinery, not what you could sell it for on an open market. You see there, those white lights we believe represent our people,' Acorna told him, pointing them out as the shape of the map changed over and over under Mac's direction. 'The maps overall represent the planet's surface at different times in its history. Mac, can you show the Captain the schematic we found earlier?'

'Yes, Khornya. It required eight presses of your hand.' But as Mac attempted to do the same thing, and he came up with several different maps in which white lights appeared, he could not return them to the same one. 'Hmmm,' he said. 'I am sure there is a pattern here if one can locate it. Perhaps you should try again, Khornya,' Mac said, stepping aside before he added an unscientific comment that surprised her. 'It seems to prefer you.'

Maybe it did. What could she do that Mac couldn't? She was telepathic, an ability she supposedly had inherited from both sets of her ancient Ancestors. This was an artifact created by those very Ancestors. Maybe the map worked with telepathy – could it show the viewers the time they needed to see based on what it knew of

246

their thoughts? Telepathy, after all, was a form of energy . . .

She wanted to concentrate on her friends but instead she projected a thought-image of the silver threads connecting this subterranean chamber and its strange device to the surface. That image appeared on the wall, still showing ragged tatters and blobs among the silver extensions as they branched out above ground.

'Hmm,' Becker said.

Acorna noticed something about the map she hadn't noticed previously.

'Look at this trunk-line here – running away from this room and downward,' she said, tracing it with her finger. 'It comes from the sea.'

'Hmmm,' Becker said again.

'I think I see a pattern here. Our site in the survey was beside what used to be a great water-fall. The *wii-Balakiire* was investigating the terrain near a former riverbed. Aari's cave and the graves were located along the shoreline of another one of the seas, if I remember the details correctly from the maps we had of the planet from the time period immediately pre-Khleevi. Water seems to be a thread that connects every disappearance for which we have enough data to make a surmise.'

'I have an idea!' Thariinye exclaimed suddenly. 'What if this supposed time force is conducted by the waters of this planet?'

Acorna had to laugh. 'Thariinye, that's what I just said.'

He looked puzzled. 'Well, of course, Khornya. But I said it better. What do you think of my idea?'

Acorna rolled her eyes but remained silent.

'I don't quite get it yet,' Becker said. 'There's no water to speak of left on the surface of this planet anymore. And that's where everybody disappeared from. So how could the disappearances be triggered by water?'

'It's just a theory,' Acorna admitted. 'But there is plenty of water down here in this ancient city, and there was enough to grow vegetation in our survey quadrant and so there may be more water out there than we know – let me see if I can get this to return to the time just before Aari and the others disappeared. What timeframe would best suit that – I know! When RK got in trouble with the carnivore plants.' She visualized the cat and the plant and when the map for that time appeared with their own small white lights and the cat's showing on the screen, she imagined the diagram of the silvery energy superimposed on it.

'You may just have a point!' Becker said. 'The silvery stuff is still all around, but it's just attached to random bits of water or moisture now – nothing to conduct it in a reasonable way. I guess it's gone a little haywire as a consequence. Which could be why people started popping off. Looks to me like if we could get the hydraulics going again at least well enough to get the energy channeled back into its old paths, it might stabilize, and if it stabilizes, well, I'm not sure how it would help exactly but seems to me we'd be closer to some answers. And maybe closer to controlling it well enough to bring some old friends home.'

'Why would anyone send time energy through water?' Thariinye asked.

'Hey, why not? How do we know what a bunch

of your crazy Ancestors were thinking?' Becker asked. 'You know all those songs the Ancestors sing about the rivers of time and the endless sea of life and so forth – maybe some Ancestral Friend took them seriously! Actually, it seems to me that if anything could hold a lot of time, water could – it's the original deal they were talking about with the saying "what goes around comes around."'

'I never thought of it that way, but then, Linyaari songs and poems are more about the tall stalks growing beside the water than about the water itself,' Thariinye said. 'Still, I fail to understand why we wouldn't know about the time-travel technology from the tales of the Ancestors. Surely, if the Hosts put so much emphasis on time transference as this room indicates, it would still be evident in the stories the Ancestors or the Linyaari tell today. I don't recall any of the Elders ever speaking of time technology among our people, not in their lifetimes nor in the days of the Ancestors. The Ancestors didn't say anything about it to you, did they, Khornya?'

'Well, I know of some references to time in the Attendants' writings, actually,' she said. 'In the glyphs we read back in the Ancestors' cave. But they seemed cryptic to me when I read them. Now, however . . . yes, it's starting to make sense. A little, anyway. I think that the truth is that this technology was entirely one for the Hosts, not something our people adopted for their own at any point. Perhaps by the time our own people evolved enough to use it on their own, this city had vanished into legend and the time-travel mechanisms along with it. Perhaps as long as its normal conduits were available, the – power – was dormant, turned off – and we never knew it was there.'

'But by the time the Khleevi finished trashing the planet, the damage they did to the water table which made up the circuitry for the time force kinda shorted it out,' Becker said. He gave a half shrug and a grimace. 'I think it's worth a try to see if we're right. Y'know, it makes as much sense as wormholes as a way to move through time and space. We know those old Hosts really got around the galaxy. Maybe this is how they did it.'

Acorna said, 'If we are right, I am worried about the consequences of it. It could take us months, even years, to reestablish the waterways on Vhiliinyar in their proper places, and Aari is in trouble now. I heard him, Captain, and I know. Something is very wrong with him, wherever he is.'

'You heard him?' Becker asked. 'Across time and all? Are you sure – what am I saying? Of course you're sure. But, do you think maybe it's just that he's lost and missing you?'

'No,' she said. 'He was afraid. He was in trouble. If he is in danger, then it is fair to assume the others are, too. We need a solution that will work now.'

'Now, huh?' Becker snapped his fingers. 'I know. Why should we wait for terraforming? We can run water lines from this lake here to the surface right this instant. I've even got a salvaged pump that would be just the ticket somewhere on the MOO, and I bet Hafiz could rustle up a drilling rig.'

'There's not enough water here to restore the entire planet's former river systems, Captain,' Mac pointed out.

'Not to do them all at once, no, but if we could get a couple of them working, string them out, see if the time force is attracted back into it again long enough for us to get back the folks who disappeared from just those areas – we can use this map deal to tell where they are now – that we can do, and it shouldn't take much time. I'll go get the hardware we'll need if you kids want to stay here and figure this thing out. We need to plot out where and when everybody is. Mac can store the data in his banks. I'll be back in a jiffy – relatively speaking. There's a tricky bit of space between here and MOO I can use as a shortcut. So, wait for me, right?'

Acorna nodded absently, and stared back over her shoulder at the wall. Could Aari wait while they tried this? Could any of the others? What if it didn't work? She couldn't let herself think of that . . . She was secretly relieved that Becker's plan would mean it would be easiest to retrieve those who had disappeared closest to the hidden lake first. That would mean Aari and Maati would be the first of the lost ones they would try to retrieve. She could not in good conscience have put her own family and friends ahead of the others who had disappeared – people like Yaniriin's wife, for instance. But she *knew* Aari was in trouble and she had felt throughout the discussion with Becker as if her skin would fly off if she couldn't do something to help him right away.

'Speaking of moisture, you guys got anything to eat or drink down here?' Becker asked.

'We have some provisions left in our packs,' Thariinye said. 'Though I did eat and drink most of mine on the climb to the ceiling.'

Becker looked puzzled.

'He means the city's ceiling, Captain,' Mac enlightened him. 'This city has been roofed. Quite a sturdy job too. Even the Khleevi damage has only breached it in a few places – such as the debris in the middle of the sea or lake.'

'Hmph,' Becker said. 'You know, that's another possibility. Whatever's going wrong could be a combination of the lack of surface moisture and contamination from the Khleevi scat in the main conductor, so to speak. Might be worth tackling that one – clean up the mess, so to speak. I figure we can't afford not to try all the possible solutions we can think of to fix this mess back up again. So, Princess, you and Thariinye might want to see about maybe purifying that lake before I get back. Just in case. Also, try to get some rest. I've got a feeling we're gonna be busy for the next little while once I return. Mac, come on back with me to the ship and I'll give you some grub to bring back. No sense starving if you don't have to—'

'No cat food, please, Captain,' Thariinye pleaded.

'Why not?' Becker asked, pretending to mis-understand as he rubbed the head of RK, who had been uncommonly quiet and thoughtful through-out the whole encounter. 'Cat's gotta eat, too. But no, I still have your garden. I'll send some fresh stuff.'

Acorna gave him a somewhat distracted embrace. 'Thank you, Captain.'

'You stay out of trouble till I get back, Princess, okay? And don't worry about Aari so much. From the looks of that map, the planet looked a whole lot better where he is now than it did when the Khleevi had him. Or than it does from where I stand at this very moment. So he's not dealing with the Khleevi and he's not stuck in some ecological disaster left behind by them. Before the big bugs got here, the way I understand it, there was nothing on Vhiliinyar that would hurt a fly, much less somebody as tough as Aari.'

But after examining this ruined city and listening to Aari's panicked mental cry, Acorna was beginning to wonder if what the Linyaari had been given to understand from their history and the Elders' old tales might have been altered to seem more peaceful and harmless than had actually been the case.

TWENTY-ONE

Maati shrieked as she plummeted into the water and felt long, twisty tentacles pulling her down. When she opened her eyes, she tried to shriek again, and swallowed water instead. The *sii*-Linyaari were certainly not a race *she'd* ever be tempted to crossbreed with. Not that that was an issue if she drowned out here.

(No one has asked you to crossbreed, *frii*, have they?) said someone very scaly, with a head full of small but lethal-looking horns. His thought in her head appeared in a bubble and sounded deep as the ocean.

(It's very rude to eavesdrop on someone's thoughts without their permission!) Maati shot back, since if she was going to drown, she didn't want to be insulted while she was doing it. (You have only yourself to blame if you don't like what you hear.)

(Look, Ma, they have legs!) said another one of the strange creatures, this one smaller and floating just below Maati.

(And just one horn, like your grandparents,) observed another, floating on the surface and touching Yiitir's horn. Maati could not see her well, but judged the being to be female by the thought-forms. Though she was beginning to worry a lot more about breathing than she was about what the strange creatures around her looked like!

(No need to get personal!) Yiitir said.

(Please,) Maarni said to the creatures crowding around her. (You don't have to drown us to see what we're like. We need to breathe to survive. We'll be happy to sit on the bank of that island over there so you can examine the differences between yourselves and us. We want to see you just as much as you want to see us. There's no need to be angry or hostile. We came to see you because we have heard of you and we wish to know more about you.)

(How can that be?) the horny-headed one asked, but as he asked – for Maati felt surely the creature had to be male – he backed away and let her bob to the surface. Once she surfaced, she found a shelf of land beneath her feet and was able to walk ashore. Maarni and Yiitir followed easily behind her. (How can you have heard of us? We have been alive but a single generation from our making. I was the firstborn, followed by others, some siblings, some of different parenting, so that we might breed. That was their intent. They thought better of it when they saw me,) he thought irritably.

Maati, safely on the shore now, lay on the beach on her stomach so she was staring face-first into the water. It seemed only polite to be on the same level with these beings. And now that she was, she saw that the horny-headed one was the most hideous of the lot. Two obviously female *sii*-Linyaari, aqua blue of skin and silver of horn, with only small bumps along the spine and top of the head, were actually quite beautiful. Their cranial bumps were surrounded with long thick strands of silvery hair floating away from their faces.

Maarni was thrilled. (Now you can see how the legends of the foam being the hair of the *sii*-Linyaari began. Aren't they fabulous?)

Maati found it easier to agree now that they had stopped trying to drown her. And while the one child in this grouping had seemed ugly to her, with his scalp full of vestigial horns instead of hair, his brother, who had the same feature, was much more attractive, perhaps because his eyes were a bit less prominent, and because he had hair like that of the females. Not that her opinion of their appearance mattered in any way. She was sure that, like all beings, they had their own ways of judging each other's attractiveness.

Seated a little farther away, Maarni was getting to work collecting data. She was nothing if not single-minded, and as soon as she had beached herself asked the group peering up from the water, (So, if your people have only recently been created, I suppose you have no legends or stories to share with me?)

(I wouldn't go so far as to say that,) the horn-headed male replied, allowing himself to wallow in the shallows and blowing a spume of water to fountain up and fall back down to the surface. (But I've a thing or two to ask you before we say any more.)

(What?) Maati, Maarni, and Yiitir all said at once.

(Just this. You,) and he nodded toward Maati, (you are a youngling, barely more than a *frii*, whereas you two are older than me, I'd judge, and I am the eldest among my kind. Yet we have never seen your kind before, and presume you must be the latest attempts. Is this true and if so, how did they manage to vary your ages so?)

Maati immediately saw the difficulty Aari had been talking about, with possibly changing the course of history with their presence, but Yiitir, who had expressed some reservations about it, too, blithely answered the *sii* being.

(We are not newly created. In our own time, we're already a race well established on the planet. Your race is no longer there, however, and we have been wondering what happened to you.)

(Couldn't tell you that since as you can see, we are here,) the male replied. (But we're few and spawning is not easy. Also, there are large predators in these waters and we are easy prey. And the water we live in, as you may have observed, is unclean . . .)

(No, it isn't,) Maarni said. (Look at it.)

They murmured among themselves, small words that made bubbles below the surface, like the bubbles that contained their thoughts when they arrived in Maati's head. One of the females ran her webbed hand along the surface, and said, (Look, Upp, no film clings to me! The water surface no longer shines with the rainbows of its destruction.)

(You have the power! The power to cure. They

257

gave you the power we were denied!) the big male, apparently the Upp the female had been addressing, said accusingly.

(Why are you so upset?) Maati asked. (We cleaned your home for you. You should say 'thank you.')

(It's not their fault, Upp,) the female with the filmless hand told her mate. (Their blending succeeded in that way, ours failed. Our four-legged parents care for us just the same.)

(And the Changing Ones consider us accidents of the lesser parts of their nature because of it,) Upp said bitterly.

(Changing Ones?)

(Our parents-who-are-not-unicorns. The shape changers.) This information appeared in a series of bubbles within bubbles, no doubt a result of the thoughts and concepts translating from the *sii*-Linyaari dialect to the modern speech Maati and the others understood.

Before anyone could say or think anything further, one of the great ships they had seen before as they journeyed on the river hove round the island and the sailors, gathered at the railing and looking very threatening, broadcasted: (You pond scum monsters cease menacing those people at once, or so help us we will beach you.) Then their thoughts turned solicitous, but in a way Maati didn't care for, (You there, guests, are you unharmed?)

Maati scowled toward the ship, angry about the threat to the *sii*-Linyaari. But Yiitir said, (We are quite well, thank you for your concern, but were enjoying a private conversation.) He said this quite as if everything, including themselves, was normal and under control. Maati's scowl broke up as she failed to control a giggle. A nervous giggle, but a giggle nonetheless. They all waved nonchalantly at the watchers on the ship.

(That won't be enough for them. If you want to learn more, and can swim, come with us to see our horned parents,) the male said, in a tightly controlled thought-whisper.

Maati felt a glimmer of hesitation from Yiitir, but Maarni dove right in. Maati did, too, and felt the impact in the water as Yiitir joined her. The *sii*-Linyaari dove deep and swam underwater as they rounded the island and headed back toward the shoreline. One of them, observing Maati's unfamiliarity with moving through the water, towed her along behind him. Once they were safely on the other side of the island, out of sight of the ship, the land Linyaari surfaced for air, then dove back under while the *sii*-Linyaari fanned their fish tails impatiently.

The *sii*-Linyaari, except for Maati's guide and helper, were dark and dappled shapes above and surrounding them. Then one of the *sii*-children swam under Maati, popping up between her legs, swimming over the top of her and dropping down to back-paddle in front of her face in a most annoying fashion.

But it turned out that the little *sii*-Linyaari was doing more than playing. As a solid wall of land loomed in front of them and she saw nothing to do but surface, the child motioned with webbed palms down for her to stay submerged, then, still back-paddling, began to twitch its small webbed fingers backward, guiding her to follow it.

The *sii*-Linyari had stopped broadcasting thoughts and Maati realized that the sailors probably possessed telepathy, too.

Ahead of her, she saw the soles of Maarni's feet disappear into what looked like an unbroken landmass, followed quickly by the flirt of two different tails. The child turned suddenly and thrust an arm into the bank and Maati saw the opening. When the child saw that she saw, it turned and slipped into the bank. Maati found it was much larger than it looked, but she still was able to guide herself with her hands on both sides for a yard or two until the space widened out enough for them to swim three abreast.

She considered herself a pretty fair survivor, having come all this way, but now her breath was running out. Could she make it, or would she drown here?

Suddenly, the tails and feet of those ahead of her turned sharply upwards. She righted herself, too, and found that with two strokes her head was once more above water. They were in an underwater grotto, deep enough to swim in, but with a good layer of air above their heads as well. They swam in silence down long stretches as the cave ceilings rose higher and higher above their heads. The water was pitch black, and very cold.

The *frii* began frolicking up the stream as they swam further in and their shrill repetitive voices broadcast their thoughts, the thought bubbles bursting after every utterance, (Going to Granny's! POP! Going to Granny's! POP!)

Up ahead, suddenly, Maati saw them, Ancestors, standing four abreast and at least twenty deep just uphill from where water met dry cave floor.

(Lookit there, Gladiis, it's our web-footed offspring, come to pay their respects!)

(And see what we brought you! POP!) cried Maati's young guide.

(I hope it's some of that nice seaweed you brought last time,) the Ancestor just behind the one addressed as Gladiis said and others showed enthusiastic agreement, ruffling air through their nostrils.

(Better! POP! We brought cousins from the future who say they're your descendants, too! POP! But be prepared! POP! They're not as pretty as we are, really funny looking! POP!)

(And very, very cold,) Maarni added through her chattering teeth as they swam up to the cloven hooves of the Ancestors.

(They are *land* creatures, with two feet and horns! POP!) Maati's *frii* friend explained before anyone else could, or the Ancestors could figure it out for themselves.

(They are, and this bears repeating,) Yiitir said, (freezing. They need to get warm and dry at once.)

The Ancestors took several steps backwards, their telepathy allowing them to march to the rear like precision dancers. Which was a good thing because they had crowded very close together and could have injured each other or at least knocked the foremost among their number into the water had they not all understood the intent to make room at the landing.

Getting out was a slippery operation for the Linyaari, since the water met the landing where the pavement sloped sharply downhill. It was all but impossible to get one's feet under one, but Maati's little guide boosted her from the rear and one of the Ancestors graciously bent his neck so she could grab hold of his mane. She, as the youngest and most agile, was first out, and helped Maarni and Yiitir next.

'Oooooh, look at them, Humiir!' the Ancestor addressed as Gladiis cried aloud with a little whinny.

'Yes, funny looking things, but kind of cute,' Humiir agreed. The other Ancestors closed around them, warming them with their heat and using horns to take the chill off their puckered and goose-bumped flesh.

'It seems to me if they'd wanted legs and horns, four were better than two,' another of the Ancestors said critically.

'Yes, but the Changers wanted the new ones to be part of each of us, Host and People of the Horn,' Gladiis replied. 'I think they're just lovely, really.'

'Hmph. I suppose we'll be seeing little feathered replicas of ourselves with wings, next thing we know,' the other replied.

'When did they make you?' Humiir asked, nudging Yiitir with his nose. 'You are an old one. That is a young one. They have not showed us your kind before. They *always* show us. When were you made?'

(My question exactly, Father Humiir,) Upp said. (Hang onto your horn. You won't believe their answer!)

Yiitir repeated his explanation about coming from the future and Humiir grunted. The others made assenting noises.

(How does that happen?) Upp wanted to know.

'It is more of the magic they call science,' Gladiis told him. 'They used their ability to change times when they brought us here too. By the time they were able to respond to our call for help, we were all but extinct. Humiir and I were the last of our kind on our old world and we were snatched from the very grip of death so quickly that death itself – in the form of two of the barbarians who had killed so many of us – were taken up with us.'

Humiir gave a braying laugh. 'You should have seen their faces! Our Hosts hauled them away and secluded them. They don't believe in killing anything, the Hosts don't, which came as a disappointment to Gladiis and me. Oh, how I wanted to get my horn into one of them!'

Maarni and Yiitir, both of the more traditional Linyaari who did not normally travel or mix with other, more violent races, gasped.

'I see they've passed on their gentle ways to you,' Gladiis said. 'But you must remember, people like those two warriors had already killed most of the other of our kind you see here. They wanted our horns, and once the Hosts saved us, we were prepared to give those murderers horn where it would heal them of their wicked ways for good!'

'What happened to them?' Maarni asked. Maati could almost see the story collector writing in a little notebook inside her head.

'The Hosts said they would study them and then put them where they could do no one harm,' Humiir said. 'They didn't care for my ideas on the issue.'

'That is too true – a pity. But back to time travel. When the Hosts heard how the others had perished, they went back to the times before the deaths and collected these folk you see here, who did not perish but came with us. All of us were brought here,' Gladiis said.

'To live happily ever after,' said Humiir dryly.

'Are you not happy, then?' Maati asked, suddenly concerned. It had never occurred to her that the Ancestors would not have been thrilled with the daring rescue and beautiful new home Grandam had described in her stories.

'A bit too citified for me,' one of the other Ancestors said.

'Not enough meadows. Too many buildings all over. We do earn our keep. Their machines create much filth and illness, for the Hosts and the planet, and we often are called upon to cleanse and heal.'

'And help them build their ideal stable form, of course,' another of the Ancestors said. 'That would be your kind, it seems.'

'I guess I'm glad they're doing it – I mean, did it,' Maati said. 'But I'm wondering the same thing as the Grandfather did earlier – why? Why breed us with two legs and horns instead of just remaining themselves and having your company. We still have you among us in our own time, though not – oh, never mind.' She didn't want to emphasize to the *sii*-Linyaari that they were already extinct in her time. It didn't seem polite somehow.

Gladiis nuzzled her fondly, and, despite the time, Maati felt so reassured and at home, being among the Ancestors with their familiar fragrance, their mixture of practicality and mystery, and the sense of kinship that was present even now, when she was questioning *why* she had been made akin to them.

'Bless you, Youngling. The last thing we would wish to do is damage your opinion of the Hosts. They are brilliant, and were valiant in our defense, and I truly believe they do mean well. They try very hard to be kind.'

'Pshaw!' another snorted. 'They think too much. That's their problem.'

'No, it's that they think only with their heads and very seldom with their hearts,' another said.

'It's amazing they do as well as they do,' Humiir said firmly. 'All that shape-shifting they do – and they have done this sort of thing before, one of them told me when he came to be healed from a bout of drunkenness. On other planets, with other species. That is where some of the other creatures on this planet are from.'

Another ancestor brayed his laughter. 'Distant cousins, I suppose.'

'The truth, dear Youngling,' Gladiis said gently, 'is that while the Hosts are, I believe, essentially good sorts, and they live a great long time, long enough certainly to have acquired wisdom, they simply are not very – stable.'

'That's a joke, *frii*,' Upp informed her. 'Stable, get it?'

'Too many of those Hosts, changing shapes all the time as if they've never found one they liked, all of them crammed into all those shifty buildings,' Humiir said. 'We couldn't stand it. Our horns were going soft and transparent with the stress. Finally we asked for a place of our own and they gave us these caves, because they could shield them from the thoughts above. They open out onto a nice bit of grassland, too. Not enough space really, no forests, no mountain meadows full of wildflowers, but no hairy warriors looking to dehorn us either. All in all, it is an improvement.'

'And here at least we are spared the chaos of their thoughts,' Gladiis said with a sigh so strong that it stirred the hairs of the little beard under her chin.

But just then Maati caught a thought – a very clear one. 'Khornya!' she heard her brother cry, and she was on her feet, pushing through the Ancestors, and searching for a way to get to him.

'Her blend was maybe a little defective?' she heard Humiir inquiring behind her. And Maarni laughed and asked another question.

TWENTY-TWO

The sea that was no longer a sea lapped at the road like a sick animal as Acorna stared into it. Dark and dirty as it was, the water lured Acorna. The sea was where the little lights that she believed indicated the presence of Aari, Maati, and the others were located.

Although she had not heard Aari again, Acorna held an awareness of his pain, his fear, somewhere in the back of her mind and it made her feel nervous and twitchy. She had to do something. The plan they had all formed together was a good one, and Becker was on his way back to the ship with Mac and RK to help him. He would return soon with supplies as he promised, but would it be soon enough? Perhaps an hour and a half had passed since she heard Aari cry out. If only she knew how to manipulate the time device better, she could arrive before whatever had disturbed him, and prevent him from suffering whatever it was that had caused him to scream to begin with.

But she couldn't figure it that closely. She was beginning to think she might be able to manipulate it to some degree however.

And she had to keep her thoughts from being too open to Thariinye. As Becker left she drew forth packets of seeds and stems she had brought in her pack and handed them to Thariinye. 'I couldn't eat a thing now, really, but that's no reason you should be hungry. Please, take mine and I will eat when Captain Becker returns. One of us may as well be well fed and rested for the work ahead. I will go begin the purification of the lake. If you rest now, you can come help me finish the job if it proves more than my horn can handle.'

Thariinye's eyes popped open with surprise, but he accepted the food gratefully. 'That sounds very sensible. After all, being a male, I will probably be called upon to help with the manual labor of installing the irrigation equipment and that sort of thing. I'll need all my strength. Maybe a nap would be a good idea, too, do you think?'

'Oh, yes. Though I don't know how you'd manage to rest with the walls flickering away and that silver thing whirling around in the middle.'

'Actually, I thought I'd find a quiet inner room upstairs, if you don't mind.'

'Not at all,' she said. It was, in fact, just what she'd wanted him to do.

When he departed, munching on the food as he climbed to the upper story, she pressed her hand to the map and thought of Aari, Maati, and the others. She was not at all sure her plan would work, but she needed to try. She pressed until she found the place where all four of the white lights were visible, three of them in the water surrounded by aqua lights, one on the shore and headed up toward the city.

Having found that place, she dared not try to adjust it further and waste more time. She had trotted quickly to the edge of the water, and stood watching it lick at the land for only a moment.

Then she stuck her toe in, felt the temperature, which was not as cold as she had feared, and waded in.

If their theory was correct, the water of this planet was the main conduit for the energies of time travel. Pollution and the disruption of its courses caused a corresponding disruption in the flow of the time force. The sea before her should be the least disrupted of all of this planet's water, since it was the closest thing to a whole body of water on the planet at the time. That was her hypothesis and she hoped it was correct.

She was about to put it to the test.

If she was wrong, she would go for a nasty swim before she purified the water and prepared it for the implementation of the rest of her plan.

If she was right, however, the wall mechanism was a control as well as an indicator of where people were and where they were sent. She was about to see if her theory would work. If it did, the others should be able to find her from what they had discussed. Meanwhile, she could save Aari from the harm that she felt sure had befallen him.

But up to her neck in filthy seawater, she could see no change in her surroundings, either in time or place. The mountain of refuse still dominated the lake, the city still loomed dead and broken beyond her, the buildings from the front street still drowned beneath the soles of her feet.

Nothing had changed. Was she wrong? And then she told herself that it was no wonder she was getting nowhere. She was not concentrating hard enough on where she wanted to go. And she had not yet committed herself sufficiently to totally submerge in this sea. So, drawing a deep breath, she jackknifed forward and plunged beneath the water.

The Hosts hurriedly left the inner chamber where the male unicorn person lay in a drugged stupor on the metal table. They had extracted from him the DNA samples they needed to test, x-rayed him, taken samples of blood, bone marrow, urine, stomach contents, sperm, and other fluids, and then left as quickly as possible.

'Gracious, what a fuss he made,' said a small winged person – currently female. Her wings were flapping very rapidly, which indicated she was upset. 'I was sending all the reassurance and good thoughts I could to him and he still back-handed me so hard I flew across the room.'

'You'd think they would have evolved past that behavior after all this time,' said a fellow with a long, serious face. 'If he is the result of our work after generations of evolution, I think we should try harder.'

'Yes, after all, it's not like we hurt him or anything. All of us were trying to calm him, but he simply kept fighting and glaring at us as if we were monsters or something.'

'But he *knew* who we are,' Highmagister HaGurdy said. 'Perhaps he isn't a final result after all. Perhaps he is only a starting place.' She sighed. 'I fear we've our work cut out for us. We should break now. It is almost time for the feast and we all need to change into something more festive.'

Not that that will take very long, thought a very junior cabinet minister, *given our nature*. He wanted to add, 'Shouldn't someone ask one of our unicorn guests to attend to him?' The unicorns were familiar with the needs for healing after studies done on the various subject offspring. Not only would they heal him of the holes drilled in him from the tests; they would also comfort him.

But Highmagister HaGurdy had left the building, followed by her cabinet, who fanned into the city in all directions. The minister had no one left to make that observation to.

The junior cabinet minister was destined to remain junior because of the direction his telepathic abilities took. He was not, as were the other cabinet ministers, a powerful and charismatic sender, the most useful sort of telepathy a politician could project.

Even his shape changes did not seem to be under his control. He changed according to whom he was with, which was also what the others did, but he seemed to demonstrate a different purpose in his changes. They changed into more dominating shapes – the better to control the beings around them. His own changes, insofar as he understood them, occurred to put his fellows at ease. Among the politicians, he appeared to be one of them, only less able, less forceful, and less impressive – easily ignored. Easily made the delegatee rather than being the delegator of tasks.

He had decided long ago that he was instinctively and incurably an empath, in other words, and there never had seemed to be anything he could do about it. Of all of them, only he had seen what the male subject had seen when he looked at them. He alone knew the reason for the man's terror, and he alone did not believe the person strapped to the examining table was somehow a failure of science.

So after a moment's hesitation, he re-entered the chamber where the subject – Aari – lay breathing his heavily drugged sleep. The junior minister administered an antidote to the sedative, released the restraints, and waited.

Aari struggled for breath against a great weight upon his chest, compressing his lungs. Confused and disoriented, he recalled meeting some people who seemed like friends, but turned out to be Khleevi. They strapped him down to torture him again. Dimly, he remembered hearing Khornya call him, trying to help. But now – he opened his eyes and after some initial blurriness, found himself staring into another pair of eyes which stared back curiously at him. Then something reached out and patted him on the cheek. It was soft but accompanied by a hint of sharpness.

'RK?' Aari asked, though the cat sitting on his chest was not quite as large, nor brindled gray as his old friend from the *Condor*. Nevertheless, he reached to pet the animal – and realized his hands were free, as were his feet, chest, and head. 'Who are you? What is this? Some sort of a cats' underground movement to free prisoners?' he inquired. 'Where were you when the Khleevi had me?'

(Back here helping to create your race, and very glad of it I am too after seeing those nightmare creatures in your mind,) his furry companion's thought answered. The cat's fur was definitely not brindled, but it was not definitely anything else. It shifted from black to red to blondish, to spotted, striped from gray through deep brown, to pale gold, even as it changed from long to short.

(You're – one of them? The Hosts?)

(I am one of them. I am Junior Cabinet Minister Grimaalkin.)

(Thank you for freeing me. It was you, wasn't it? I am Aari.)

(I know who you are. I know you wish to leave before the others come back to vivisect you in the interests of making a kinder, gentler race to inhabit this planet. Come, let us go find the unicorn people and they will heal your wounds.)

The cat jumped down and Aari sat up too suddenly, felt dizzy, and had to catch himself with the edge of the table before standing. At that point he realized he was naked. His shipsuit was neatly folded and stored under the table.

(Vivisect?) Aari asked, wincing as he donned the suit. (Not really? Surely not!) After all, these were the kindly Hosts. He had heard them, vaguely in some unnoticed quarter of his mind, decry violence.

(Oh, they wouldn't mean to,) Grimaalkin assured him. (And they would ask the unicorns to heal you, of course, but what they would do to you wouldn't make you happy. A couple of the unicorns already have come very close to not surviving the experiments. Good thing they have the healing power they have. On other planets, I understand, races with other abilities have not always survived our wish to improve their stock by blending it with our own.)

Aari braced himself on the table and stood, more firmly this time. (I have to get back to my own time. And my friends, as well. Can you help us?)

(Certainly. Any idiot can run the time transport.) The cat bounded from the chamber. When Aari did the same, a young man with long ginger hair, overlong eyebrows, and a sparse mustache that was longer than his face stood in front of the wall. He was wearing only a white coat, such as all of the scientists had worn, and his bare legs and feet – heavily covered with curling red hairs – looked incongruous with the coat. But his thoughts came to Aari in Grimaalkin's voice.

(When is your true time?) he asked.

(Not so fast,) Aari answered, and was taken aback when Grimaalkin chuckled.

(I meant in years, not in speed,) the cat/man said.

(So did I. I was using a figure of speech I learned from a friend. It means, in this instance, please don't rush me, for you are moving more quickly than I am prepared to do. I was not alone. My little sister and two companions came here with me. They are in the lake. I need to collect them before we leave this place – or, rather, this time.)

(That presents no problem. The lake is a very

good place to begin a time transport. I don't care much for it when I'm in cat mode but I like a good swim otherwise. Since the unicorns have been here to keep it clean, the sea is a good place to be, if you can stay clear of the sea unicorns.)

(I believe my friends are with the sea unicorns,) Aari replied.

(Then you are wrong. I am not too fast. We haven't a moment to lose. It may be too late already. Quickly now, tell me when you are from so I may set the transport. Then as soon as we find your littermate and friends, we can activate from the lake. Hurry!)

Aari gave him a year, but that meant nothing. Finally, at Grimaalkin's urging, he described the area and era from which he and his friends had been transported. Grimaalkin, working furiously, changed the shape of the map to look like post-Khleevi Vhiliinyar.

Then the junior cabinet minister turned to Aari and said, (Now. Follow me!) Before Aari could blink, Grimaalkin blurred back into a cat and raced for the inclinator to the ground floor.

(Wait! It's all very well for you. You belong here. But someone will see me.)

(Not tonight! Feast night! They'll all be there, or at least be too busy with their own changing to notice you. Come on!)

Aari ran after the cat as fast as he could, down the hill toward the docks and the sea once more. In the middle of the sea, he saw the island his friends had been heading for. He saw the boat, too, floating upside down in the water. He took a deep breath to steady himself – surely his friends were fine. They *had* to be fine.

(I hope we're not too late,) Grimaalkin answered Aari's alarm with more urgency of his own. (If you think my fellow cabinet members are bad, you should see their offspring by the unicorns!)

In one fluid motion the little ginger cat grew longer, paler, broader, and bumpier, and with a flash of white buttocks dove into the water. Aari, shipsuit and all, dove in after him, and both began swimming toward the upended boat.

Then, suddenly, he was swamped by an upsurge of water that left him gasping and floundering.

He felt a touch and opened his eyes. Acorna swam to him – and through him – and when he surfaced, she was gone.

He was in a dark wet place which shook constantly, as if with horror.

(Is this your time?) Grimaalkin asked. (No wonder you were so scared!)

Acorna plunged beneath the surface of the lake and felt it – somehow – deepen beneath her. She opened her eyes and saw the filthy sea giving way to a younger, cleaner wash of water below. She turned to head back for the surface, her eyes open, and saw what she thought were jellyfish swimming above her, transparent, indistinct, ghostly. She was heading straight for one and she swerved to avoid it. It had been further off than she thought, however, for as she neared collision with it, she saw it was a man – her man. She cried out, swallowed water, reached to embrace him . . . and lost him.

And then she was on the surface of a busy harbor. Where the column of stinking debris had been was a lovely little island. Fish swam around her and farther away ships sailed busily back and forth. A few yards from her, on shore, was the living version of the dead city from which she had just come.

And Aari? She dove several more times, calling him, calling Maati, but there was no trace of him, nor the other figure, his companion. Had it been Maati? Were they dead? Had she seen their ghosts? Phantoms? Shivering with more than the cold of the water, she swam ashore, wiping herself and squeezing the water from her hair and clothing as best she could.

Then she climbed the hill to the building she had left just moments ago, yet many, many years in the future.

She had no idea what she would find here, except that she had a hard time imagining it could be as fearsome as all of the things she had gone through already in her lifetime – not as terrible as the Khleevi, or as wily as Baron Manjari, his crazy daughter Kisla, and her guardian Count Edacki Ganoosh, or even as formidable as General Ikwaskwan.

Aari had sounded terrified to her, but she was not reading any terror in the air now, as she walked toward the city. According to legend and history, this time on Vhiliinyar should have as sentient beings only the Hosts, the Ancestors, and the earliest beginnings of her own race. The history of Vhiliinyar according to Grandam had been remarkably placid for the most part. No wars, perhaps a few natural disasters, but nothing as deadly as the events and creatures Acorna had encountered in her own time.

If something back here had harmed her love, if it was intent on harming Maati, Yiitir, and Maarni, then it would find her ready and willing to take it on. Theirs had been a peaceful mission, to rebuild what had been destroyed through no fault of their own. Her people had endured about all of the hardship anyone could stand and she didn't intend that they should be subjected to more. And she was perfectly willing to explain that point of view to anyone who disagreed, regardless of what race they came from.

She was in such a state by the time she stormed into the building with the time device that she felt ready for anything . . . except for what she got, which was a silent, deserted building with no one to challenge and no one challenging her.

The changes in the rest of the city meant nothing to her at the moment. Her sense of ire was so aroused that her sense of wonder failed to register all the vehicles whizzing by and the beautiful music playing in the streets.

She rode down the inclinator from the ground floor to the floor containing the time device in her own time.

This area was eerily as she had left it – lit up and unoccupied. Not quite as silent. From somewhere she heard a pounding, as of construction or machinery starting up.

And there was one other change too. A door she had never noticed before made an opening in the wall of shifting glyphs. She peered through it into some sort of medical or laboratory facility. A shiver ran through her that had nothing to do with her wet condition.

The metal table in the middle of the room beckoned to her from a memory that was not hers. She walked to it. A few curly silver hairs lay upon it, a drop of blood. Kneeling so that she was level with the table, she sniffed deeply. Aari. This was where he had been when he called. The hairs were his hairs. The blood was his as well.

But where was he?

What had happened to him?

Was he hurt somewhere, needing her touch to heal him? She reached out to him mentally – and heard nothing.

She searched the room, the walls, and then started on the adjacent room. In the back of her mind was Aari as she had seen him in the water, wondering what he was doing there. She passed the time map and saw that it surprisingly reflected Kubiilikaan as it had been before her dive into its shrunken sea. Deserted, subterranean, befouled, and damaged. She grinned suddenly. Aari had escaped back to their own time! They had passed each other time traveling, using the seawater as a conduit. He would be waiting for her when she returned! She should have trusted that he would find a way back to her! There had never been any need for her to travel at all.

But what about the others?

The map was no help – it seemed to be locked in its current incarnation.

She was ready to pay attention to the thumping now, and she returned to the corridor, heading as if pulled toward it to the entrance to the Ancestors' caverns. The stone floor shook as if a major earthquake rocked the building's foundations.

Acorna saw the release for the passageway door recessed in one of the flagstones and pressed it. As the door raised, hooves flashed past her nose.

She backed away, then peered downward.

'Ha! Got it!' An Ancestor had backed up on the top step and attacked the closed door with all the strength of its hooves and hindquarters.

'Hello?' Acorna said.

'It's another one, Gladiis!' the Ancestor exclaimed. 'What in creation does she want, do you suppose?'

'Khornya!'

The Ancestor was all but knocked aside by Maati as she leaped from the top step straight into Acorna's arms, knocking her over backwards.

'Oh, Khornya, you came! You came! I should have known! I heard the most awful cry from Aari and – where is he? Is he okay?'

'I think so, yes,' Acorna said, smoothing Maati's hair and hugging her tightly. 'It looks as if someone hurt him, but not badly. Somehow he got away before I could rescue him. Inconsiderate of him, don't you think? So I'll have to rescue you instead, I suppose. Are Maarni and Yiitir with you?'

'Yes, uh huh. They're here. They're fine. But before you rescue us, first, come on, you have to meet Grandmother Gladiis and Grandfather Humiir and the others, and Upp and the *frii* and their family.'

Leaving the door open, Acorna allowed herself to be led below and found herself surrounded by Ancestors. Maati introduced her to the ones she had named. All the while Maati was pulling her by the hand deeper inside the cavern. Here Acorna could smell and hear the sea echoing against the walls. She also made out the faces of Maarni and Yiitir. They looked well, happy even. Acorna breathed a sigh of relief.

Maati started to drag Acorna past them to the water. 'Upp? *Frii*? *Sii*-Linyaari? I have someone I want you to meet!'

'Maati, they're not here,' Yiitir told her.

'Not here? Where are they? Did they go back to sea?'

'I don't think so,' Maarni said. 'One moment they were swimming below the landing, the next they were gone. They're very quick, you know, and it's dark here so I could be mistaken, but it seemed very sudden – even for them. The *frii* was doing one of his leaps from the water and it looked to me as though he vanished in midair.'

'Oh, no!' Acorna said. Now she understood what had happened with Aari also. He hadn't been trying to time travel when she met him in the water. Her own journey had precipitated his – probably before he was ready. He must have been looking for Maati and the others – and the *sii*-Linyaari, also in the water, had time traveled, too.

281

Maati caught her thought and laughed. 'Aari is going to be unhappy with Khornya! She tried to rescue him and messed up his precious space-time continuum!'

'Oh, Maati,' Acorna said. 'I fear you may be right!'

TWENTY-THREE

Halfway through the tunnel to the surface, Mac said diffidently, 'Captain, with all due respect, I detect a flaw in your logic in this situation.'

'Now that is totally inconceivable,' Becker told him. 'You must be malfunctioning. What flaw?'

'You have a com unit. Why would you fly all the way back to MOO when they could fly what you need here in half the time, even considering your shortcut?'

'Because—' Becker stopped. 'Because . . . they wouldn't know where to get what we need.'

'Some of the finest engineers in the universe are in Mr Harakamian's employ, Captain. They are reputed to be very competent.'

'Yeah, but the Linyaari only want me here. Not them.'

'That is not the case if one is speaking of Linyaari engineers. Of which there are many on MOO.'

'Yeah, but in case you haven't noticed, the Linyaari have a funny habit of disappearing from this place.'

'Then perhaps we should attempt to stabilize

the time diffusion in the landing area and nearby surroundings.'

'For which we need the equipment they'd be bringing,' Becker said, one word at a time to emphasize that this time it was Mac whose logic was flawed.

'Captain,' Mac said. 'I may shut down from pure shock. Do you mean to tell me you no longer have aboard the *Condor* a half a dozen pumps of various sizes, hoses, and the other items necessary to make an irrigation system, albeit one of limited size?'

Becker stopped and scratched his mustache. 'You got a point, Mac. I congratulate myself on upgrading your memory. I'll go ahead to the ship and start digging the stuff out. Meanwhile, if you return for Acorna and Thariinye now, we'll have more people to haul stuff back there. As soon as we have this first area built and get it tested, then we can have the other Linyaari come down from the sky and help us with the work while we're waiting for the supplies from MOO.'

'Other Linyaari, Captain?'

'Yeah, see, they sent a couple of shuttles here but one of them disappeared, so the other one, which was supposed to help me, dropped off the equipment they brought and returned to the mother ship.'

'Should I not come along and ensure that you do not disappear, Captain?'

'I'll walk back in my own tracks, son. It's an old Becker trick taught to me by my pappy who was taught it by his'n.'

'I do not entirely understand you, sir.'

'Good. Good. I'd worry more if you did. Now off you go. RK, you with me or with him?'

The cat looked from one to the other. There was no real choice to make. Becker was flesh and blood and winced and complained when RK dug his claws in. Mac was not. RK followed Becker. It was about time to re-mark his territory anyway.

'Mr Harakamian, there's a relay from Vhiliinyar. Captain Becker wishes to speak to you personally.'

Hafiz graciously indicated that the underling should activate the nearest com link. He was in his personal garden, surveying the progress of his Kardadistanian Rhodamians, whose bright red blossoms were being coaxed into bloom by his gardening staff.

'Hafiz? Becker here,' a disembodied voice said from the direction of Hafiz's favorite water feature, a four-tiered cascade plummeting from the exalted height of twelve feet from his artificial mountain. Only half of it was material. The other half was hologram and turned off when no one was in the garden. Frugality was a virtue (though one he practiced infrequently of late), even when turning an artificial moon into the showplace of the universe.

'Yes, Captain. If my beloved niece is there, may I speak to her please? I thirst for the sound of her voice.'

'I'll have her call when she gets here. Mac went

285

back to get her and Thariinye. Meanwhile, we need your help.'

He sighed. Too often these days people needed his help. Too seldom did they offer lucrative favors in return. But he had the faith of his forefathers that all his good works would be repaid tenfold in the fullness of time. He just wished time would fill out more quickly. His heir and his board of directors had begun expressing concern about the state of his accounts lately, and questioning the vast withdrawals he had been making from corporate holdings.

Karina wafted in. 'Haffy? Is it Acorna? Has she news?'

'Hi, Mrs H.,' Becker said. 'Like I was just telling Hafiz, we need some help down here. While they were rooting around in the caves here on the old home world, Acorna and Thariinye found this old city.'

'Excuse us, Captain, Mr Harakamian,' Yaniriin, who was part of the relay, cut in. 'With all due respect, gentlemen, our Council was very reluctant to allow an offworlder such as Captain Becker to set foot on our world and even more reluctant to allow him to access certain highly classified areas. Please do not describe what you have seen to others over the com unit, Captain Becker. I know Mr Harakamian will understand the need to maintain security.'

'Uh – right,' Becker said. 'Sure, Yaniriin, whatever you and the Council say. Anyway, Hafiz, Mrs H. – she, Acorna I mean, discovered this – er – object which is probably responsible for the disappearances. Our belief is that it may have been screwed up by the Khleevi decimating the planet's water supply. There is a – uh – hidden water source we can tap if we can get some irrigation equipment down here pronto to help stabilize the uh – process which is being triggered by the object which is making all the people go bye-bye. Yaniriin, was I confusing enough to suit you?'

'That was admirably obfuscated, Captain Becker, thank you.'

'Captain Becker, have I not made it clear that we will be fully restoring the planet's resources as soon as the survey is completed to the Linyaari Council's satisfaction? That aspect of the work is still some months away, however. Suitable equipment has been ordered but is not expected to arrive for several weeks. At any rate, it would not be employed until the terraforming process has been implemented.'

'Yeah, yeah, but that's not what I'm talking about. I'm talking about this *object* that made the people who were doing the survey to begin with disappear. We need the equipment now if we're going to get them back. We need a lot of it.'

'I regret that we do not have that sort of thing on hand at all times,' Hafiz said, growing a bit irked at Becker's insistent tone. Most people were quite diffident to Hafiz Harakamian these days, and he was at a stage in life when he could choose to feel insulted if the diffidence was lacking. 'From what you have been allowed to tell me,' he continued in an offended tone, 'there is no guarantee that such equipment as you seek will be of any use whatsoever. You have only a little idea that it *could* help.'

'Maybe, but do you have a better idea?'

Silence followed.

It was no use. Becker tried every argument he could think of, and appealed to Yaniriin as well, but Hafiz, remembering the last balance sheet he had seen, was unmoved. He had tried and tried to help the Linyaari and so far all he got was demands for privacy and more privacy . . . and no return as yet was – returning.

'I think this conversation is now at an end, Captain Becker. You and the others must do the best you can with the lavish resources the House of Harakamian has already provided.'

'Uh-huh. Yeah. Wait. Just a sec. Don't hang up. I have an incoming call from Thariinye.

'What? Huh? Yeah? Oh, holee sh – I mean, damn. I should have known.'

'I am signing off now, Captain Becker. I have an empire to run, after all,' Hafiz said with great dignity to the general vicinity from which Becker's voice issued.

'No, no, don't. At least, I wouldn't, if I was you. That was Thariinye. He's on the way up to the ship with Mac, but they used the com unit to give me the news. Hafiz, Acorna's gone.'

'Gone? How so gone?' Hafiz demanded with indignation and suspicion brewing dangerously in his voice.

'Disappeared. After Mac and I left she told Thariinye she was going down to the – uh – body of water I mentioned, to purify it, because it was

– I'm sorry, Yaniriin, a filthy polluted swamp. Which we figure is part of the problem with the workings of the object. And why it's behaving erratically and making people disappear. The absence of water and the contamination and what not. Acorna figured that out herself, so my guess is she did this on purpose. She was real upset about Aari being missing. Claimed she'd heard him hollering for help.'

'But if the solution to this problem is untried, if you have not the equipment, why would she risk herself before a certain solution is at hand?'

'I dunno. She's a sweet girl, but kinda dumb sometimes. At least, she leads with her heart, not her head. I bet she figured she had some adoptive relatives who, once the situation was explained to them, would do anything within their power to help her return, and to bring back the others. Naïve of her really. Y'know, I tried to teach her better but she has this sentimental idea about people. Maybe wherever she is, she's getting some sense knocked into her now.'

Hafiz felt as if someone had just knocked something into him, but he was trying to control his tone, his demeanor, so as to conceal this from Becker. Then he turned and saw Karina. Her gauzy lavender robes were kilted to her waist, her dimpled knee bent to force the blade of a shovel into the soil surrounding his beloved exotic flowers. Her hair had come loose from its bindings and her tongue stuck out a bit from between her sharp little white teeth and her luscious lips.

'What in the name of the Three Prophets and

289

the Three Books are you doing, my beloved Djinn of Energetic Endeavor?' Hafiz asked, his intended tones of authority emerging in an alarmed squeak.

'If you won't have anyone else do it because we're pinching pennies, Haffy, then I will personally dig up the irrigation systems in all of our gardens and send them to the Captain to save our dear Acorna. After all, if there is no Acorna, there is no need for any of this, is there? I will keep digging, although I feel quite faint already from hunger and overexertion.' She said this as she flicked a teaspoonful of dirt to one side and panted heavily, leaning against the shovel handle as if she might swoon.

Hafiz modulated his voice and spoke in a tone that must have been much like that of one of the Three Prophets of his faith declaiming the Law. 'Very well, Becker. Acorna must be saved. So let it be written, so let it be done. I have spoken. My people will strip my gorgeous gardens and we here will drink from common reservoirs and cease washing our clothing or our bodies until you have completed your task and our Lady of the Light and her people are safely among us again.'

'Okay. That's great. We'll be on the lookout. Make it snappy though, will you? Gotta dash.' And the insolent junk man terminated the connection without so much as a verbal *salaam*.

Hafiz had no time to get his feathers ruffled by that, however. Karina picked that moment to swoon gracefully toward the ground. Naturally, he found it necessary to cushion her fall. When he had assured himself she had sustained no damage, he summoned every able-bodied staff member in his employ and began the destruction of his newly planted gardens. He consoled himself with the thought that he could use the equipment on order to replace that which he was sacrificing.

TWENTY-FOUR

Maati was now completely serious, her face set and her voice trembling to keep it from rising to a shrill whine. 'How can they all be gone again? Oh, Khornya, it's not *fair*. Aari can come back if he wants to, can't he? I know we had a big fight and I acted like everything was his fault and I didn't care about him but he can't be gone already! I just got him back and I wasn't done with him yet!'

'I know the feeling exactly, Maati, but you mustn't think it was your fault. Those people up there,' she jerked her head sharply upwards. 'They did something to him—'

'Did they hurt him?'

'I don't think they did, at least not very much, but the way they treated him must have reminded him of the Khleevi. You know how brave he is. Nothing else would have bothered him so much as that. I suspect he was trying to find you when I arrived. And I think that my arrival somehow or other sent him forward to our own time. Aari is probably waiting for us back in our own time, worried sick about us. So now we've got to get back again ourselves.'

'Very sensible, my dear,' Yiitir said. 'But how?'

292

'If I can get it to work the way it did in our time, I can set the device on our own period, then come back to the sea where we will – how can I explain this? – think ourselves back there while using the water to conduct our thought-energy and combine it with whatever it is that drives the time switching device.'

Yittir shook his head. 'I can't see how that would work.'

'Neither can I,' Acorna said. 'And it might not, but it worked to get me here. It is the only way I know to get back. I feel we have to try it.'

'You can't go back up there,' Maarni said. 'If the people who hurt Aari capture you, what will they do to you?'

'Oh, really, *yaazi*,' her lifemate said. 'This is the Hosts we're speaking of, not the Khleevi. They won't hurt the girl. Will they?' He addressed the last to the Ancestors.

'They will *not*,' said Humiir, tossing his head so that his mane flew in a magnificent manner.

Acorna realized that the Ancestors intended to go with her, and that was not what she had in mind. 'Don't worry. They all seem to have gone for the day. I'll be fine. I'll just slip up there, set the machine, and when I give the signal, my friends and I can dive into the water. The worst that can happen is it won't work and we'll all have to dry off again.'

Finally the unicorns agreed to stay below in case the three Linyaari needed help, but they made Acorna agree to leave the passage open between their cavern and the upper stories of the building.

Even though she knew the building was empty, she found herself creeping back along the corridor and slipping into the room dominated by the quicksilver swirl. At least there had been no need to turn on lights. They had left the entire first two floors glowing from the walls and ceilings too, Acorna saw now. Even the floors brightened with each footstep. In its own eerie way, it was beautiful.

The control room was still deserted, and the map was as she had seen it before. She stood before it, memorizing every detail. It looked subtly wrong to be their own time, and there were details Aari could not know about the present time – the tunnel, for instance.

She took a deep breath, and concentrated hard on the subtle alterations that would indicate the area as she had left it with Thariinye, Mac, Becker, RK, the tunnel, the city. When the map was as she thought it should be, she sent the thought to Maati and the others, (Okay, jump in the water. I'll be right behind you.)

She wouldn't be, not exactly. First she was going to return the map to its former state, and then she would find Aari before taking him back to their own time. But there was no need to upset Maati and the others by telling them that.

(We'll wait,) Maati said. (You might get lost.)

Maati knew her all too well, it seemed, but fortunately, the others did not. (Don't be difficult, child,) said an Ancestral voice, followed by a distant splash.

Acorna concentrated hard and the map briefly

showed in miniaturized three-dimensional detail the landscape she had left ahead of her.

She sighed deeply. The others should be safely back with Becker and Thariinye now. If they weren't, well, they could be fetched along with the other missing people, but Acorna was pretty sure she'd done the necessary work to return them. She listened closely, hoping to hear the Ancestors' thoughts indicate if her friends had vanished or not. Instead, she heard voices right behind her.

'You see what I told you? He got loose! And now he's messing about with the time device and he's sure to get lost and there goes the future of our race!'

Acorna turned from the map and faced such a large group of people that she was amazed she hadn't heard them arrive. That's what she got for listening with her mind instead of her ears.

'Highmagister, that is no male.'

'Even better!' the woman said. Her hair was a blue-white flame wound with sparkling stones that matched those on her dinner gown. Behind her ranged what appeared to be an entire party's worth of guests. 'We have his contribution – with hers, we will insure the future of our descendants.' Belatedly she smiled at Acorna, saying, in thought-speak (Hello, dear lady, I am the Highmagister HaGurdy and I believe in your time we are known to you collectively as the Ancestral Hosts although, of course, we are actually your Ancestors as well. Have you come to find your friend? He must still be in the next room. Come along and we'll take you to him.)

(He has gone. He managed to escape in spite of what you did to him.)

(Oh dear. Well, he was very excitable, and rather more timid than he appeared.)

If thoughts had color, Acorna's burned crimson. (He was not timid, you fool! He is among the bravest of our people. He endured and survived torture at the hands of the worst enemy the universe has ever known. It is to your discredit, not his, that you reminded him of that experience so strongly that he relived it while enjoying your hospitality. Why, you aren't fit to parent another race. You aren't even fit to entertain the Ancestors! Maybe they were better off where they were! Hosts, indeed!)

(Why, you ill mannered, ignorant young ingrate!) the Highmagister said. (You are too stupid to realize that we are called the Hosts because we are each host to many different forms, not simply because we have invited a few unicorns to share our planet. Do you think this is the first time we have done this?)

(No,) Acorna said. (I've already been told that you've bred your different shapes with other peoples on other worlds and then moved along. If your behavior was as thoughtless and careless of the rights of others there as it has been here, I'm not surprised you've moved a lot. Probably you've been thrown off the other planets.)

The Highmagister changed form as Acorna watched, finally stabilizing as a towering creature with wild black hair, a sharp beak, and long scarlet claws. The sleeves of her gown and a black cloak were suddenly swept back by an invisible wind turning them into wings as she ordered, "Someone get that creature a sedative and prepare her. Her mind is obviously not going to be an asset in creating our descendants, but her body is a perfect match for the male's and we might as well use his material with hers.' Four other Hosts began to close the distance between themselves and Acorna. They didn't have to change. They were already large and frightening looking enough.

Acorna was trembling with shock at herself and just how angry she had become.

'Aari is my lifemate and his seed is welcome to my body but only as a gift from him personally. You will not use us in this way, without our leave and against our wills,' she said firmly.

But though her words were brave, she felt quite alone, with Maati, Yiitir, and Maarni gone forward in time and Becker and the others unreachable. Her intent had only been to return her friends home, then locate and join Aari and do the same.

'You are too ignorant to make a decision in this matter,' the bird-woman told her coldly.

'I am not ignorant at all. I know that my race was formed somehow but – according to my people – it was not by some third-hand forced fertilization from the people who rescued our venerated Ancestors. I begin to wonder if your sort ever had anything to do with our beginnings. The stories of my people say that both sets of our parents were good and honorable.'

She stated the truth as she saw it as forcibly as

possible, hoping someone else would recognize it. The reactions of the others were unknown to her as she spoke, however. Her whole being focused on broadcasting her outrage. Nothing was left in her mind to receive impressions from the Highmagister or her people.

The bird-woman flew at her and the other four Hosts closed in on Acorna.

As they rounded the silvery column, Acorna surprised herself by dipping her chin, putting her head down and preparing to sink her horn into the first Host who laid hands on her.

But her head snapped up again at a sound that seemed to be drums. 1-2 3, 4. 1-2 3, 4.

The Hosts scattered as a tight phalanx of Ancestors marched through the party guests and into the room. They halved the Hosts' ranks down the middle, one half to the left, the other to the right of the column. When they stopped, the determined Ancestors, their chin whiskers twitching with the intensity of their purpose, stood between Acorna and the Hosts. Each half of the crowd was separated from the door by Ancestors standing sideways. When someone came too close, he or she was bumped, gently but firmly, right back into place. One of the Hosts changed into a small four-legged being and ran under the belly of the Ancestor restraining him, only to be met by another Ancestor's horn and the inquiringly raised brow and narrowed eyes of a third Ancestor.

(This has gone far enough,) Humiir broadcast. (Highmagister, for all your words, it seems to have escaped your grasp that this child is our daughter and granddaughter and great-granddaughter – the daughter, granddaughter, and great-granddaughter of us all, as her life-mate was our son, our grandson, and our great-grandson. If this kinship is not enough to grant her gentle treatment at your hands, then we must keep you from disgracing yourself by delivering her from you until other, wiser heads can prevail.)

While he spoke, Gladiis said, (Khornya, my dear, Areel is the largest, swiftest, and strongest of us all. Climb upon his back, and he will carry you far from this place. Your friends are safe, and you must run far and hide well until we are able to persuade the Highmagister or her political opponents to see reason.)

(But you—?) Acorna began.

(We are in no danger. These are not evil creatures, merely misguided and overconfident of their role in the destinies of others. And obstinate! I'll bet you thought you got that from our side of the family!)

Acorna threw her arms around Gladiis's neck in an impulsive hug, but Gladiis nudged her to Areel. She threw her leg across the Ancestor's back, bent low to grasp his neck, and simply held on as he soared from the room over the heads of Ancestors and Hosts alike. One leap to the center, one to the door, one from the door to the cavern entrance and down he went, his muscles surging beneath her, and she swayed as she learned to harmonize her movements with his as he bore her away down the dark corridors.

Dimly she was aware of pursuit. Areel's pounding hooves echoed down the stone passageways, and as they thundered through each section, its walls lit behind them, as if their flight heralded light for the underworld.

Never had Hafiz given such a large house party under such restricted circumstances!

All animal life on the Moon of Opportunity now lived under the bubble of his palace, sharing the public baths, the food, the drinking water, the air and energy resources he had insisted on retaining. Hundreds of pumps, hundreds of thousands of kilometers of plascene conduits and pipes, thousands of valves and connectors had stripped MOO of its life-supporting facilities, laid waste to its gardens, its newly planted forests and meadows, its housing for staff and guests alike. He certainly hoped the inconvenience was temporary.

Almost all of the Linyaari who were not missing were now on Vhiliinyar. Within the confines of Becker's few hundred feet of hose, they busily transplanted the irrigation systems that had once watered Hafiz's lavish gardens. Instead of islands of lush blossoms and serene pools and splashing fountains, the systems now spread across the disfigured face of the Linyaari homeworld.

The conditions he endured to accede to the Linyaari demands, and Becker's, made Hafiz feel that he had been reduced to his days of impoverishment, that he had come down in the world. He had no desire to attempt his holograms. After all, without the pumps, hydraulic energy was not available and his other energy sources must be conserved for the necessary life-support systems to keep the MOO functioning, despite the temporary lack of gardens and plantings. The only bright spot was that Karina apparently found a certain spice of adventure in their newly bland existence. The atmosphere of tension, the crowded conditions, the need to steal moments of privacy from the people constantly seeking the assistance of the Harakamians, brought out the outlaw in his darling, and stimulated her inner strumpet in a way that relieved his own tension at totally unexpected times and in altogether inappropriate, but interesting, places. So he was not altogether displeased by the situation. But he felt it was only good negotiating strategy to appear terribly put out. That way no one would be under the illusion that all of this effort and inconvenience on his part would be without a substantial price.

Therefore the acting head of the Linyaari Council on MOO approached Hafiz nervously.

'Uncle Hafiz,' the Council head began, since from their first meeting, Hafiz had insisted that since Acorna was his niece, her relatives by extension were his relatives. 'Your pardon for this intrusion,' she continued. Karina Harakamian rose from Hafiz's massive desk, on which pillows had been incongruously spread, pulled her lavender silk up over her plump shoulder, dimpled at the Linyaari Council head, and fled with a giggle. Her departure left a panting and slightly disheveled Hafiz to climb down off his desk and sit in the chair behind it, trying to wipe the smirk from his face and settle his features into impassiveness.

'What is it?'

'We have a most important delegation arriving from narhii-Vhiliinyar. Their vessel requires re-fueling followed by immediate departure for Vhiliinyar.'

'Has this delegation no need to rest and refresh themselves for a night or two? Not,' he added, 'that we are not rather crowded at the moment and our hospitality thus much poorer than our usual standards. But we would endeavor to make them comfortable.'

'Speed is of the essence, Uncle Hafiz. And this – delegation – requires absolute privacy, so we further request that only Linyaari people partici-pate in the docking, refueling, and departure procedures.'

Hafiz sighed. Once more, he felt he was being insulted with mistrust, but he was nevertheless inclined to be magnanimous at this moment. He waved his hand dismissively. 'So let it be done. It is all as one to me.'

As the Council head turned to go he added, 'If you see Madame Harakamian on your way out, would you tell her I have not yet finished instructing her as to my wishes, and require her presence again?'

'Certainly, Uncle Hafiz,' the Council head agreed with a grave bow of the head, all the while wondering why, when Uncle Hafiz was so stern, Auntie Karina laughed and smiled so often.

Maati, Maarni, and Yiitir swam unguided and alone back out the darkened tunnel to the sea.

Maati was pretty sure the time thing had worked, because once they hit the water, the Ancestors vanished, and she knew they couldn't have actually *gone* anywhere so quickly. But Khornya was not with them, as she had promised to be.

The older people were slightly confused, though Maarni pretended she knew exactly where she was going. The water seemed higher to Maati than it had been before, and there was stuff floating in it – not really dirty stuff, because their horns of course would purify the water around. But bits of metal and wood, glass, and plas that she felt, but couldn't see very well.

She hoped with every stroke that the *sii*-Linyaari would return to the tunnel with Aari. It was spooky in here without them.

Once they got up to where the Ancestors lived, the walls lit up, but here they were left with only the sound of the water ricocheting around the high cavern ceiling. It reminded Maati of the sound inside her ears now that they were wet, all scritchy, pinging, and poppish.

But finally, after what seemed a very long time, she saw some brightness in the distance. She bumped into Maarni as the woman stopped in place, listening. There was a sound like the beating of a monster's heart coming from beyond the tunnel.

'What *is* it?' Maati hissed, whispering.

Yiitir swam around his wife and on toward the light. 'Girls, girls, it's a pump. A large pump. My goodness, all our little escapades have made the two of you quite skittish. Some sort of work is taking place in the harbor.'

'Well, don't reveal yourself in the open until you know what it is,' Maarni cautioned. 'It could be the Khleevi for all we know. Or the Hosts. There's no guarantee Khornya landed us at the proper moment.'

Maati gathered herself and swam even further than Yiitir. (Sure there is. Khornya wouldn't have sent us unless she was sure.) She broadcast her thoughts, (Aari? Khornya? Thariinye? Anybody out there?)

For a moment is seemed as if the whole planet held its breath and she repeated, more feebly, (Anybody? It's me, Maati, and Yiitir and Maarni are with me.)

(*Maati!*) The answering cry came from not just one, but many Linyaari consciousnesses, including one very special one in particular.

(Where have you been, brat? I've been – I mean, the Council has been worried crazy!)

(Thariinye, I've been hiding just to make you mad) she teased. (And so have Maarni and Yiitir. No, we've been time traveling and we met the *sii*-Linyaari and ancient Ancestors and everything – did Aari come? Are the *sii*-Linyaari here? And Khornya? Is she here?)

(No, but one thing at a time, irritating Youngling. Where are you?)

She swam out to sea through the opening,

which was now much shallower below and much larger above. Bouncing up and down in the water, she waved her arms. (Here! We're here! Come bring a boat and get us. I am soooo tired of being wet!)

TWENTY-FIVE

With three more pairs of hands to help, Becker was able to expand the safety ring of irrigation far enough to accommodate landing area for two ships and three more shuttles. There had been no further Linyaari disappearances, and they had begun to retrieve their missing, so it was starting to look like their theory – he grinned to himself here – held water. When Hafiz's equipment began arriving, soon after Maati and the others had been fished out of the sea, the network rapidly expanded.

At the suggestion of and with the help of the Linyaari engineers, the hole that had allowed the debris from the surface to collapse into the sea was expanded so that lines could be run up the column connecting the planet's surface to the water of the ancient sea. This allowed a second network of irrigation troughs to feed directly from there.

Maati, Yiitir, and Maarni helped Becker locate the place where they had disappeared with Aari. This was the first place Acorna had wanted to make safe and, although three of the missing had returned, it was still the area closest to the lake site. Becker thought this was where Aari would probably return, and maybe Acorna, too.

'It's amazing how much closer this is when we use your shuttle,' Yiitir remarked. 'It took us a great deal of time and effort to walk from here to the city, didn't it, ladies?'

Maati and Maarni agreed. Maati was pleased that the lines now made the site of the former waterfall safe. And the shuttle lost when Becker first arrived had reappeared over an irrigation ditch dug across the site where it had vanished. Amazingly, all hands were still on deck. It had been a triumphant moment for all of them.

Maati could scarcely believe they had been back only a day and a half – too much activity had been packed into the time for it to seem possible. They worked round the clock – digging, pumping, and laying hose, lines, and valves. Fortunately, there were machines that did most of the digging, with Mac pitching in where more finesse and intelligence were required than brute force.

Suddenly Maati heard Yiitir, who had been busy consulting with the engineers, exclaim to Maarni, 'The Ancestors are coming! They're on their way from MOO right now! According to our dispatcher, they insisted they were needed right here.'

'I can scarcely see the Ancestors in all this mess!' said Miryii, one of the engineers. 'It will break their poor, old hearts to see their former planet reduced to this.'

'They're a tougher lot than you might suppose,' Yiitir assured him.

When the ship carrying them landed, the Ancestors and their Attendants asked immediately to be taken to the Vriiniia Watiir and to the falls. At that point they demanded, quite shrilly, that a deep pond be dug immediately at a site they selected. Then it had to be filled immediately as well, never mind that the filling left the underground lake so low that some of the pumps could no longer pump to their irrigation lines. When the Linyaari attempted to explain this to them, the Attendants turned them away, said that the grandparents were weary from their trip, that the filling of the pond was well done and necessary, and that they could all go away and do their work elsewhere.

Since there was a great deal to do and enough equipment still functioning to start running a line toward where the crew of the *wii-Balakiire* disappeared, everyone but Maarni, Yiitir, Maati, and RK did as the Attendants suggested. Maati asked the Attendants if they could stay the night with the Ancestors.

The Attendant in rumpled lime and fuchsia looked like she was about to deny her request when the Ancestor with a blanket that color said, 'Yes. Yes, we would like the company of these great-grandchildren. They have recently been among *our* Ancestors and we would like to hear of them.'

And so they all talked, and slept and – it seemed to Maati – waited.

Areel was the fastest and most powerful thing Acorna had ever traveled on, short of a space shuttle. And he *felt* even faster than one of those. He galloped so fast that the wind tore at her face and her hair, and once they were outside, clods of earth flew up and pelted her legs and sides. She still rode low over his neck, but once they were out of the tunnel, she hung onto his mane instead of riding with her arms around his neck.

She could run very swiftly herself, but how wonderful it must be to run like this. The Ancestors of her time deemed themselves too ancient or too important for this kind of race, but Areel gloried in it.

His endurance was greater than that of any living thing she had ever known. They ran far beyond the outskirts of the city, with pursuit still hot behind them. Looking back, she saw the Hosts following, flying, running, some on two legs and some on four. She wasn't sure, but others seemed to be running on six legs or more. In and among them ran the Ancestors, trying to discourage them. She heard snatches of the thought-talk between them that flew into her mind, only to be whisked away as Areel's feet ate up another furlong.

Finally, only two Hosts pursued them. The rest simply abandoned the chase. Acorna was exhausted just from riding, and she knew Areel must be even more tired than she was, though his pace never faltered. 'Great-Grandfather, we have to stop. You must rest or you'll surely die. And I have *got* to relieve myself.'

'Aaaaaah,' Areel said, taking care of his own need as she dismounted. She found herself so stiff and sore that she fell, and she had a much harder time than she would have imagined rising to her feet again. Areel, finished with his own task, inclined his head. 'Take my mane, child. There. I have never had a rider before, but you made yourself no burden. Now, quickly. I will graze as you do what you must. You grab some grass as well.'

She did as he said and pulled up handsfull of grasses rather than waiting to graze. She wished they had stopped near running water. Her mouth and throat were terribly dry from the rush of air filling them as Areel ran. But he was saying, 'They come. Hurry. To me.'

And behind them she heard the thought-broadcast, (Halt! Stop! We need you! Come back immediately!)

Nothing there to make her change her mind, although eventually, if they could reach a place where there was some tactical advantage, she would have to try to negotiate.

But not now. Behind her she saw a huge black bird and a vast, fast, gray beast with a white patch covering its back and front legs. She climbed back aboard Areel and they were off again.

The landscape grew familiar and she wondered where she had seen it. In her dreams perhaps? She had had such sweet dreams as a child of a home-world she never knew. And by the time she found out that the homeworld must be Vhiliinyar, that world had been destroyed. So perhaps this was a site from her dreams.

Or was it something more recent?

That was it! Hafiz's holo-projection of Vhiliinyar when it was done. This was a place she had seen there, except that when she saw it on the vid, it was from a different perspective.

Now Areel splashed into a great broad river, swimming toward the other side, when a huge blue-eyed leviathan swam up behind them. From its fin, a white garment fluttered.

'The co-parent of the *sii*-Linyaari,' Areel informed her. 'And the first to disown our watery children when they were not as well-formed as had been hoped by the Hosts. For myself, I thought they were quite attractive in their own unique way.'

The leviathan was much faster than Areel in the water, and the huge black bird caught up with them quickly, too.

Meanwhile they were being swept downstream.

'Great-Grandfather, I know this place. There is a waterfall not far from here, a very steep one, and you will not be able to avoid it. I'm going to jump off now. You swim to shore and save yourself.'

'You will be killed!'

'Perhaps not. I have seen this place. I think I can swim to a spot I know and avoid the rocks,' she said, but it was a vain reassurance to save Areel from dying with her. She had seen the holo of the waterfall, true, but she had no idea where the rocks were. The holo had prettily covered these up with decorative sprays of spume.

'Even if you escape death or injury, the Hosts will recapture you,' Areel said.

'Then you and the other Ancestors will just have to rescue me again,' she said. 'I have faith in your ability to do so. Thank you, and farewell.'

311

And she slid off his reassuring bulk into the water.

She made an arrow of her slender body and swam with the current, shooting toward the falls more quickly than even the powerful leviathan chasing her could swim.

The water became rougher, stiff white ruffles around rocks with only small patches of silver-green water maintaining the flow to the falls. She was so busy dodging rocks she forgot her pursuit, forgot to see if Areel made it to the far shore or not, and even forgot about the fall itself.

Until the instant when she hung over the edge, looking down and down and down over a sheet of spraying white water into a white trimmed green pool below, and then she was diving, for she would not let herself fall uncontrolled to her death, not if she could help it, plunging straight for the pool. She heard a high shrill sound in her ears and it occurred to her halfway down that she was hearing her own scream.

TWENTY-SIX

Acorna dived deep, deep, deep into the pool and then, laying her hands to her sides, shot to the surface like a rocket. Flicking the hair from her eyes and the water from both, she peered through the blurs the drops made and saw an Ancestral form on the bank. 'Areel! You made it! And so quickly.'

'Who are you calling, Areel, Youngling? And these days I don't do *anything* quickly,' the Ancestor replied. And then she was seeing double, triple, and in even more multiples as all sorts of Ancestors herded together beside the pool.

'Khornya!' cried four Linyaari voices, and Acorna swirled in the water to see Maati, Thariinye, Maarni, and Yiitir watching her from the shore and waving. Maati dived in and came out to meet her, pulling her to shore by the hand. 'I don't get it!' the girl exclaimed. 'How did the Ancestors *know*? They had us dig this pool, then we all just sat and waited for you to pop out of it!'

'Hmph,' snorted the lime and fuchsia bedecked Ancestor. 'That's for us to know and you to find out, if you're a very studious and clever girl, Youngling.'

'Still, Grandmother, you must admit it's a good thing Khornya came to inquire about our ancient writings, or you and the other Ancestors might not have recalled the prophecy in time to fulfill it.'

'Nonsense. It was a prophecy. Of course we fulfilled it,' snapped the first Ancestor. 'Now that the girl's had her soft landing, let's desalinate this frogpond and have us a nice cool drink. Nothing in this Friend-forsaken place to eat or drink. I'd take a bite out of one of the Khleevi themselves if they were here, I'm so disgusted with what they've done to our Home.'

RK hopped onto Acorna's shoulder and began grooming her wet face and hair, which made verbal conversation difficult. Maati and the others led her back to a shuttle, and then down to the tunnel. On the way, she called Yaniriin and asked him to patch her through to Hafiz.

'It is good to hear your voice, child of my heart,' Hafiz said. 'You are safe? Well?'

'Yes,' she said, rejoicing in her salvation. But then Acorna's voice was slowing down and she found it hard to respond to the questions he asked her. She didn't need to ask her own question. Aari had not returned. He was not here. Had he been, there would be no need to ask. He would have been with the others at the pool. She would have heard him in her mind the instant she had surfaced in her own time.

She didn't allow herself to brood, however. She knew that wherever he was, he would find a way to return to her. Or she would find him. It was just a matter of time.

As the irrigation systems hydrated more and more of the sites where Linyaari explorers had vanished, Acorna helped to retrieve the missing Survey teams by working with the time machine, locating the appropriate dots of light, and helping the crews make sure that the fresh water flowed where the people were landing in this time.

Neeva and the crew of the *wii-Balakiire* returned with their pockets loaded with detailed drawings and notations about the planet as it had been before the Khleevi, with soil, plant, and grass samples – even examples of insect life.

When their collecting met with the admiration of the hydraulics crews, Melireenya said, 'We simply treated it as another diplomatic expedition, gathering all the information we could about our surroundings. We knew where we were, although we didn't know when – the area was totally unpopulated, which was certainly not the case shortly before the Khleevi came.'

'You must have been there sometime between the period when ancient Kubiilikaan disappeared and the period when our people became more populous,' Yiitir told her. 'Of course, we now know the city didn't actually disappear. It was deliberately buried and covered over with meadow.'

'We've been studying the writings on the walls of the old city, and when he has time, Maak has helped us with his translations,' Maarni said. 'And we've made copies of the glyphs and their meanings—'

'Which she just happens to have in her shipsuit pockets,' Yiitir said with a wry smile. 'In case you'd like to see. Along with the holos of the grandchildren.'

Maarni stuck out her tongue at him.

The crews were busily realigning the hydraulics to cover the distance between the sea and the former base camp. Neeva, Khaari, Melireenya, Hrronye, Maati, Thariinye, RK, Yiitir, Maarni, and Acorna remained within the protected area atop the buried city. Already the increased flow of fresh clean water was causing small, healthy plant life to pop up all over the sites they had irrigated. Tiny star-shaped white and yellow blossoms, furry coverings of lichens on blasted stone, even a bristle of grass formed a meadow of sorts. Here the lot of them sat, munching on packaged leaves and seeds, while Maarni pulled out her findings and smoothed them on the ground for all to examine.

'You see here, this falcon-headed glyph with a woman's body? Up to this point she is in the guise of the Leader, or Highmagistrate and scientist/ mage.'

'Highmagister,' Acorna supplied. 'She was called Highmagister HaGurdy.'

'Yes. Oh! I see. That's what this character here means. It's a proper name. Thank you, Khornya. Well, as you can see, here she is wearing the coat of high office and that light around her head indicates power. We see in this panel what looks like the punishment of a Linyaari criminal, significant because until this point, no other Linyaari appear in any of the glyphs.'

'That was no criminal,' Acorna said. 'That's Aari. She wanted to use him as a shortcut to building our genetic structure. But she tried to do it without his consent.'

'Ahhhh – well, yes, that begins to explain things.' Maarni waited, in case Acorna had anything further to add. She had not spoken or projected thoughts to anyone since her return about what had happened to her on her journey. While she did not appear to have been injured in any way, her attitude of thoughtful withdrawal worried her friends. These comments were the first any of them had had from her indicating what had happened in the Hosts' chambers once she had returned Maarni, Maati, and Yiitir to their own time.

'The figure that was Aari simply disappears and is not seen again in any of the glyphs. However, the female Linyaari figure who appears here – why, that must be you, Khornya!'

'Yes,' she said simply.

Maarni said, 'I want you all to know that I obtained permission from the Ancestors and the Attendants to share this information with our people. Prior to this time, even this record has been kept as the sacred secret of the Ancestors. I believe in light of what we know from our personal experience that perhaps from the most ancient Ancestors to the present ones, they were wise enough that they did not wish their descendants to think badly of half of their lineage.'

'So the stories Grandam told me and the ones told to her were the versions the Ancestors edited to make them suitable for children?' Maati asked.

'Yes,' Maarni told her. 'The Ancestors place a high value on peace and contentment, as do most of us, and knowing about the – tempestuous side of the family – would be upsetting to some and perhaps have had a bad influence on some of the youngsters. Now the Ancestors feel that the truth has come out, but that our race has endured times that make us long more than ever for peace and contentment. Enough time has passed that much can be forgiven. Perhaps, also, the Hosts don't seem so bad when one knows about the Khleevi.'

'No,' Acorna said, closely scrutinizing one of the star-shaped blossoms as she spoke. 'Though it seems more of a betrayal when it comes from those who are kin than those who are clearly enemy and alien.'

'You see here now the story I told you of the origin of the falls. At least we thought it was the origin of the falls, but it seems the story was actually a creation story of the pool. The version we found on the walls shows the falcon with the woman's body and all of these other strange-looking creatures, interspersed with Ancestors, chasing what looks like a two-headed Ancestor –'

'That would be Great-Grandsire Areel with me on his back,' Acorna said. 'The Ancestors intervened when Highmagister HaGurdy would have used me to replace Aari in her experiments.'

'Here,' Maarni's finger stabbed at a picture of the two-headed unicorn with a wave halfway up his body to indicate the river. 'We see the pursued creature – Areel and Khornya, in the water but not until here –' she tapped a later picture, where a pool surrounded by Ancestors received the body of a falling Linyaari superimposed on what was clearly supposed to be a waterfall, 'do we see that there is a cascade there. This glyph must have come from a private story of the Ancestors . . .'

Behind her, a standing figure cleared her throat. 'After your visit, the Ancestors recalled the prophecy of Grandam Gladiis. It was she who saw you fall into the future, to be saved from the waters of the past by those of the present day. Everyone thought Grandam Gladiis had gone a bit gaga when she made her prophecy, but the Ancestors decided differently when they heard of the time machine. Once they knew that you'd gone missing, they realized that they were the ones to do the saving, and you were the one to be saved and they – er – sprang into action, after their fashion, that is.'

Acorna smiled broadly for the first time since she'd returned and Maati smiled even more broadly in appreciation of it. 'Once more I benefit from their wisdom and insight,' Acorna said.

Maarni said, 'And as you can see here, once this waterfall glyph appears, the light disappears from around the bird-woman's head and she is always shown with wings folded. Here she and her fellows help with the birth of the Linyaari – you can see a line of them there. But then there follows a glyph – this one, which says that all lab-conceived Linyaari were sent immediately to the Ancestors for nurturance for their first few years. Later, those who wished to returned to the city for their education. But you see from this other figure

– this one here, the woman with the bear's head, that the bird-woman's power was diminished and soon she is shown entering one of the ship glyphs. More and more of them disappear. There are three panels of what appear to be grown Linyaari inside the city building towers and carrying sun-shapes on their shoulders along with the Hosts.'

'Those are the globes at the top of the buildings!' Thariinye said.

'Other Linyaari figures,' Maarni continued, 'meanwhile, are shown building the ceiling and covering it over with soil and trees. Even the sea is divided between the upper world and the lower.'

'And then the last of the Host figures are shown entering the ship glyphs and are not seen in further drawings. For a time the city is shown to be lit by the globes with some of the Linyaari involved in technological activities below, while others, in ships much as we know them now, are shown coming and going from the planet, and engaged in a different level of technical activity on the surface. Here is the final glyph of the city, indicated by the column with the rayless globe, no longer accompanied by Linyaari figures. And this symbol here,' she tapped a horizontal doorway, 'which appeared earlier in the open position between the caverns and the city, is shown locked, or sealed shut.'

Acorna turned to the Attendant who had spoken earlier. 'Do the Ancestors recall any other apocryphal material about a Linyaari like Aari entering at any other time?'

The Attendant shook her head. 'I'm sorry, Khornya. No. If they remember anything, I will notify you at once.'

'How about the *sii*-Linyaari?' Maati asked.

'After the initial glyphs, they are not mentioned again,' Maarni said. 'Of course, we know now it's because they vanished in time.'

'Oh, I hope they didn't go to a time when the water was too foul for them to live,' Maati said. 'But – but they should have come out at the same time as Aari, right? So he could have purified it for them.'

'The entire sea? Always?' Yiitir shook his head. 'Doubtful, I'm afraid.'

With a roar, the *Condor*'s shuttle landed nearby and Becker alighted. RK yawned, stretched himself off Maati's lap, and sauntered over to greet the Captain. 'We have the water in place, Princess, if you want to go work the way-back machine and see if you can find Aari and the *aagroni* and the rest of your scientists and bring 'em back alive.'

Before becoming involved with the rescue efforts, Acorna had barely known many of the people who disappeared, but that had changed. Now she carried a palm-held computer stocked with pictures, anecdotes, resumés, preferences, passions, and stories from loved ones about each person. Now she felt she knew each of them much better than she had known any of them to begin with. If she was to use psychic energy to help locate and bring them home, she had to know who they really were.

She found the base camp location, near the old graveyard and Aari's cave. Then she concentrated mostly on the *aagroni*, Kaarlye, and Miiri, at first, then on Lareel and Liimi, Faarli and Paari, Seela and Kewmii.

As she concentrated, she held her hand against the map and watched carefully. Her reward was fourteen white lights widely dispersed from the original area, which no longer bore the topography of the ruined planet, but instead included rivers, streams, foothills, and forests as well as pastures. Other lifeforms, indicated by lights of different colors and intensities, moved among the white lights. Why were they so scattered? That was going to make them much more difficult to bring back.

The heavy shielding that had confounded the surveillance ships when Acorna and the others first explored the caverns and city had been partially removed. Through the breach, Acorna was able to send the Linyaari engineers at the base camp a picture of where each white light was, so they could distribute their irrigation ditches appropriately. But if these people kept moving, it would be hard to bring them home.

Once she located the lost survey team members, she returned with Becker to the base camp. By the time they arrived there, so had several of the missing people. She saw at once why they had been so scattered when she'd seen them. They were scientists. They'd been collecting specimens, of course. Their hands were full and pockets stuffed with all manner of plant life, and any animal small or cooperative enough to come along. The *aagroni* and Kaarlye and Miiri arrived with three species of birds nesting in their manes and some small furry rodent-like creatures in their shirts. Miiri was leading what looked like some kind of baby deer, while Kaarlye had a pair of bear-like creatures clinging to each hand. The *aagroni*'s shirt was stuffed with the Vhiliinyar equivalent of rabbits, squirrels, chipmunks, and a large bird, a gooselike creature which had fouled – or perhaps fowled? – the inside of the *aagroni*'s shipsuit.

The *aagroni* didn't seem the least bit unhappy about that, however, nor did he seem particularly surprised to find himself once more on post-Khleevi Vhiliinyar surrounded by his fellow Linyaari, Becker, and Mac.

'It's about time you brought us back,' he told them. 'I hope you can send us back to the past again soon. We'll take proper enviroshelters for the animals and collection bags for the plants next time.'

The *aagroni* wanted to go back out again right away, but finally agreed that other lost people had to be found first. Though he didn't like it.

TWENTY-SEVEN

Acorna was a patient person, but by now she was more frustrated than she could ever recall being. In between searching for the teams, while the equipment was being moved from site to site, she searched the time map for Aari. It hadn't been that difficult to find a location similar to the one she had memorized in the past, the one he had left behind when he fled. But the area on the map contained no little lights of any sort, neither white nor aqua. So she concentrated as hard as she could and kept searching but she couldn't seem to find the right time or place in the space-time continuum.

The night after the base camp team was located, however, she saw, at last, a collection of aqua lights in the sea as it had been above ground. The crews were moving the hydraulic equipment to another site and no one manned the pumps tonight. When a ship came to collect the *aagroni* and his team, Neeva and her crew had gone along, as did some of the other recently returned people. Yaniriin's lifemate was among them, and eager to see him once more.

Becker camped with the engineering team and even Maati had returned with her parents to MOO. Acorna was glad Kaarlye and Miiri were safe but didn't like to face them, feeling as she did, irrationally responsible that Aari was lost again.

She kept the screen where she could see the blue-green lights, and walked down to the sea. The water level was much lower now, and the buildings which had been covered were once more exposed and had resumed their proper place as dock-front real estate.

At least now, when she walked into the water, it was clean and clear.

She dove, submerging herself totally, thinking of the aqua lights and Aari. As she surfaced, she knew she was not alone.

(Sister! POP!) a horn-headed sea creature with humanoid features cried a friendly greeting that had a bubble around it. The bubble popped when the words emerged.

(Hello. I am called Khornya,) she told him – and the small ones and the females with wavy long hair who bobbed around her. (I believe you know my lifemate, Aari? Is he here? I have been searching and searching for him.)

But myriad little bubbles popped 'No!' 'Not here!' 'No longer!' 'Gone!'

'Where?' she cried. 'When?' and 'how long?' but the *sii*-Linyaari couldn't say. They could only describe what had happened to them from their point of view. The waves around them rose and the waves fell. They had fetched up in a sea covered with darkness, and Aari had gone away and not returned. They, however, had been sent here, where the suns still shone and the sea was warm. Only a few people ever appeared on the shore and some sort of building was going on, but that was of no concern to them.

Where Aari had gone, they couldn't say, but they wished him well and considered him a brother and good friend.

'If he returns, we'll tell him you were asking for him,' the horn-headed Upp said.

A small *sii*-Linyaari swam after her. 'Perhaps he went with your brothers and sisters on one of the ships, Khornya!' the *frii* said. 'He liked the ships. I could tell. And several left the planet after he swam ashore.'

'Thanks, little one,' she said, and continued swimming ashore herself. The spaceport was deserted. There were no ships for her to take now, even if she knew where he had gone. Was it possible Aari had discovered a way to use a ship to return from here to their own time? Wherever he was, he knew where – and *when* – she could be found. And she knew he wanted to find her again as much as she wanted to find him. But why had he had to leave just then? Just when she was so close to finding him? If only he had waited just a little longer.

But he hadn't. He was gone. Lost to her again. After all this effort, all this pain.

She was so good at helping people, at finding a way through their problems. Now that it really mattered so very much to her, now that she had needs of her own, she had failed. Bad timing, her uncles would say. Oh, yes! Very bad timing indeed. She felt flattened, somehow empty now.

It was so lonely without Aari beside her – more lonely than she ever had been before they came together. Intellectually, she realized she wasn't alone. She had her friends, her adoptive human family, of course; but it wasn't the same. They were not hers in the way that Aari was.

She pulled herself ashore and shook off a few droplets. What should she do now? Aari wasn't here to find, and she had no other way of seeking him in this world and time. She tried to shake off the weight of bewilderment and frustration, the load of disappointment and sadness bearing down on her. She would not give into the loneliness. Would not give into grief. She had accomplished some of what she came here to do. She *knew* now that Aari was alive and uninjured. She *knew* he cared for her and longed for her as she did him. He was strong, intelligent and resourceful and had gained some knowledge of the time-travel device. He'd be fine. Really. Of course he would.

So for the moment, she simply had to trust that, since she could not find him, he would find her.

She was easier to locate than he was, after all. *She* wasn't lost in time and space. Even if she was not on-planet when he came looking for her, someone on Vhiliinyar would always know where she was. He knew who and where and when to ask about her. He'd find her, now that he'd found a way to start looking for her.

And, he could just keep looking for a while, she

supposed. After all, that's what she had done. A little flash of anger ran through her when she thought about his absence from this place after all she'd gone through to get here. It gave her the power to go on, to climb the hill, to return to the machine, to reset it for her own time.

She would use the water still clinging to her body to return.

Aari was an adult male. He had been in far more threatening situations than this one and had escaped without her. She had no way to continue after him from here, and she had the needs of others to consider. She did not, after all, wish to bring the *sii*-Linyaari forward to shallow seas and darkness again.

But then, as she activated the machine, she realized that perhaps she wouldn't be so easy to find after all. When the terraforming of the old homeworld began, everyone would have to leave. If Aari returned to Vhiliinyar to look for her then, he would arrive on the rapidly mutating surface of the deserted planet – and that could be deadly.

The wall of reason and good sense she had just finished building to sustain herself crashed down upon her, crushing her spirit with the sheer weight of it, and leaving her with the sense she and Aari could be truly lost to each other, perhaps for all time, and nothing she had done or could do right now would make any difference.

Arriving back in her own time, she found her feet and eyelids as heavy as her spirit. What she really should do was sit for a moment and try to think this through one more time. But sitting turned into laying down on the cold floor of the building, and her thought turned into a deep disturbing dream.

She had been under the impression that all of the Ancestors had returned to narhii-Vhiliinyar, but when she opened her eyes in her own time, she was surrounded by unicorns.

'You are very troubled, Great-Granddaughter,' said the lime and fuchsia Grandmother.

'Of course she's troubled, old girl. She misses her lifemate and doesn't know where the boy's gone off to.'

'It's not just that,' Acorna said. While the two speakers were standing, many of the Ancestors lay on the floor, as if searching for something to graze upon. Acorna opened the pockets on her shipsuit and pulled out all of the food she had to offer.

'That is not necessary, Great-Granddaughter. Our Attendants fear we will take harm from this journey and so overfeed us to the point of bursting to counter any ill-effects. You were saying it was not just that you missed the boy. If it is not that, then what makes you so sad?'

'It's the terraforming. As soon as all of the teams have been located, we will all be leaving the planet while it is terraformed to restore the mountains and other contours, to replant and replenish the water, to restore the atmospheric layers.'

'Yes, so that Vhiliinyar that was will be again!' one of the Grandfathers crowed. 'I am looking forward to that!' Then his enthusiasm faltered. 'But you are not, are you?'

'Not any longer. Because when they do that, it will utterly change everything, the city will be destroyed and so will the time map. In fact, even if we tried to move it to MOO, it would do Aari no good. He will not be able to find his way back here again if the time device is gone. Or, at least, that is what I fear. And I cannot find him. The *sii*-Linyaari say he is not with them, that he may have gone off planet with our people of the pre-Khleevi past, before the city was buried. Without his light on the map of this planet, I cannot search for him. I cannot hope to find him, and he will be unable to find his way home again.'

'My dear,' the lime-and-fuchsia-draped Grand-dame said. 'He is a grown man. When the *sii*-Linyaari last saw him, he saw them to safety, then walked away on his own two feet. Since you cannot find him in time, it is probable that he is in space.'

'But what if he's not? Or even if he is, he will not be able to return when he's ready!'

'Not the way he left, anyway,' a Grandfather said. 'But perhaps there are other ways, ways you don't know. Or at least not yet. Calm yourself, child. Maad, what is that song you used to sing the Younglings? This one needs sleep. And good dreams.'

When she awoke, the Ancestors were gone and Becker had the next team ready for her to find. Two more teams after that, and the shuttles came for them. She wanted to slip away, to return to the machine, but perhaps Becker knew what was on her mind. He kept a close eye on her and made sure she boarded the *Condor* ahead of him. RK stayed very close to her. She returned to the quarters she had shared with Aari and found the coverings they had used, taking comfort in his scent lingering on them. Snuggling into them, she didn't feel quite so alone.

TWENTY-EIGHT

'Never in the history of our people have we held a high Council meeting of such importance, and certainly never have we held a Council of importance elsewhere than our own world, and with folk other than our own kind in attendance.'

The temporary Council head, one Kaalmi Vroniiyi, had a strong and sonorous voice that filled the ballroom of Hafiz's palace.

'However, here with us tonight are those who have involved themselves in our causes and our welfare, who have endangered themselves and their own livelihoods to help us when we were set upon by enemies. We have decisions to make in some cases, only because they have made choices possible where previously acceptance of disaster would have been our only course.

'We stand with feet on two worlds. Our dear friend and adopted kinsman, Uncle Hafiz, who has given us his home for this meeting, who has succored us during our disasters and grief, who has aided in the rescue of those of our number when in danger, has offered us his help in restoring both of our homes. One for our private spiritual use and one for public trade. While there is some long-range benefit to Uncle Hafiz's firm, in the meantime he has had to strip his beautiful and delicious gardens to help rescue some of us from time-traps caused by the Khleevi occupation of our beloved Vhiliinyar.

'He has offered to restore Vhiliinyar to its former pastoral and sylvan glory in return for a loan that our descendants will still be repaying his descendants many *ghaanyi* from now.

'And yet, recently, some of us have had, thanks to the Khleevi, unusual experiences which have shown us that things change. Even our beloved Vhiliinyar has not always been as many of us remember it. Sleeping, at its heart, for instance, is an ancient but in some ways very modern city. It waits for us to awaken it and use it. Within this city is an enormously powerful and dangerous instrument, that can be used to destroy the fabric of existence or, potentially, to mend the tears in that same fabric and bring continuity and harmony.

'The Khleevi, and I am happy to say the *late unlamented Khleevi*, thanks to the valor of some of our people and to our non-Linyaari friends such as Captain Becker, Uncle Hafiz, Colonel Nadhari Kando, and others, have been perhaps our greatest challenge, but at the same time they have been our greatest teachers.

'These lessons have not been easy ones. One of our sons, our brothers, was so horribly mistreated by them that he bears scars still despite reunion with his family and the love of an extraordinary daughter of the people. And we have lost many others of our people to their terrible tortures.

'And we, who feel we always do the best thing, are always good and always kind, left these people behind. Furthermore, when Aari came out alive, we were not all accepting of his return.

'Though unwilling to wage war ourselves, we allowed our friends and allies to wage it on our behalf. Now that both our planets have suffered from the conflict, we have professed ourselves to be willing to allow them to rebuild for us, to heal our worlds as instantly as we would heal a small cut, with no effort on our part.

'But will this truly be healing? Some of us think not. Some of us feel that allowing Uncle Hafiz to beggar himself on our account is bad for us all. We feel that a more gradual rebuilding of both planets is called for, a pay-as-we-go process in which we interact with and learn from those who contribute their skills to our homes' rebirth.

'Uncle Hafiz has ordered much that is needed to terraform our planet but we are here to decide the fate of that process. Do we want instant terraformation or do we, perhaps, wish to rebuild a mountain here, rededicate a stream there, allow Dr Hoa to improve our climate so that the seas refill, the rivers run, the meadows flourish in a gentle fashion? Meanwhile, thanks to the genius of our Ancestral Hosts, we have found a way to reclaim some of our lost species. As habitat becomes available for them, we may reintroduce them to the present time.

'One other factor enters into this equation before you, the Linyaari people, give the Council the benefit of your wisdom. That same son so injured by the Khleevi has become lost in time and of all our lost people, he is one who cannot be found. He leaves behind a mother and father who also were lost, a little sister who has only just come to know her sibling, and a lifemate who is our own dear Khornya, from and through whom we have gained the help we needed to survive our late catastrophes. Aari is only one male, you may say, just one Linyaari when many are needing their homes. So, shall we abandon him again? What say you?'

Before anyone else could answer, the ballroom was stunned into silence by the pounding of hooves, 1-2, 3, 4. 1-2, 3, 4. 1-2, 3, 4. As the Ancestors, the best kept secret of the Linyaari people, marched in synchronized formation into the room and with one voice brayed, 'Nay. We say nay. We will not lose him again as long as there is hope he may survive. We will never again willingly sacrifice the life of any of our people – or our friends – as long as there is hope they may survive. For the needless death or abandonment or even mistreatment of any one of us causes a plague of grief, pain, and anger beyond the power of the horn to heal, a poison to the waters of our souls. Be it known that this is the advice and the vote of we, your many times great granddames and grandsires, collectively known as the Ancestors.'

The vote was taken. Acorna shakily voted nay with the entire hall.

As the Ancestors marched back out again, the lime-and-fuchsia-clad Grandam stopped before her for a moment and Acorna threw her arms around the Ancestress's neck, thanking her profusely.

335

'Oh, nonsense child. We have always had plenty of time for truly worthwhile people. And now you and the other Younglings will have time and space to move mountains, cry yourselves rivers, and generally grow into the present. I suggest that you enjoy it, while you leave being relics of the past to us. We have a lot of experience at it.'

And with that, they marched from the room.

GLOSSARY OF TERMS AND PROPER NAMES USED IN THE ACORNA UNIVERSE

Aagroni – Linyaari name for a vocation that is a combination of ecologist, agriculturalist, botanist, and biologist. *Aagroni* are responsible for terraforming new planets for settlement as well as maintaining the well-being of populated planets.

Aari – A Linyaari of the Nyaarya clan, captured by the Khleevi during the invasion of Vhiliinyar, tortured, and left for dead on the abandoned planet. He's Maati's brother. Aari survived and was rescued and restored to his people by Jonas Becker and Roadkill. But Aari's differences – the physical and psychological scars left behind by his adventures – make it difficult for him to fit in among the Linyaari.

Aarkiiyi – Member of the Linyaari survey team on Vhiliinyar.

Aarlii – A Linyaari survey team member, firstborn daughter of Captain Yaniriin.

Acorna – A unicorn-like humanoid alien discovered as an infant by three miners – Calum, Gill, and Rafik. She has the power to heal and purify with her horn. Her uniqueness has already shaken up the human galaxy, especially the planet Kezdet. She's now fully grown and changing the lives of her own people, as well. Also called Khornya.

Ancestors – Unicorn-like sentient species, precursor race to the Linyaari. Also known as *ki-lin*.

Ancestral Hosts – Ancient spacefaring race that rescued the Ancestors, located them on the Linyaari home planet, and created the Linyaari race from the Ancestors and their own populations through selective breeding and gene splicing.

Andina – Owner of the cleaning concession on MOO, and sometimes lady companion to Captain Becker.

Attendant – Linyaari chosen to serve the Ancestors.

Balaave – Linyaari clan name.

Balakiire – The Linyaari ship commanded by Acorna's aunt Neeva in which the envoys from Acorna's people reached human-populated space.

Barsipan – Jellyfish-like animal on Linyaari home planet.

Becker – See Jonas Becker.

Calum Baird – One of three miners who discovered Acorna and raised her.

Condor – Jonas Becker's salvage ship, heavily modified to incorporate various 'found' items Becker has come across in his space voyages.

Declan 'Gill' Giloglie – One of three miners who discovered Acorna and raised her.

Delszaki Li – Once the richest man on Kezdet, opposed to child exploitation, made many political enemies. He lived his life paralyzed, floating in an antigravity chair. Clever and devious he both hijacked and rescued Acorna and gave her a cause – saving the children of Kezdet. His recent death was a source of tremendous sadness to all but his enemies.

Dharmakoi – Small burrowing sapient marsupials known to the Linyaari, now extinct as a result of Khleevi war.

Edacki Ganoosh – Corrupt Kezdet count, uncle of Kisla Manjari.

Enye-ghanyii – Linyaari time unit, small portion of *ghaanye*.

Feriila – Acorna's mother.

Fiicki – Linyaari communications officer on Vhiliinyar expedition.

Fiirki Miilkar – A Linyaari animal specialist.

Fraaki – Linyaari word for fish.

Geeyiinah – One of the Linyaari clans.

Ghaanye (pl. *ghaanyi*) – A Linyaari year.

Gheraalye malivii – Linyaari for Navigation Officer.

Gheraalye ve-khanyii – Linyaari for Senior Communications Officer.

Giirange – Office of toastmaster in a Linyaari social organization.

Giryeeni – Linyaari clan name.

GSS – Gravitation Stabilization System.

Haarha Liirni – Linyaari term for advanced education, usually pursued during adulthood while on sabbatical from a previous calling.

Haarilnyah – The oldest clan amongst the Linyaari.

Hafiz Harakamian – Rafik's uncle, head of the interstellar financial empire of House Harakamian, a passionate collector of rarities from throughout the galaxy and a devotee of the old-fashioned sport of horseracing. Although basically crooked enough to hide behind a spiral staircase, he is fond of Rafik and Acorna.

Haven – A multigeneration space colonization vehicle occupied by people pushed off the planet Esperantza by Amalgamated Mining.

Highmagister HaGurdy – The Ancestral Friend in charge of the Hosts on old Vhiliinyar.

Hraaya – An Ancestor.

Hrronye – Melireenya's lifemate.

Hrunvrun – The first Linyaari Ancestral Attendant.

Iiiliira – A Linyaari ship.

Iirtye – Chief *aagroni* for narhii-Vhiliinyar.

Ikwaskwan – Self-styled 'admiral' of the Kilumbembese Red Bracelets.

Imaara – An Ancestor Attendant.

Jonas Becker – Interplanetary salvage artist; alias space junkman. Captain of the *Condor*. CEO of Becker Interplanetary Recycling and Salvage Enterprises Ltd – a one-man, one-cat salvage firm Jonas inherited from his adopted father. Jonas spent his early youth on a labor farm on the planet Kezdet before he was adopted.

Kaarlye – The father of Aari, Maati, and Laarye. A member of the Nyaarya clan, and life-bonded to Miiri.

Ka-Linyaari – Something against all Linyaari beliefs, something not Linyaari.

Karina – A plumply beautiful wannabe psychic with a small shred of actual talent and a large fondness for profit. Married to Hafiz Harakamian. This is her first marriage, his second.

Kava – A coffee-like hot drink produced from roasted ground beans.

KEN – A line of general-purpose male androids, some with customized specializations, differentiated among their owners by number, for example KEN637.

Kezdet – A backwoods planet with a labor system based on child exploitation. Currently in economic turmoil because that system has been broken by Delszaki Li and Acorna.

Khaari – Senior Linyaari navigator on the *Balakiire*.

Khetala – Captured as a small child for the mines of Kezdet, later sold into the planet's brothels. Rescued by Acorna, and now a beautiful young woman.

Khleevi – Name given by Acorna's people to the space-borne enemies who have attacked them without mercy.

Kii – A Linyaari time measurement roughly equivalent to an hour of Standard Time.

Ki-lin – Oriental name for unicorn, also a name sometimes associated with Acorna.

Kilumbemba Empire – An entire society that raises and exports mercenaries for hire – the Red Bracelets.

Kirilatova – An opera singer.

Kisla Manjari – Anorexic and snobbish young woman, raised as daughter of Baron Manjari; shattered when through Acorna's efforts to help the children of Kezdet her father is ruined and the truth of her lowly birth is revealed.

Kubiilikaan – The legendary first city on Vhiliinyar, founded by the Ancestral Hosts.

Kubiilikhan – Capital city of narhii-Vhiliinyar, named after Kubiilikaan, the legendary first city on Vhiliinyar, founded by the Ancestral Hosts.

LAANYE – Sleep learning device invented by the Linyaari that can, from a small sample of any foreign language, teach the wearer the new language overnight.

Laarye – Maati and Aari's brother. He died on Vhiliinyar during the Khleevi invasion. He was trapped in an accident in a cave far distant from the spaceport during the evacuation, and was badly injured. Aari stayed behind to rescue and heal him, but was captured by the Khleevi and tortured before he could accomplish his mission. Laarye died before Aari could escape and return.

Laboue – The planet where Hafiz Harakamian makes his headquarters.

Lilaala – A flowering vine native to Vhiliinyar used by early Linyaari to make paper.

Linyaari – Acorna's people.

Liriili – Former *viizaar* of narhii-Vhiliinyar, member of the clan Riivye.

Lukia of the Lights – A protective saint, identified by some children of Kezdet with Acorna.

Maarni – A Linyaari folklorist, mate to Yiitir.

Maati – A young Linyaari girl of the Nyaarya clan who lost most of her family during the Khleevi invasion. Aari's sister.

Mac – Android and member of Becker's crew on the *Condor*.

Madigadi – A berry-like fruit whose juice is a popular beverage.

Maganos – One of the three moons of Kezdet, base for Delszaki Li's mining operation and child rehabilitation project.

Makahomian Temple Cat – Cats on the planet

Makahoma, bred from ancient Cat God stock to protect and defend the Cat God's temples. They are – for cats – large, fiercely loyal, remarkably intelligent, and dangerous when crossed.

Manjari – A baron in the Kezdet aristocracy, and a key person in the organization and protection of Kezdet's child-labor racket, in which he was known by the code name 'Piper.' He murdered his wife and then committed suicide when his identity was revealed and his organization destroyed.

Martin Dehoney – Famous astro-architect who designed Maganos Moon Base; the coveted Dehoney Prize was named after him.

Melireenya – Linyaari communications specialist on the *Balakiire*, bonded to Hrronye.

Miiri – Mother of Aari, Laarye, and Maati. A member of the Nyaarya clan, lifebonded to Kaarlye.

Misra Affrendi – Hafiz's elderly trusted retainer.

Mitanhyaakhi – Generic Linyaari term meaning a very large number.

MME – Gill, Calum, and Rafik's original mining company. Swallowed by the ruthless, conscienceless, and bureaucratic Amalgamated Mining.

MOO, or Moon of Opportunity – Hafiz's artificial planet, and home base for the Vhiliinyar terraforming operation.

Naadiina – Also known as Grandam, one of the oldest Linyaari, host to both Maati and Acorna on narhii-Vhiliinyar, died to give her people the opportunity to save both of their planets.

Naarye – Linyaari techno-artisan in charge of final fit-out of spaceships.

Nadhari Kando – Delszaki Li's personal bodyguard,

rumored to have been an officer in the Red Bracelets earlier in her career.

Narhii-Vhiliinyar – The planet settled by the Linyaari after Vhiliinyar, their original homeworld, was destroyed by the Khleevi.

Neeva – Acorna's aunt and Linyaari envoy on the *Balakiire,* bonded to Virii.

Neeyeereeya – The most populous of the Linyaari clans.

Ngaen Xong Hoa – A Kieaanese scientist who invented a planetary weather control system. He sought asylum on the *Haven* because he feared the warring governments on his planet would misuse his research. A mutineer faction on the *Haven* used the system to reduce the planet Rushima to ruins. The mutineers were tossed into space, and Dr Hoa has since restored Rushima and now works for Hafiz.

Niciirye – Grandam Naadiina's husband, dead and buried on Vhiliinyar.

Niikaavri – Acorna's Grandmother, a member of the clan Geeyiinah, and a spaceship designer by trade. Also, as *Niikaavre*, the name of the spaceship used by Maati and Thariinye.

Nyaarya – One of the clans of the Linyaari.

Nyiiri – The Linyaari word for unmitigated gall, sheer effrontery, or other form of misplaced bravado.

Order of the Iriinje – Aristocratic Linyaari social organization similar to a fraternity, named after a blue-feathered bird native to Vhiliinyar.

Paazo River – A major geographical feature on the Linyaari homeworld, Vhiliinyar.

Pahaantiyir – A cougar-like animal native to Vhiliinyar.

Palomella – Home planet of Nueva Fallona.

Piiro – Linyaari word for a rowboat-like water vessel.

Piiyi – A Niriian biotechnology-based information storage and retrieval system. The biological component resembles a very rancid cheese.

Qulabriel – Hafiz's assistant.

Rafik Nadezda – One of three miners who discovered Acorna and raised her.

Red Bracelets – Kilumbembese mercenaries; arguably the toughest and nastiest fighting force in known space.

Renyilaaghe – Linyaari clan name.

Riivye – Linyaari clan name.

Roadkill – Otherwise known as RK. A Makahomian Temple Cat, the only survivor of a space wreck, rescued and adopted by Jonas Becker, and honorary first mate of the *Condor*.

Shahrazad – Hafiz's personal spaceship, a luxury cruiser.

Shenjemi Federation – Long-distance government of Rushima.

Siiaaryi Maartri – A Linyaari Survey ship.

Sii-**Linyaari** – Legendary aquatic race also developed by the Friends.

Sita Ram – A protective goddess, identified with Acorna by the mining children on Kezdet.

Standard Galactic Basic – Standard language used throughout human-settled space.

Stiil – Linyaari word for a pencil-like writing implement.

Techno-artisan – Linyaari specialist who designs, engineers, or manufactures goods.

Thariinye – A handsome and conceited young space-faring Linyaari from clan Renyilaaghe.

Theophilus Becker – Jonas Becker's father, a salvage man and astrophysicist with a fondness for exploring uncharted wormholes.

Thiilir (pl. *thilirii*) – Small arboreal mammals of Linyaari homeworld.

Thiilsis – Grass species native to Vhiliinyar.

Twilit – Small, pestiferous insect on Linyaari home planet.

Vaanye – Acorna's father.

Vhiliinyar – Original home planet of the Linyaari, destroyed by Khleevi.

Viizaar – A high political office in the Linyaari system, roughly equivalent to president or prime minister.

Vilii Hazaar Miirl – An officer in the Linyaari space fleet.

Virii – Neeva's spouse.

Vriiniia Watiir – Sacred healing lake on Vhiliinyar, defiled by the Khleevi.

Wii – A Linyaari prefix meaning small.

Yaazi – Linyaari term for beloved.

Yaniriin – A Linyaari Survey Ship captain.

Yasmin – Hafiz Harakamian's first wife, mother of Tapha, faked her own death and ran away to return to her former lucrative career in the pleasure industry. After her accumulated years made that career much less lucrative, she returned to squeeze money out of Hafiz in the form of blackmail.

Yiitir – History teacher at the Linyaari academy, and Chief Keeper of Linyaari Stories. Lifemate to Maarni.

BRIEF NOTES ON THE LINYAARI LANGUAGE

by Margaret Ball

As Anne McCaffrey's collaborator in transcribing the first two tales of Acorna, I was delighted to find that the second of these books provided an opportunity to sharpen my long-unused skills in linguistic fieldwork. Many years ago, when the government gave out scholarships with gay abandon and the cost of living (and attending graduate school) was virtually nil, I got a Ph.D. in linguistics for no better reason that that (a) the government was willing to pay (b) it gave me an excuse to spend a couple of years doing fieldwork in Africa and (c) there weren't any real jobs going for eighteen-year-old girls with a B.A. in math and a minor in Germanic languages. (This was back during the Upper Pleistocene era, when the Help Wanted ads were still divided into Male and Female.)

So there were all those years spent doing things like transcribing tonal Oriental languages on staff paper (the Field Methods instructor was Not

Amused) and tape-recording Swahili women at weddings, and then I got the degree and wandered off to play with computers and never had any use for the stuff again . . . until Acorna's people appeared on the scene. It required a sharp ear and some facility for linguistic analysis to make sense of the subtle sound-changes with which their language signaled syntactic changes; I quite enjoyed the challenge.

The notes appended here represent my first and necessarily tentative analysis of certain patterns in Linyaari phonemics and morphophonemics. If there is any inconsistency between this analysis and the Linyaari speech patterns recorded in the later adventures of Acorna, please remember that I was working from a very limited database and, what is perhaps worse, attempting to analyze a decidedly non-human language with the aid of the only paradigms I had, twentieth-century linguistic models developed exclusively from human language. The result is very likely as inaccurate as were the first attempts to describe English syntax by forcing it into the mold of Latin, if not worse. My colleague, Elizabeth Ann Scarborough, has by now added her own notes to the small corpus of Linyaari names and utterances. It may well be that in the next decade there will be enough data available to publish a truly definitive dictionary and grammar of Linyaari; an undertaking which will surely be of inestimable value, not only to those members of our race who are involved in diplomatic and trade relations with this people, but also to everyone interested in the study of language.

NOTES ON THE
LINYAARI LANGUAGE

1. A double vowel indicates stress: aavi, abaanye, Khleevi.

2. Stress is used as an indicator of syntactic function: In nouns stress is on the penultimate syllable, in adjectives on the last syllable, in verbs on the first.

3. Intervocalic *n* is always palatalized.

4. Noun plurals are formed by adding a final vowel, usually *-i*: one Liinyar, two Linyaari. Note that this causes a change in the stressed syllable (from LI-nyar to Li-NYA-ri) and hence a change in the pattern of doubled vowels.

    For nouns whose singular form ends in a vowel, the plural is formed by dropping the original vowel and adding *-i*: ghaanye, ghaanyi. Here the number of syllables remains the same, therefore no stress spelling change is required.

5. Adjectives can be formed from nouns by adding a final *-ii* (again, dropping the original final vowel if one exists): maalive, malivii; Liinyar, Linyarii. Again, the change in stress means that

349

the doubled vowels in the penultimate syllable of the noun disappear.

6. For nouns denoting a class or species, such as Liinyar, the noun itself can be used as an adjective when the meaning is simply to denote a member of the class, rather than the usual adjective meaning of 'having the qualities of this class' – thus, of the characters in *Acorna*, only Acorna herself could be described as 'a Liinyar girl,' but Judit, although human, would certainly be described as 'a Linyarii girl,' or 'a just-as-civilized-as-a-real-member-of-the-People' girl.

7. Verbs can be formed from nouns by adding a prefix constructed by [first consonant of noun] + *ii* + *nye*: faalar – grief; fiinyefalar – to grieve.

8. The participle is formed from the verb by adding a suffix *-an* or *-en*: thiinyethilel – to destroy, thiinyethilelen – destroyed. No stress change is involved because the participle is perceived as a verb form and therefore stress remains on the first syllable:

> *enye-ghanyii* – time unit, small portion of a year (ghaanye)
> *fiinyefalaran* – mourning, mourned
> *ghaanye* – a Linyaari year, equivalent to about 1 1/3 earth years
> *gheraalye malivii* – Navigation Officer
> *gheraalye ve-khanyii* – Senior Communications Specialist
> *Khleev* – originally, a small vicious carrion feeding animal with a poisonous bite; now

350

used by the Linyaari to denote the invaders who destroyed their homeworld.

khleevi – barbarous, uncivilized, vicious without reason

Liinyar – member of the People

linyaari – civilized; like a Liinyar

mitanyaakhi – large number (slang – like our 'zillions')

narhii – new

thiilir, thiliiri – small arboreal mammals of Linyaari homeworld

thiilel – destruction

visedhaanye ferilii – Envoy Extraordinary

A LIST OF OTHER ANNE McCAFFREY TITLES
AVAILABLE FROM CORGI BOOKS

THE PRICES SHOWN BELOW WERE CORRECT AT THE TIME OF GOING TO PRESS.
HOWEVER TRANSWORLD PUBLISHERS RESERVE THE RIGHT TO SHOW NEW RETAIL
PRICES ON COVERS WHICH MAY DIFFER FROM THOSE PREVIOUSLY ADVERTISED IN
THE TEXT OR ELSEWHERE.

08453 0	DRAGONFLIGHT	£5.99
11635 1	DRAGONQUEST	£6.99
10661 5	DRAGONSONG	£5.99
10881 2	DRAGONSINGER: HARPER OF PERN	£5.99
11313 1	THE WHITE DRAGON	£6.99
11804 4	DRAGONDRUMS	£5.99
12499 0	MORETA: DRAGONLADY OF PERN	£6.99
12817 1	NERILKA'S STORY & THE COELURA	£5.99
13098 2	DRAGONSDAWN	£6.99
13099 0	THE RENEGADES OF PERN	£5.99
13729 4	ALL THE WEYRS OF PERN	£6.99
13913 0	THE CHRONICLES OF PERN: FIRST FALL	£5.99
14270 0	THE DOLPHINS OF PERN	£6.99
14272 7	REDSTAR RISING: THE SECOND CHRONICLES OF PERN	£6.99
14274 3	THE MASTERHARPER OF PERN	£6.99
14631 5	THE SKIES OF PERN	£6.99
14762 1	THE CRYSTAL SINGER OMNIBUS	£8.99
14180 1	TO RIDE PEGASUS	£5.99
13728 6	PEGASUS IN FLIGHT	£6.99
14630 7	PEGASUS IN SPACE	£6.99
13763 4	THE ROWAN	£5.99
13764 2	DAMIA	£5.99
13912 2	DAMIA'S CHILDREN	£5.99
13914 9	LYON'S PRIDE	£6.99
14629 3	THE TOWER AND THE HIVE	£5.99
09115 4	THE SHIP WHO SANG	£5.99
08661 4	DECISION AT DOONA	£4.99
08344 5	RESTOREE	£5.99
10965 7	GET OFF THE UNICORN	£6.99
14436 3	THE GIRL WHO HEARD DRAGONS	£5.99
14628 5	NIMISHA'S SHIP	£6.99
52973 7	BLACK HORSES FOR THE KING	£4.99
14271 9	FREEDOM'S LANDING	£6.99
14273 5	FREEDOM'S CHOICE	£6.99
14627 7	FREEDOM'S CHALLENGE	£6.99
14909 8	FREEDOM'S RANSOM	£6.99
14099 6	POWER LINES (with Elizabeth Ann Scarborough)	£5.99
14100 3	POWER PLAY (with Elizabeth Ann Scarborough)	£5.99
14621 8	ACORNA (with Margaret Ball)	£5.99
14748 6	ACORNA'S QUEST (with Margaret Ball)	£6.99
54659 3	ACORNA'S PEOPLE (with Elizabeth Ann Scarborough)	£6.99
14749 4	ACORNA'S WORLD (with Elizabeth Ann Scarborough)	£5.99

Transworld titles are available by post from:

Bookpost, PO Box 29, Douglas, Isle of Man, IM99 1BQ

Credit cards accepted. Please telephone 01624 836000
fax 01624 837033, Internet http://www.bookpost.co.uk
or e-mail: bookshop@enterprise.net for details

**Free postage and packing in the UK. Overseas customers allow £1 per book
(paperbacks) and £3 per book (hardbacks).**